SEASIDE

Lovers

Seaside Summers
Love in Bloom Series

Melissa Foster

ISBN-13: 9781941480441
ISBN-10: 1941480446

Cover Design: Natasha Brown

WORLD LITERARY PRESS
PRINTED IN THE UNITED STATES OF AMERICA

A NOTE FROM MELISSA

If this is your first Love in Bloom book, all of my love stories are written to stand alone, so dive in and enjoy your next fun, sexy, and oh-so romantic adventure!

The best way to keep up to date with new releases, sales, and exclusive content is to sign up for my newsletter.
www.MelissaFoster.com/news

ABOUT THE LOVE IN BLOOM BIG-FAMILY ROMANCE COLLECTION

Seaside Summers is just one of the series in the Love in Bloom big-family romance collection. Characters from each series make appearances in future books, so you never miss an engagement, wedding, or birth. If this is your first Love in Bloom novel, you have many more loving, loyal heroes and sexy, sassy heroines waiting for you!

Download a free Love in Bloom series checklist here:
www.melissafoster.com/SO

Get **free** first-in-series Love in Bloom ebooks and see my current sales here:
www.MelissaFoster.com/LIBFree

Visit the Love in Bloom Reader Goodies page for downloadable checklists, family trees, and more!
www.MelissaFoster.com/RG

CHAPTER ONE

PARKER COLLINS SHOVED a handful of M&M's in her mouth, eyes glued to *Saw III*. A burst of light illuminated the pitch-black media room, followed by a scream of terror. Christmas, her four-year-old English mastiff, sacked out beside her on the couch, pushed his big head beneath her legs as darkness shrouded them again. Another shrill scream brought her big chicken of a dog deeper into her leg tunnel.

"Whoever said dogs were a *man's* best friend was an idiot. *My* best friend." *Especially now that Bert's gone.* A few tears slipped down her cheek.

Christmas whimpered, pulled his head from beneath her legs, and licked her from chin to eyes, getting every last one of her tears and coming back for more. He'd been lapping up her tears for two weeks, ever since she'd lost her friend, mentor, and the only family she'd ever known. Bert Stein had suffered a massive heart attack while Parker was in Italy filming her latest movie, and she'd been moving on autopilot ever since: picking up Christmas from his housekeeper in Los Angeles because Bert had been watching him while she was away,

1

attending Bert's funeral, *trying to remember how to breathe*, and finally, coming to her house in Wellfleet to mourn—and, she hoped, to mend a fence Bert was never able to with his estranged brother.

Holing up in the bay-front home she'd built for the Collins Children's Foundation, where no one would look for her, was the only way she could grieve without negative ramifications. God forbid an A-list actress went out looking like an average woman whose heart had been ripped from her chest. Rag magazines would pay big bucks for pictures of her puffy, tired eyes and I-don't-give-a-shit tangled hair. She could just imagine the headlines: *Parker Collins's New Drug Addiction,* or *Unplanned Pregnancy for Parker,* or anything else that would sell magazines. Nobody cared that she'd never even smoked a cigarette, that she needed to have sex in order to get pregnant, or that she'd gone so long without, she wondered if her best parts even worked anymore.

She pressed her hands to Christmas's droopy cheeks, kissed her bewildered boy's snout, and reached for the bottle of tequila she'd been nursing. She'd never had tequila before tonight, but it was the perfect addition to her chocolate–horror movie grief remedy. After pouring herself another shot, she tossed it back in one gulp, savoring the warmth as it slid down her throat and drowned her sadness.

She set the glass beside her on the couch and shoved her hand into the jumbo bag of peanut M&M's that had consoled her throughout the evening—because a big lazy dog was great for licking tears, but nothing quenched sadness like candy-coated chocolate. And tequila. *Definitely tequila.* Her fingers scraped the bottom of the bag. *Damn it.* She tossed the empty bag to the floor. Christmas hung his head over the side of the couch and whimpered.

"Don't judge me. It can't be that bad." She leaned forward to assess the damage, knocking an empty pizza box to the floor, and reached for the coffee table to stop the room from spinning. "Whoa."

Another scream brought her eyes to the movie, then toward the movement in her peripheral vision, where a shadowy figure blocked the entrance to the media room. It took her alcohol-drenched mind a minute to realize the tall, broad man filling the doorway wasn't supposed to be in her house. Panic spread through her veins, catapulting her to her feet. Christmas darted to the stranger with a friendly *woof.*

"Oh God." She reached for the wall to steady the spinning room, fighting to push through her drunken haze. She'd seen enough movies to know she was going to die in the media room of this lonely house, wearing chocolate-stained sweatpants—or more accurately, ice-cream-, tequila-, pizza-sauce-, *and* chocolate-stained sweatpants—while her dog made a new friend of her killer.

"Stay back. He's a killer. One command and you're dead!" Not likely with her loving dog.

The man sank to one knee, his face hidden by her big, traitorous dog.

"Yeah, I can see that," he said casually, as only a coldhearted psycho killer could.

Searching for a weapon, she grabbed the tequila bottle, only too late realizing it was spilling down her wrist. She flipped it upright, wishing this was a movie and someone would yell, *Cut!*

A piercing scream drew their attention to the heart-pounding terror on the projection screen. Suddenly the room was showered in light. Parker's eyes slammed shut against the sensory invasion, then flew open to get a look at the man who would probably find fame as the *Parker Collins Killer.*

Her breath caught in her throat, and her hand flew to her frantically beating heart, as she took in the Greek god rising to his feet before her. His smoldering dark eyes nearly brought her to her knees. *Grayson Lacroux.*

"Grayson?" *Do I sound scared, drunk, or like I want to jump your bones?* Probably all three, which wasn't good. Grayson had won a two-year contract in a design competition last summer, and for the past ten months he'd been designing artwork for the Collins Children's Foundation. As the founder of CCF, Parker headed up the project, and they'd exchanged hundreds of emails—emails that felt intimate and meaningful and had pulled her through too many long, lonely nights to count.

"What are you doing here?" She cringed at how breathless she sounded. Even in her drunken state she knew it had nothing to do with her initial fears and everything to do with the towering male across the room.

His lips curved up as he surveyed the room. She'd come straight down to the media room in full-on holing-up mode after arriving from LA. Her open suitcase lay in the middle of the floor, lace and silk seeping over the sides. The clothes she'd worn on the flight were strewn across the hardwood floor. One pink high heel peeked out from beneath an empty bag of Twizzlers; the other was nowhere in sight. An orgy of fun-size candy bar wrappers and M&M's littered the floor.

"I might ask you the same thing." His voice was low and rich and made the room feel fifty degrees hotter.

Maybe that's the tequila.

"I came to take measurements for the railing and heard a noise. I didn't know you were here."

Measurements? She couldn't think with his dark, assessing gaze trained on her as he crossed the room. Each step was a declaration of power and control—the same air of confidence he relayed in his emails. Parker was used to beautiful people, but holy mother of hot and sexy men, Grayson brought manliness and sex appeal to a whole new level. An *enticingly tempting* level. She was five nine, and he had several delicious inches on her. His bulbous biceps and massive breadth made her feel more delicate than she was. His tousled, thick dark hair and unwavering air of command made her knees wobble. She took a deep, unsteady breath and backed against the wall to stabilize those wobbly knees, but he stepped closer, assaulting her senses with his musky, and somehow summery, scent.

Nope. Definitely not the tequila. The man was a walking heat wave.

He eyed the tequila bottle in her hand, and his eyes filled with amusement. "Having a little party?" He plucked a sticky piece of candy from her hair and held it between his large finger and thumb with a cocky grin.

A crazy-hot cocky grin that sent dirty thoughts about his mouth rushing to the front of her mind. "Not exactly," she mumbled.

"You've been avoiding my emails."

She'd been avoiding email, voicemail, and *life* since Bert's funeral. Grayson was on her callback list, along with her agent, a few foundation staff members, and about a dozen so-called friends.

"I...Um..." *Can't really think clearly.* She lifted the tequila bottle. "Care to join me?"

His gaze dragged down her tank top, bringing her nipples to attention and reminding her she'd taken off her bra. As if on cue, Christmas *woofed*, Parker's pink lace bra dangling from his mouth. Grayson's eyes brimmed with heat, making her want to put him on a totally different kind of *to-do* list.

He'd been the subject of her late-night fantasies for so many months she felt like she already knew him well enough for him to own that list.

This was bad.

Very, very bad.

Parker didn't have that kind of *to-do* list. She *did* relationships. Or rather, *didn't* do them, based on her dating history.

Ugh! Her head was too fuzzy to try to untangle the web of lust she'd weaved with every email, every intimate glance into his private world of family, friends, and his love of his craft. Grayson worked with heavy metals, as evident from his insanely perfect physique, which no gym in the world could produce, and his designs were excruciatingly unique and beautiful. Parker had probably driven him crazy making changes, but if she had, he'd never let on. She loved reading his descriptions about why he designed certain pieces and how he felt when he was creating them. Sometimes he wrote about missing his family, or about bonfires and outings he'd gone on when he flew home to work with his brother on specific designs for CCF. She'd been careful not to ask personal questions, so she wouldn't feel inclined to share her personal life, but she had secretly clung to each of his tales, treasuring the emotions he'd so eloquently shared. She'd made excessive design changes just to keep those intimate glances of him coming.

And now he was here, all six-something feet of him, close

enough to see and touch and taste—and between her grief and his godliness, she was clearly losing her mind.

She pushed past him, grabbed the lingerie from Christmas, and tossed it into her suitcase. "Lie down."

Christmas walked in a circle and plopped onto a pile of clothes with a huff.

Parker grabbed a shot glass from the bar, determined to remain in her inebriated state so she could deal with all the testosterone flinging around the room, and sank down to the couch. "Coming, big guy?"

HELL YEAH, I'D totally be into coming. Grayson scrubbed his hand down his face to try to clear that thought from his brain and sat down beside Parker, silently reminding himself that she was technically his boss *and* a client. That was only one reason he should stop thinking about how incredibly sexy she was. They'd been emailing for almost a year, and he'd sensed affection brewing between them, even if neither one had directly addressed it. Three weeks ago she'd sent him an email pulling him from the foundation project to design a railing for this mini-mansion and had followed it up with a note about being *excited to finally get together in person*—and he hadn't heard from her since.

Another reason he needed to keep his sexual urges at

bay—because he really needed to find as many reasons as possible right this very second—was the inebriated state and slightly red, puffy eyes of the scrumptious blonde currently reaching across his lap. Her hair tumbled sexily over her bare shoulders as she fished for something between the leather sofa cushions. There was no ignoring the feel of her pert nipples against his thigh, making him hard and hungry for what he shouldn't have. *At least not tonight, with all that alcohol muddying your thoughts.*

She crawled off his lap and held up another shot glass. "Voilà! Fill 'er up!"

Needing the alcohol to calm the inferno inside him, he gladly filled their glasses and handed her one. She wrapped her delicate fingers around his, giving him ideas about what else he'd like to see those slender digits wrapped around. Her blue eyes filled with determination, which he also found incredibly sexy.

"Don't tell anyone you saw me like this."

Seriously? Who did she think he'd tell? "I'll cross putting an article in the paper tomorrow off my list."

She pushed her face to within an inch of his. His eyes fell to her luscious lips as more erotic thoughts raced through his mind. He was skating on very thin ice.

"*Parker* can't do things like cry, or curse, or eat an entire jumbo bag of M&M's and watch horror movies until her eyes nearly bleed without being judged. Only Polly can do that."

"Polly?" He reached for her glass, figuring she'd had enough and needed more babysitting than his sexual urges did at the moment.

She pulled her glass out of his reach with a devilish glint in her eyes and *clinked* it to his. "To Bert. I miss him *so* much I ache." She downed the drink in one swallow.

Bert? Jealousy clawed at him. He shifted his gaze away from her, taking in the room again. *Tequila, chocolate, pizza? Two weeks of radio silence. Aw, hell. Hallmarks of a rough breakup.* That thought bugged the shit out of him, so he moved on to another. Maybe this was her typical go-to stress release after filming and Bert was her...*director?* No way she'd *ache* for her director. Unless...*Christ*, something else, *anything* else. No matter how hard he tried, he couldn't get past his first assessment. Had their emails only *felt* personal? It was difficult to assess a lot of things over email, so it wasn't out of the realm of possibility that he'd misinterpreted the depth of their friendship, regardless of the heat simmering between them now.

As she refilled their glasses, he realized she'd never mentioned her dog. He'd talked about his family and friends, and if he'd had a dog, he sure as shit would have mentioned it. Who would leave out their dog? Feeling like a complete numskull, he realized she'd never mentioned her family, either. Had he been sucked in by her musings over how pretty the countryside was and how she wished *he* was there to see it?

And her off-the-cuff remarks about how acting would be easier if the other actors were as confident as *he* was?

Another look around the room told him he was an idiot.

This is a post breakup breakdown. So much for babysitting. He could deal with a lot of things, but picking up the pieces from some other guy's mistakes was not one of them. He downed the shot, thankful she'd refilled their glasses.

"Bert?" he mumbled to himself, thinking about how he'd like to wring the asshole's neck—right after he wrung his own for being such a fool. Parker was America's sweetheart. Right up there with Julia Roberts. While he'd been slowly falling for the sweet, gorgeous woman a million miles away, she'd probably been out with dozens of Hollywood heartthrobs. He didn't like knowing he'd misinterpreted their friendship, but he only had himself to blame for that. But he didn't appreciate being blown off or having his time wasted. He couldn't move forward with the railing designs he'd sent her over the past two weeks without her approval—and she'd obviously been too wrapped up in whoever the fuck Bert was to answer a single email.

It was time for him to leave.

She turned her big, tear-filled baby blues on him, making him sorry he'd come by to get the final measurements for the railing. "Bert was the best man on the planet. He was—" Tequila spilled over the top of the glass. "Oh, gosh! Darn it! I…"

"I've got it." Grayson pushed to his feet, needing to put distance between them anyway, because regardless of his not wanting to still be attracted to her, every fiber of his being had been consumed with her for months. He found a towel behind the bar.

Christmas lumbered over, sniffed the spillage, and went back to lying on the pile of clothes, leaving Grayson to mop up the mess—and scrub out his urge to be an asshole and walk out the door, leaving her alone to deal with her breakup woes. Hearing about some guy—other than him—that she thought was *the best man on the planet* was nowhere on tonight's agenda.

"Maybe you've had enough." He tossed the wet towel on the bar, grabbed another and wet it down.

"Oh no." She shook her head, waving a finger at him. "No amount of tequila is enough right now. I've never had tequila before, and you know what? I like it. It's delicious. Numbing. Truly helpful right now."

He wiped down the coffee table with the clean, wet towel and tried to keep the distaste from coming out in his voice. "I'm sure there are plenty of other guys to take his place."

Her mouth gaped.

He turned away and tossed the towel on the bar, having no patience for women who pretended they didn't know they were pretty. "You're Parker Collins. Tons of guys want y—" He turned around and nearly bowled her over. His arm circled her waist to keep her from falling. "Whoa. You okay?" Apparently she wasn't only a skilled actress, but she also had wicked ninja skills.

Tears slid down her cheek, conflicting with the anger in her eyes.

"Bert Stein wasn't a *guy*. You shouldn't assume. You're…infuriatingly *male*." She twisted from his grip, downed another shot, and sank down to the couch again. More tears fell, turning the anger in her eyes to sadness and filling him with guilt.

Grayson's compassion overpowered his hatred of drama. He had a younger sister, and if she was this sad and a guy was with her but didn't try to help, he'd pummel the asshole. He sat beside Parker and gave himself over to five minutes of hell. "All right, I'll bite. Who was he?" *And by the way, why didn't you tell me you were here? I wouldn't have barged in.*

She reached for the tequila, and he reached for her hand. Their eyes connected. Hers were so full of conflicting emotions—heat and sorrow—it stirred all the affection he was trying to push aside. He kept ahold of her hand and guided her back from the edge of the couch, taking her emotions more seriously, unwilling to let her fall any further into the blankness alcohol had to offer. He knew about that crutch all too well, having dealt with his father's alcoholism a few years ago.

"Tell me about Bert," he said in a softer tone. At Bert's

name, Christmas's head popped up. The dog surveyed the room, then lowered his chin to his paws again and closed his eyes. At least Bert knew she had a dog.

"He was my...*everything*," she said just above a whisper. "And now he's gone."

His heart ached at the sadness in her voice, pushing the jealousy in him to the pit of his stomach. When she lifted her eyes, another tear slid down her cheek, forcing that ache a little deeper.

"Gone, as in he went somewhere?" Grayson asked, hoping she hadn't lost her lover forever. "Or gone as in, *gone?*"

"*Gone*. He was like a father to me, and two weeks ago he passed away." She swallowed hard, more tears spilling from her beautiful eyes.

His breath hitched in his throat. *A father?* They'd emailed for nearly a year. How could he not know about someone so important to her? Now he was not only an idiot, but an asshole for assuming she was overreacting to a rough breakup.

She turned away, causing a torrent of emotions in him. The desire to pull her in to his arms until her sadness subsided obliterated every other thought. He gathered her close, soothingly stroking her back, remembering the gut-wrenching devastation he'd experienced after he'd unexpectedly lost his mother to an aneurysm. He closed his eyes with the memory, pushing his own painful past aside, and pressed a kiss to the top of Parker's head.

"I'm so sorry," he whispered. He held her until her breathing evened out and her tears stopped. He wiped her tears with the pads of his thumbs, wishing he could do something more and knowing time and compassion were the only things that would help.

"You came here to grieve?"

She nodded. "Flew in this morning."

"What about your family? Don't you want to be with them?" When he'd lost his mother, he'd needed family as much as he'd needed air to breathe. "Friends?" he asked hopefully.

"There's only me." Her eyes shifted to the dog. "And Christmas."

You're going through this alone? I should have fucking known you had no family. As painful as that thought was, he realized she'd had no reason to include family in their email conversations. Maybe he hadn't misinterpreted everything after all. Despite his waffling on the meaning of their interactions, his protective urges surged forth, driving his need to ease her heartache. He slid his hands to either side of her neck, brushing his thumbs over her jaw as he lifted her face so she had no choice but to meet his gaze. She was vulnerable and hurting, so different from the strong, sunny actress the world knew her to be. But grief didn't care about social status, and neither did he. All he saw was the woman he'd spent almost a year thinking about night and day looking at him with sad, soulful eyes. Despite the warning bells going off in his head about their professional relationship and his potential misinterpretation of their emails, he wanted to hold her all night, to kiss her until her pain subsided, and to protect her from ever being hurt again.

He fought the urge to kiss her and said what remained true regardless of whether he'd misinterpreted their relationship or not. "And me, Parker. Now you've got me, too."

CHAPTER TWO

PARKER AWOKE SATURDAY morning to Christmas's wet tongue slurping her face. She groaned, and the sound vibrated in her skull, making her regret turning to her new friend, Tequila, last night. She rolled over, and Christmas pressed his nose in to her cheek, urging her to get up and feed him. She blinked a few times and realized they were no longer in the media room, but on her bed. She couldn't remember coming upstairs. In fact, she couldn't remember much past—*Oh shit! Grayson.*

She bolted upright, sending a rush of blood throbbing behind her eyes. Groaning again—and immediately regretting it—she closed her eyes and reached beneath the covers, praying she wasn't naked. *Whew.* Her eyes flew open with relief. She still had on her sweats and tank.

Oh no. My sweats? The ice-cream, chocolate, tequila-stained sweats? Images from the night before snuck into her mind: Grayson looking like sin and pleasure all wrapped up in more than six feet of deliciously rugged man. His eyes filling with amusement as he plucked candy from her hair, and a

MELISSA FOSTER

minute later, brimming with heat. The kind of heat that made her feel sexy and feminine. She closed her eyes again, hoping she hadn't acted on those feelings.

She remembered telling him about Bert, and on the heels of that memory was the recollection of being in his arms and his soothing voice and reassuring words making her feel a little less lonely. *If only I could remember if he made me feel less lonely in other ways, too.* She'd never actually had drunken sex, but she'd been so wrapped up in Grayson's emails soothing her for all these months, who knew what she would do when her brain was drenched in tequila and grief.

Christmas shoved his nose into her thigh, jerking her from her thoughts.

"Sorry. I know you're hungry."

Forcing herself to her feet, she waited for the pounding behind her eyes to settle, then padded down to the kitchen to get Tylenol and coffee and to feed Christmas. While Christmas ate, she meandered through the house looking for signs of drunken debauchery.

The living room cushions hadn't been moved, and the hardwood floors were free of naked butt prints. *Whew! At least we didn't christen this room. Only about fifteen more to go.* She looked up at the high ceilings and sent a little thank-you to the powers that be. She hadn't expected to come to Wellfleet to grieve for the most important person in her life. She'd planned on returning to LA after she finished filming, spending a week or two with Bert, and *then* coming to Wellfleet to see…

Oh no. She'd been so upset over Bert, she'd forgotten she'd sent Grayson an email a few weeks back asking him to return to Wellfleet and make a railing for the house. She wanted a prettier railing, that much was true, but she'd really looked forward to spending time with him to see if what she'd felt for him all these months had been real and whether there might be something more between them. After last night, she might as well kiss those thoughts goodbye.

She made her way down to the media room, searching for clues about last night. The pit of her stomach went hot at the thought of having sex with the gorgeous, confident man who wrote lovely emails—and saw her looking like hell, heard her rambling, and wiped her tears. What a mess. She was never a mess. Ever. She was organized, on top of her lines, and she rarely took time off from acting, going from one film to the next with just enough time to prepare. Acting was a good distraction from the life she wasn't living. People in her circles were more interested in what she brought to the table or what being seen with her could do for their careers, making friends and relationships transient at best. But while she had acting and hiding in her whirlwind life down pat, she had no experience with grief. She'd been only a year old when she'd lost her mother. Bert's unexpected demise had thrown her completely off-balance, and poor Grayson had witnessed it.

She touched her cheek, remembering the feel of his rough

thumb as he brushed away her tears. The intimate gesture had taken her by surprise. But it was the memory of the caring look in his eyes that had her frozen in place now, standing just a few feet from the media room. Had he really looked at her like that, or was the alcohol skewing her memory? What was worse than thinking she'd seen a caring look in his eyes, was suddenly remembering wanting desperately to kiss him. What if she *had* kissed him but couldn't remember it? What if she'd tried to do more and he'd had to fight her off? Or worse. What if he didn't fight her off?

No more tequila. Ever.

Christmas bounded down the stairs and nudged the back of her knee, sending her stumbling into the media room. Her eyes widened at the spotless room. She blinked a few times, wondering if she'd dreamed up the whole night. Maybe Grayson hadn't even been there. She took in the pristine hardwood floors and leather couches, the clean wooden bar where the nearly empty tequila bottle sat square in the center. *Nope.* She hadn't made up that part. She remembered the towels Grayson had used to clean the coffee table and looked for them behind the bar. No dirty towels. She must really be losing her mind.

My suitcase! Her heart slammed against her ribs. She definitely remembered her clothes and candy strewn around the room. *Shitshitshit.* She tore upstairs to her bedroom and found her suitcase sitting on the armchair by the windows. She opened it, hoping and praying he hadn't—*Oh no*. He'd folded her clothes. She tipped open the hamper, melting a little when she saw two soiled bar towels. But that moment of reveling in his thoughtfulness was shattered when she realized there was only one reason a man would ever go to so much trouble.

She must have slept with him.

She didn't know what pissed her off more, the embarrassment of having probably attacked him, or not remembering one single second of it. That thought made her want to crawl back into the tequila bottle *and* get on the next flight out of town.

How could she ever face him again?

She couldn't. There was no *how* involved.

Chastising herself for being so reckless, and for being too drunk to remember what was probably the best sex she'd ever have in her entire life, she showered, dried her hair, and began the process of becoming Parker Collins.

Foundation, blush, eyeliner, lipstick—*sigh*—fake eyelashes. She hated fake eyelashes. So what if hers were too blond? Couldn't she just go back to being Polly Collins for a little while? Her agent had chosen Parker as her Hollywood name. It wasn't like she tried to hide her true identity, but the world knew her as Parker Collins, and she had never publicly talked about being Polly. Polly had become her reference to living a *normal* life. Not that her life had been normal before. But being Polly meant living life as a non-celebrity. How many times had she told Bert she wanted to go back to being Polly? When she was sick of the paparazzi, or had cramps, or was too exhausted to care if she went to the grocery store looking good enough for anyone other than herself.

Bert's voice sailed into her mind. *The world adores Parker Collins, and that makes it possible for you to give back to the children of the world. Polly's the strength and courage that drives you, but she has the power to undermine Parker in the eyes of your fans. Polly is yours forever, but she can never be theirs.*

Swallowing past the lump in her throat, she put on the damn eyelashes and grabbed her keys. Time to buck up and visit Bert's bastard brother.

GRAYSON WALKED ALONG Parker's side yard carrying the new designs for her railing he'd drawn up late last night, trying to get his thoughts together before knocking on her door. He'd told himself he needed to catch up with the beautiful, leggy blonde to try to nail down the final design for the railing. But while that might be true, it wasn't what had kept him up all night wishing he could reverse time and rewrite the last ten months. If he could, he would damn well make sure he knew about Bert well before he passed away, and that she had no family, and a great dog, and all the other personal things she'd probably kept hidden. And he would have been with her immediately after she'd lost Bert so she didn't have to deal with that loss alone.

She'd put up a tough front last night, even with the tears she'd shed. Grayson had suffered grief, and he knew how it could knock a person to their knees. She'd fallen asleep with her head on his shoulder while they were talking, or rather, while she mumbled and he tried to follow along. Little of what she'd said made sense, but then again, not much of what he'd felt since then had made sense either. He tried to convince himself it wasn't his place to try to be there for her, especially knowing he might have misinterpreted their dealings for nearly a year. Besides, shouldn't she have an entourage of people caring for her? But she didn't, and Grayson had never been good at being dissuaded from something he wanted. And regardless of whether it made him a fool or not, he wanted to be there for Parker.

Christmas bounded around the corner of the house, favoring his right paw, and *woofed* with delight at the sight of Grayson.

Grayson knelt to love him up. "Hey there, buddy."

The dog licked his cheek. Then the big lug buried his snout in Grayson's crotch.

"Nice to see you again, too." Grayson redirected the dog's nose. "Where's your mama?"

Christmas plopped down on his butt by Grayson's feet, giving him a chance to inspect the dog's giant paw. He picked a piece of what looked like taffy from between the pads, and the dog licked his cheek again.

"Christmas!"

At the sound of Parker's voice, Grayson and Christmas looked toward the front yard. Parker came around the corner of the house and stopped cold at the sight of Grayson. He preferred the dog's eager reaction.

Christmas, obviously used to seeing Parker looking like a million sexy bucks, *woofed* and sprinted over to her. Grayson wasn't quite as quick to collect himself. He rose to his feet, mouth dry, trying not to gawk as he took in her high heels and long, tanned legs, which disappeared beneath a pair of expensive-looking navy shorts. She wore a demure white blouse, and her long blond hair lay sexily over one shoulder. The whole ensemble was topped off with a floppy white sun hat and enormous sunglasses.

"Hi," he said, having trouble reconciling this primly put together actress with the dressed-down, grieving woman he'd been with last night.

She shifted her large designer bag to the crook of her arm and nervously petted Christmas. "I...I didn't expect to see you here."

"I probably should have called." *I was worried about you.* "I thought we could take a few minutes to go over the design ideas for the railing."

Her eyes darted nervously to the water, the house, the dog,

everywhere but at him. "I...I can't. I have to...um...go into Brewster." She turned and hurried toward the front of the house.

Grayson fell into step behind her, admiring the view of her perfect rear end and mulling over the brush-off she was clearly giving him. Assuming she was pissed at last night's unannounced intrusion, he said, "I'm sorry about barging in last night."

"*I'm* sorry about last night," she said with her back to him as she let Christmas in the house.

"You have nothing to be sorry about. I didn't realize you were in town. Otherwise I wouldn't have used my key."

She didn't respond. He'd obviously been mistaken last night when he'd thought the heat between them was more than just drunken lust. He should give her the designs to review and leave. But he couldn't shake the feeling that behind those sunglasses she was hurting, and if what she'd said last night was true, she was suffering alone. Plus, she'd said something about meeting a *bastard* today, and that wasn't sitting well with him.

"Parker, about last night..."

She clicked the remote to the garage, revealing a shiny silver Lexus. Damn, he hadn't thought to check the garage last night. The house had been pitch-dark when he'd arrived to recheck the measurements for the railing, and then he'd heard a noise downstairs and he'd thought someone had broken in.

This no-eye-contact thing she had going on was beginning to annoy him. He'd gone ten months without eye contact, which had made the design process more difficult. But he'd resisted the urge to ask her to Skype or FaceTime, because he had a feeling if they did, all those emotions he was feeling would come tumbling out. He'd proven he sucked at reading her without eye contact, and he wasn't about to take a chance of being wrong about anything else where Parker was concerned. Without a word, he lifted the sunglasses from her face.

"Grayson. What...?" She put her hand in front of her face and turned away.

He gently turned her toward him. There wasn't enough makeup in the world to hide the worry and sadness swimming in her eyes. It didn't matter if she wanted him around or not. He wasn't leaving.

"Parker, I didn't come to go over the drawings. I was concerned about you."

Her lips parted, as if she was going to respond, but she lowered her eyes in silence.

"I know you're sad about Bert, but you can talk to me. I've dealt with loss like this before."

She finally met his gaze. "You have?"

"Yes, when I lost my mother. I know how hard this is, and if you're embarrassed about drinking or the candy, or whatever, don't be."

"Thank you." Her eyes went glassy. "I'm sorry about your mom."

"Me too. I really do understand, so if you need a friend, I'm here."

"I appreciate that," she said softly. Her cheeks flushed. "And thank you for cleaning up last night. You really didn't have to do that."

"Well, it was either that or pick more candy out of Christmas's paws."

She smiled, and it loosened the knot in his gut.

"I think I found taffy in his paw this morning."

"No, you didn't."

"Sure did. And, um...*Christmas?*" He cocked a brow, relieved to see her tension easing. "We've been emailing for almost a year. How did I not know about your big lovable dog?"

"Sorry. I don't talk about my life much, and he wasn't on location with me. He always stays—*stayed*—with Bert when I was filming." Her eyes warmed. "Bert gave him to me for Chanukah."

"You're Jewish and you named your dog Christmas?"

"I'm not Jewish, but Bert was, so we celebrated Chanukah. One year I said it might be nice to have Christmas. The next day he gave me my boy and said, 'Now you can have Christmas every day.'" She blinked away the dampness in her eyes.

"I think I would have liked Bert."

"I...I think he would have liked you, too. Can I ask you something?"

"Anything." *Just keep talking.*

Her lips twisted in an adorable, confused expression. "Did we...?"

"Did we...?"

She rolled her eyes. "Last night. Did we...you know?"

A laugh escaped before he could stop it. "No, we didn't. Christ, Parker. Don't you think you'd remember that?"

She lifted one shoulder.

"Trust me, sweetheart. If we had, not only would you remember every blessed moment of it, but you'd think about it for days afterward. Weeks. Maybe even months."

"Please." She laughed, and the delightful, feminine sound was like music to his ears.

He couldn't resist sliding his hand around her waist and teasing her. "Well, since you asked so nicely."

Her fingers curled around his forearm, and her eyes turned midnight blue. The air between them sizzled, as it had last night. Maybe he hadn't misinterpreted a damn thing. He fought the urge to lean in and kiss her. She licked her lips seductively, jolting him back to reality. She was worried they'd hooked up and he was about to kiss her? *Christ.* He didn't want to be *that* guy.

He forced himself to step aside before his desires took over. "Last night you mentioned something about meeting a *bastard* today. Is that where you're going?"

"I said that?" She crossed her arms, unfolded them, and crossed them again.

"I guess that means yes?"

"I can't believe I said that." She leaned against the car. "What else did I say?"

Not wanting her to face *any* bastard alone, he circled the car and climbed into the passenger seat. "We can talk on the way there. I'll get a ride back to town from Hunter."

Her jaw gaped. "I...Grayson. Really?"

Hooking his seat belt, he leaned across the driver's seat and smiled up at her. "Want me to drive?"

"What?" She looked at the key fob as if she'd forgotten she was holding it. "No. I'm capable of driving. I just..." She let out a frustrated sigh and climbed into the car, eyeing him as she pushed the start button. The engine purred to life. "You're really coming with me?"

"You're really meeting a bastard?"

She looked at him as if he already knew the answer and was fighting the urge to roll her eyes.

"Okay, then." She shifted the car into drive and pulled out of the garage.

"I didn't mean to scare you last night."

She clicked the garage remote, closing the doors behind them. "You didn't scare me."

"Okay, so honesty obviously isn't your thing." He settled

29

into the leather seat as she pulled onto the road. "I didn't scare you, and you didn't try to kiss me."

She gasped. "I did not!"

He lifted a shoulder, and she gritted her teeth. She was too cute not to toy with, at least a little. "Parker?"

"What?" she snapped. "I did not try to kiss you!"

He laughed. "So, want to go with honesty, or...?"

"Why are you even in this car?" A playful smile curved her lips, and he knew she was coming out from under the embarrassment of thinking they'd slept together. Not to mention that he loved knowing she'd thought of him that way. "Honesty! Of course. You're—"

"Infuriatingly male? I know, you told me that last night."

She cringed. "Oh God, really?"

"Yup. And trust me, you don't want that to change."

"You're big on the whole 'trust me' thing, aren't you?"

"I'm a pretty trustworthy guy. So, why don't you tell me where we're headed?"

She ignored the question, and as they drove by Mayo Beach, she pointed to the gazebo across the street that Grayson had built for the competition last summer, and just beyond, the sculpture his brother Hunter had made.

"You and Hunter are so talented," she said.

"Thanks. So are you."

She shot him a confused look. "You've seen my movies?"

"Well, only the porn, but that counts, right?"

She punched his arm, and he rubbed it, feigning a pout.

"I never did porn."

"Now I'm confused. Are we back to the lying game?" he teased.

She punched him again, and he caught her hand and kissed the back of it. He had no idea what had made him do it, but she sighed, and it was just about the sweetest sound he'd ever heard.

"You're—"

He cut her off. "Infuriat—"

"No," she said with a smile. "I mean, you are that, but I was going to say *different.*"

"Different? Is that good or bad?"

"The jury's still out." She slid him a look he couldn't read.

"Okay, then." That was better than a cold shoulder. "Tell me about this bastard you're going to see."

"Abe Stein. He's Bert's brother and only living relative." Her tone went serious. "They hadn't spoken for more than fifty years. And I just...They only had each other, and they let that go. I want to try to, I don't know. Fix it."

"Does he know you're coming?"

She shook her head as she pulled onto Route 6 and headed toward Brewster.

"I was afraid he might not see me. He might not even know Bert passed away, so there's that little bit of heartache I get to dole out. I mean, Bert was pretty well-known in the photography world, so there was a good amount of press when…"

"Then he probably knows." He was glad he'd come with her. A surprise visit with Bert's estranged brother sounded like trouble in the making. "What makes you think he wants to fix whatever it is you're trying to fix?"

"I'm pretty sure he won't. Bert tried to reconcile with him, and Abe never gave him the time of day. He returned every letter Bert ever sent. But that didn't stop Bert from hoping they'd work through it one day, and that made it feel important to me. Well, that and the fact that Bert left me a key to his safe-deposit box containing the returned letters, a few pictures, and a single piece of paper with the address of the resort where his brother is living. I didn't realize the address was for Ocean Edge Resort until later, when I searched it online, and then it took several phone calls to put the pieces together and figure out what it meant. After throwing Bert's name around to the staff and the manager, Abe's name finally came up, and the pieces fell into place. But Bert must have wanted me to have all that for a reason, right?"

"I don't know about that, Parker. Maybe he just left you the letters because it sounds like you were the closest thing he had to family. Do you know anything else about Abe?"

"Just that he's loaded, and Bert described him as a self-righteous, self-absorbed bastard who swindled their father out of his company and drove his own wife and daughter away years ago."

"Seriously? You must be a glutton for punishment. Are you sure you want to do this?"

She looked at him out of the corner of her eye. "Bert once told me that I reminded him of his niece. He trusted me with this for a reason. I have to do it."

Like hell. He wasn't so sure he liked this Bert guy anymore. What kind of man leaves a woman a trail of meat to a hungry lion? Change of plans. Work could wait. He wasn't about to let her see this guy alone. "Then I'll go see him with you."

"Grayson." Her shoulders dropped.

He covered her hand with his. "We both know I'm infuriatingly male, so don't even try to dissuade me. This is what friends do. They support one another, through tequila, tears, and curmudgeonly old bastards."

Her brows knitted. "I'm not really used to friends like that. You don't have to."

"I want to. End of discussion."

She opened her mouth, and he was sure she was going to make a remark about his male attitude, so he cut her off. "And you're enticingly female. Deal with it."

She pulled into the gated community of Ocean Edge Resort and Golf Club, magnifying the difference between the circles in which they traveled. Parker sat up straighter, drew her shoulders back, and inhaled deeply, blowing it out slowly.

All of the worry and teasing he'd seen in her eyes slipped away, replaced with a mask of pleasant calm as she morphed into the confident Parker Collins the world knew and loved right before his eyes.

He wondered if she ever got lost between who she really was and the woman she was expected to be.

CHAPTER THREE

PARKER TOSSED HER hat into the backseat and grabbed her bag, trying to ignore the perplexed look in Grayson's dark eyes. At least that look made it easier for her to climb back into her actress armor, unlike the warm, caring look he'd been giving her that made her think it was okay to let her guard down and feel like a normal, grieving, twenty-eight-year old. Not that any of his looks in between caring and perplexed made anything about being near him easy. He was kind, caring, tough, and stubborn, and she needed a will of steel to battle her mounting attraction to him.

As she stepped from the car she stole another glance. His black shirt stretched tight across his broad chest. His low-slung jeans looked like old favorites, worn in the knees and frayed at the edges. Everything about him said he was comfortable in his own skin. She'd been that way once. Even when she'd been moving from house to house in foster care, she'd been comfortable with who she was as a person. But that was before she'd found fame. She no longer had the luxury of being herself, and she wasn't sure she knew who the famous Parker

Collins really was. But she'd been blessed with a life others would kill for, and she needed to get out of her selfish head and get on with what she came here to do.

She met Grayson's assessing gaze, which felt hot and sexy and made her feel a little dangerous. Who was she kidding? She wasn't a dangerous type of girl. She was a play-by-the-rules, do-what-she-was-told kind of girl, as evident by everything in her life...besides last night.

She should probably warn Grayson, or at least offer an explanation about running hot and cold and the way she'd have to act while she was out in public, but what could she say? *I can't risk bad press, and I'm trying to hold my shit together long enough to get through this terrible, awful meeting?* That would make her look like a fake. She already felt that way most of the time. She didn't need him to know it.

The impressive resort, expensive cars, and the smartly dressed valet heading their way were reminders of why she'd climbed out of her grief-induced horror-movie-watching, junk-food-eating stupor this morning. Parker knew how to play this game well, so she did what she did best and shifted her eyes away from Grayson, focusing on the valet.

Sometimes she hated being a celebrity.

Most of the time.

Almost always.

Especially right now.

"Thank you," she said, handing the valet her key fob,

along with a few large bills.

Grayson stepped closer, warmth returning to his dark eyes as he searched hers. "Are you okay?"

No. I'm in serious need of a hug, and a drink, and a mountain of chocolate. I need Bert, too. Her heart squeezed at the thought. *Can you please bring him back? Just long enough for me to say goodbye and hug him one last time?*

Pushing all those truths aside, she said, "Yes. Thank you," too curtly for his kindness, and she hated herself for it. But being Parker under these circumstances took effort.

He held her stare for a few silent beats and placed his hand on her hip. "You sure?"

She was used to being pawed at and hit on, but no one touched her like this—as if they cared and didn't need permission to do so. She realized that after last night, he'd seen more of the *real* her than anyone else ever had, other than Bert. Grayson had gotten a glimpse of Polly.

Fighting the urge to step into his arms, she said, "Yes. Thank you."

He glanced over his shoulder at the resort, his hand slipping from her hip. She felt better when he was touching her, but she held her head up high, ready to take on her most torturous role yet.

Parker had access to private beaches, elite clubs, daily spa treatments, and just about anything she could ever want, in any city she visited. But she'd never felt comfortable in them, and no amount of money or celebrity could give her what she truly craved: the love and security of family. Bert had been her family, but now...

She pushed those thoughts aside, feeling like she'd spent her life pushing things aside, as they crossed the marble floor on the way to the elevators. She felt the eyes of several people on her. She'd never get used to the icy chill those first seconds of recognition brought with them, reminders to be on alert, ready for anything from people seeking autographs and pictures to handsy men and jealous women.

Relief came when the elevator arrived and the doors closed behind them. Short-lived relief. Grayson's big body made the confined space seem even smaller. He smelled like sand and surf and sinful pleasures, and his scent was permeating her skin, bedding down in her nasal cavities. And he was standing too close, making it harder to remember a single reason why she should fight her attraction to him.

As if she wasn't nervous enough about meeting Abe?

He touched her hip again, sending sparks through her veins and holding her transfixed with his penetrating gaze. He was clean-shaven, which made her thoughts travel to places they shouldn't, like wondering what his smooth cheeks would feel like against her inner thighs.

"Hey," he said with a voice as enticing as melted chocolate. "You sure you're okay? It's just us in here. You can relax."

Right. With your sexy voice making me want you and my

brain telling me it's wrong for no apparent reason at all and a bastard waiting a few floors up?

"Just don't judge me, okay? Just us or not, I can't risk bad press, which sucks, but it's part of my life." Why was she snapping at him? It wasn't his fault she wanted him.

His brow wrinkled. "I don't give a rat's ass about who you have to be, or how you have to act for anyone else. I respect your career, and I'll do what I can to protect your image or whatever it is you're worried about. But I only *care* that *you're* okay with how you feel inside, *for yourself*, not for anyone else's sake."

How can I be okay? I'm nowhere near okay. Especially when you say something so caring and sweet and romantic it makes me want to climb into your arms and stay there for a month. She swallowed that confession and said, "I'm fine, and I *am* relaxed."

His eyes narrowed, and he stepped distractingly closer. His hand slid around her waist, pulling her against his hard body. He lowered his face until she could feel his hot breath on her lips. Holy mother of God, she couldn't breathe.

"What...?"

"Helping you relax," he said with a sinful curve to his lips before he slanted his beautiful mouth over hers in a deep, sensual kiss.

The first stroke of his tongue took her from shocked to *whoa, this is nice.* The next catapulted her from *nice* to she had no idea what, because her brain stopped functioning. His lips were soft, the kiss was hard, and he explored her mouth like he owned it, sending spirals of ecstasy whizzing through her. She'd forgotten what it felt like to be kissed *for real*, not as part of a scene, and oh Lord, did she want more. She went up on her toes, trying to intensify the kiss, completely unaware that the elevator had come to a stop on Abe's floor. Grayson stepped back, his hand still a searing heat at her waist.

"Better?" *Calm. Cool. Collected.*

So unfair.

She lifted a hand to her tingling lips. "Mm-hm."

As the doors began to close, he held them open. She wished he'd let them close and would kiss her again. He brushed the pad of his thumb just below her lower lip, probably fixing the lipstick his incredible mouth had smudged. She had the crazy urge to lick his thumb. To pull it into her mouth and tease it with her tongue.

"I'll be more careful of your lipstick next time." The firm press of his hand on her lower back brought reality in again.

He guided her out of the elevator and down the hall on noodle-like legs. She stopped a few feet from Abe's suite to allow her synapses to begin firing again, as she remembered why she was there. When she'd called the resort and found out that Abe lived there, she'd been surprised to hear he had a round-the-clock nurse and failing health.

"What's wrong?" Grayson asked.

"I'm nervous. That was…" *Insane.* "Intense. And unexpected and probably inappropriate. But"—she motioned around his broad chest—"that's all your maleness coming out and trying to help. *I think.*"

"It was," he said easily.

Well, nothing like clarification. It would have been nice to hear something about how *maybe it had started that way, but…Ugh! Okay, so you're not interested in me? Do you exude sex and desire around all of your friends?* She shook her head to try to focus on why she was there. What if Abe refused to see her? What if he yelled at her? What if he said horrible things about Bert? But Grayson was too distracting, and all her thoughts tumbled out.

"I've met with high-powered filmmakers, directors, and producers, and I'm even more nervous meeting Bert's brother. Abe despised him, and I don't know what to expect, or if he even knew about our relationship. How could he? Bert said they hadn't spoken in forever. And I'm rambling. I've already told you all this. And you kissed me. You kissed me like…like…" *Shutupshutup!* "Nerves. Sorry."

Grayson placed his strong hands on her shoulders, and his piercing, confident stare silenced the voices in her head. She waited with bated breath for him to rescue her. To say she didn't have to do this so she could run back into the elevator, maybe steal a kiss *or fifty*, and hole up in her house again until she forgot about seeing Abe altogether. Why, oh why, did

Grayson make her feel like she could let down her guard? It was so much easier to push through everything when she was in *Parker* mode.

"You're doing this for Bert," he reminded her solemnly. "And you're doing this for yourself. You can do this, Parker, and I'll be right here by your side if you need me."

She wanted to kick him in the knees for not refusing to let her go through with it, but how could she when she'd insisted in the car that she needed to do this. When his hand found her back again and gave her a nudge toward the door, she forced herself to straighten her spine and told herself this was just another role. A role she'd brought on herself.

She slid a practiced smile into place as the door opened, revealing a tall, svelte, older woman with cold blue eyes.

"Yes?"

Parker had expected a plump, homely nurse, not a beautiful white haired woman with perfect makeup, wearing a tight black skirt and a sharp white blouse. Grayson's hand pressed a little more firmly on her back, and she was thankful for the support.

"Hi. I'm Parker Collins, a friend of Abe's brother, Bert Stein."

The woman didn't waste any smiles, or any breath, as she waited for Parker to continue speaking. Given her flat affect, Parker wondered if she'd even known Abe had a brother.

"Is Abe available?" She should have called, but she hadn't

expected there to be a guard nurse on duty.

"Please come in." The nurse stepped aside and waved toward a Victorian-style couch by the windows. "Have a seat and I'll see if he's available. Ms. Collins and…?"

"Friend," Grayson said casually, and guided Parker across the silent room. Long velvet curtains, an antique claw-footed desk, a Victorian-style armchair, and a grand piano gave the room a hands-off museum feel.

When the nurse disappeared behind two heavy wooden doors, Parker whispered, "Friend?"

"The focus shouldn't be on me. I'm here for you, not for him."

Her heart soaked that right in, a sliver of happiness to calm her worries.

The nurse took a long time before she returned, gracing them with the same icy expression.

"Mr. Stein will see you now, but he's had a long morning. Please keep it brief."

"Yes, of course. Thank you." Parker rose to her feet, but they refused to move.

"You've got this," Grayson said loud enough for only her ears.

His supportive hand returned to her back, and he guided her across the floor. He pushed open the heavy wooden door and stepped into the unusually warm room with her. Parker's eyes were immediately drawn to the frail old man lying in a hospital bed. She hesitated, her heart aching at his similarities to Bert. He had smallish eyes, a hawklike nose, and a sharp chin, but where Bert had been a bit plump and spry, even at eighty-six, Abe was all skin and bones. His knobby knuckles looked too big for his bony fingers. Compassion replaced her nervousness.

"Well? Are you going to come in or stand there all day?" Abe grumbled in a tone too demanding to have come from the ailing man before them.

"Yes, sorry," she said. The energy coming from Grayson was like that of a guard dog protecting his charge as they moved toward the bed, beside which medical machines silently displayed numbers and graphs.

"Mr. Stein, I'm Parker Collins, a friend of Bert's. Or I was. I'm so sorry for your loss."

His gray-blue eyes shifted toward her, stopping short of where she stood. His sparse white brows drew into an angry slash. "I didn't lose anything."

She wondered if he was lucid and worried he'd misunderstood what she'd said. "Maybe you aren't aware that your brother Bert passed away?"

He waved a frail hand and scoffed. "I know that."

Her stomach plummeted at his rancor. *So you're just a jerk?* Grayson's jaw clenched.

No one said this would be easy. Thinking of Bert, she forced herself to continue speaking. "I know you two didn't get along, but—"

"Who were you to *him*?" He clutched the blanket in fisted hands.

His use of *were* gave her chills, but the way he snarled after growling the word *him* made him look less like a grumpy old man and more like the Big Bad Wolf. Families didn't hate this deep. They couldn't. It wasn't natural. She debated walking out and forgetting the whole thing, but Grayson's hand pressed against her back, and she drew strength from his support, forcing herself to try again.

"We were very close. He helped me get started as an actress." She blinked away the frustration and grief simmering inside her and added the most meaningful part of their relationship, hoping Abe might soften. "We were like family."

"Family," he mumbled, turning away and chewing on the word, as if it tasted foul. "I had family once. If you and Bert were like family, I pity you."

Tears of anger burned her eyes. She couldn't believe this bitter man was related to the loving, kind man who had been her most cherished friend for the last decade. Grayson stepped forward, and she reached for his hand, giving him an *I've got this* look, which paled in comparison to the turbulent expression he threw back as his fingers curled around hers.

She took one last stab at civility. "I would like to talk, to understand what went wrong. Maybe we can get through it, if you'll just give me a few minutes. Then I'll get out of your way."

"Who says you're in my way?" Abe snapped. "Christ Almighty, you kids think you can waltz into someone's life and *change* it? What makes you think I want to get *through* anything?"

Grayson squeezed her hand, drawing her attention. The slant of his eyes, the firm set of his jaw, and the angry tilt of his head told her he wanted to slay the old man, but he wouldn't. He was silently asking for her approval. That touched her deeply. He'd not only volunteered, but he had pushed his way into coming with her, and he wanted to step up to the plate *for* her? She didn't even know how to process his selflessness.

She mouthed, *It's okay.* His eyes narrowed, shifted to Abe, and he remained silent, giving her the courage to keep going.

"Bert was a wonderful, warm man, and I cared about him very much." Parker's voice shook. *So much for years of acting.* She was failing miserably. Probably because she wasn't acting. This was real. This was for Bert. "You missed out on so many years together. I wanted to share some of that with you."

Abe Meaner-than-a-Snake Stein waved his gnarled hand again. "*Pfft.*"

"Hey," Grayson snapped. "She's come all this way to talk to you. The least you can do is treat her with respect."

"Grayson!" she said in a harsh whisper.

Abe lifted his chin in a silent grimace for an interminable

moment. Parker was sure her heart was going to beat right out of her chest.

Just when she was ready to walk out the door, Abe turned toward them and said, "Noted."

She didn't know what to make of that, but her nerves were fried, her patience was gone, and she was sure she'd made a huge mistake.

"I'm sorry to have bothered you." She turned to leave. *I need another calming kiss. Stat!*

"Tomorrow," Abe said firmly. "Same time."

She turned and gaped at the old man. "I'm here *now*."

This time Grayson was the one who shook his head, warning her into silence.

"Tomorrow," Abe repeated. "Don't be late."

CHAPTER FOUR

IT TOOK A colossal effort for Grayson to hold his tongue as he and Parker left Abe's suite and headed for the elevator. Parker was visibly shaken, but she kept her game face on much better than he did. Grayson clenched his teeth so hard he was afraid they'd crack, hoping to remain silent long enough to calm himself down before he cursed a blue streak and told Parker what he really thought of Bert for leaving the letters that led her here.

The second the elevator doors closed, Parker grabbed his face and pulled him into a scorching-hot kiss, turning all that anger into white-hot desire. He backed her up against the wall, pressing his hard frame into all her supple curves. She clung to the back of his neck, filling his lungs with her sexy moan and setting loose all the pent-up lust he'd been holding back. His hands moved over her hips, around her waist, up her back, earning another sexy sound that brought his mind to dark, erotic places. He rocked his hips against her, and when her nails dug into his flesh, it yanked him from his steamy fantasies. She felt so good, tasted so sweet. He wanted her now, here. He wanted more of her, more than he'd ever wanted from any woman before, because beneath his hunger for sex and seduction was the passion to protect her with everything he had. She was vulnerable, sad, and angry, and he couldn't take advantage of that; he had to protect her from himself. Now.

He drew back, kissing her more tenderly, and finally, reluctantly, pulling his mouth away completely. She pressed her fingers harder against the back of his neck.

"Kiss me, Grayson," she pleaded.

The ache in her voice shot straight to his heart, shredding his control, and he claimed her again, deeper, harder, wanting her to feel what he felt for her, setting free ten months of pent-up emotion.

When the elevator stopped, he reluctantly pulled back again. Parker's eyes fluttered open, and he couldn't look away, wondering what had caused the unexpected—and exquisite—assault.

She cleared her throat, fidgeted with her blouse, her shorts, tucked her hair behind her ear, and when the elevator doors opened, she said, "That should help you relax."

Holy fucking hell, was she for real?

He matched her quick pace as they crossed the lobby. "Is that what that was?"

"Uh-huh." Her eyes remained trained on the doors as they pushed through and stepped outside. "Wasn't that why you kissed me?"

It had started out that way, but he'd enjoyed every second of it.

She slipped on her sunglasses, walling off her emotions, and motioned to the valet. Damn, he should have taken care of that, but his blood was still pooling below his belt.

The hot afternoon sun had nothing on the charged sexual tension sparking between them as they waited in heated silence for the valet to bring her car. He was acutely aware of the leers from nearly every male on the premises. Jealousy clawed at him, an unfamiliar and frustrating emotion, but hell if he could do a damn thing about it. He struggled to tune out the ogling men, fighting the urge to claim her with another flaming kiss, because if he did, he was afraid he wouldn't stop there. It didn't help that she kept touching her lips, as if she was battling the same excruciating resistance. He shoved his hands in his pockets to keep them from acting on their own. If only he could turn his brain off, too.

When the valet brought the car, he whipped out his wallet and handed him a few bucks, then opened the passenger door and motioned for Parker to get in. When she didn't, he removed her sunglasses so he could see her eyes—which were so full of lust it nearly stole his voice.

"You're safer with my hands and mind occupied."

Her breath *whooshed* out. "I...Um..."

He guided her into the seat and closed the door, wondering how he'd resist her when they got *out* of the car.

PARKER'S MIND SPUN. She'd kissed Grayson in the elevator to calm her nerves as much as his, because he'd looked like he was ready to blow and she'd been on the verge of exploding with disappointment and anger. But after a second, as with their first kiss, she'd stopped thinking at all and had succumbed to the greediness burning inside her, taking as much of him as he was willing to give.

On the way back to Wellfleet, his eyes were trained on the road, giving her a moment to really look at him. His thick, inky black hair looked finger-combed. The muscles along his chiseled jaw jumped to a frantic beat. His sleeves strained across his rigid biceps. He held the steering wheel so tightly his knuckles blanched. He was so different from the men she knew. Actors tended to be slimmer all over, less masculine, prettier. There was nothing *pretty* about Grayson. Even his name was rugged. On looks alone, he was all sharp edges and bulbous, hard muscle. But she'd already gotten a glimpse of his tender side, and when he spoke to her, there was nothing rough about his rich, soothing voice. Like the emails he'd sent her, every word felt important, made just for her.

His eyes darted to her, catching her staring.

"You okay?" He looked at the road again.

Um, not really. "Sure."

"What's going on in your pretty head? Just spit it out. It's better that way."

"I wasn't…I don't…"

"You were, and you do," he said with an air of seductive authority.

"Fine," she snapped. "I was admiring you. Okay?"

His lips curved up in a gratified smile. "Fine with me."

"Of course it is. Just tell me this—do you kiss all your friends?"

He shrugged and shifted a brief, serious stare to her before returning his attention to the road. "Don't you?"

Unexpected disappointment gripped her. "No, I don't kiss all my friends. Not that I have that many, but…No. That's weird. Why would you do that?" She should shut up, but her brain was spinning and her pulse was racing, making it impossible for her to keep anything inside. "That felt like an intimate kiss. A lover's kiss, not a friendly kiss. I don't even kiss like that when I'm acting."

He chuckled, which infuriated her.

"You're *laughing* at me?"

"Relax," he said so casually she wanted to slap him.

She was too busy fuming over the idea of him kissing other women to say a word.

"You never asked *how* I kiss my friends."

She scoffed but couldn't suppress her relief. "You're an

ass."

"Probably. If you're asking if I kiss my friends the way I kissed you, the answer is no. That was a kiss reserved for only my *special* friends."

She rolled her eyes. "Of which you probably have a harem."

He opened his mouth to respond, and she held up her hand, silencing him.

"Don't say a word. I don't want to know."

He shrugged again. "You did great in there with Abe, by the way."

"Why didn't you stop me from going in?" *I hate the idea of you kissing other women!*

"Because you *needed* to do it."

"Right." He had no idea what she needed; that much was clear. "There is no way I'm going back tomorrow. That was so stressful. No stinking way. Never."

"Yes, you are. Tomorrow, same time, just as he asked."

"No, I'm not. You don't know me very well yet. I'm *not* going back."

"I know you well enough."

She picked that apart as they drove back to her house. He had gotten a pretty blatant glimpse of her losing her mind last night, but that didn't mean he *knew* her. And she'd told him about Bert, and he knew she had a big slobbery dog, which not many people knew. But that wasn't really knowing her, either, was it? She cringed inwardly, recalling that he'd also seen her morph into her actress persona. Okay, so maybe he'd gotten a fairly good glimpse at parts of her, but still. He didn't *know* her.

He pulled the car into the garage, and before she could gather her thoughts, and her bag, he opened her door and offered a hand to help her out. The designs he'd had with him earlier were in his other hand. She'd totally forgotten about them.

She looked at his outstretched hand, realizing she was as attracted to the gentleman in him as she was to the stubborn guy who'd jumped in her car and the possessive man who'd taken her in that incredible first kiss in the elevator and pressed her against the wall. *Oh, that was nice. You felt so goo—*

He took her hand and pulled her to her feet. "Friends help friends from cars. You overthink everything, don't you?"

"No." *You just get me all hot and bothered.* She snagged the keys from his hand and unlocked the door to the house, hoping he couldn't tell that she was still having trouble cooling her jets.

Christmas *woofed* and bounded over. She loved him up, kissed the center of his big head. He pushed from her hands and lunged at Grayson. Grayson laughed as Christmas's paws landed on his chest. Why did seeing him with her dog make her heart go all sorts of crazy?

"Hey, buddy. I missed you, too." He let Christmas lick his

face, and her heart melted even more. Christmas gave him one last lick and trotted out to the yard.

Grayson followed her into the house. "Overthinking. That's why you're always making design changes. It'll hold you back."

"Like you know anything about that?" She wasn't about to admit she'd constantly made changes so she could read more of his thoughts on designs and the process he went through to come up with the final products. Or that when he wrote about his family, every word seemed like it came straight from his soul. No way was she going there. Their emails felt intimate in ways she was embarrassed to admit.

He arched a brow. "Overthinking?"

"Being held back," she clarified. There had been a brief time, as a teenager, when she'd been bitter and angry and wanted someone to blame for her landing in foster care. But there was no one to blame but Mother Nature. Eventually she'd moved past those ugly emotions and realized that at least she hadn't been born to a drug addict who lived on the streets. But she heard a hint of that bitterness in her tone now, and it made her sick to her stomach.

She put down her bag, and when she turned, she smacked into his chest. His enticing scent filled her senses, making her even more aware of just how many things she liked about him. "Sorry."

"I'm not."

"No. I mean…" *You're not?* That made her falter. "I meant I'm sorry for snapping at you. I'm edgy because of Abe. I wish I could just forget that he was Bert's brother and move on, but I can't. He's so unlike Bert that it's hard for me to remember they're family. But they *were*, and the things he said pissed me off. I didn't expect to get so upset." She closed her eyes and breathed deeply.

"Don't overthink it," he said with the same calm confidence he seemed to do everything—except when it came to protecting her around Abe.

Or kissing me.

"You're doing something that means a lot to you," he reminded her. "But that doesn't mean it means a lot to him. It'll take time to break through to him, but you need to try."

"Why should I bother?" She wasn't sure she could go through another visit.

He looked at her for a long moment, holding her steady gaze before answering. "Because you care."

He said it like it was a fact, and he was right. She'd never forgive herself if she gave up now, but that he knew that momentarily bewildered her.

"I'm going to leave these design ideas for you to look over." He set the drawings on the counter. "Just give me a holler when you're ready to talk about them."

"You're leaving?" She sounded as panicked as she felt. She was used to him being there, distracting her from missing

Bert. And, okay, she liked him. A lot. *A whole lotta lot.*

He cracked a sexy smile that went all the way up to his eyes and simmered. "I do have a life."

"Oh, right." She waved a hand, feeling like an idiot. "Of course you do. I'm sorry. I'll look these over and give you a call."

"Great." He turned toward the door, and the pit of her stomach sank.

When he turned back, hope sprouted in her chest.

"I know you're going to overthink the whole Abe thing again, so I'll say it once more so you don't have to. We're going back tomorrow because Bert was important to you, and you'd never forgive yourself if you didn't at least try to fix their mess."

She crossed her arms and lifted her chin, pretending he hadn't nailed her with his assessment. "You think you know me so well."

He shrugged again, apparently his go-to answer. Or maybe it was his way of letting her know she'd never really given him the chance to get to know her, which stung, because in all those months they'd been emailing, she'd absorbed everything he'd given—which was a lot—and she'd closed off her most intimate secrets.

"You think you're so smart, all stable, and wise, and in control." *And able to leave so easily. Shutupshutupshutup.* She tried to laugh it off, as if she were teasing, but she didn't want him to leave her alone in that big, empty house. And she didn't want to go back and see Abe tomorrow. But he was right. She was going to, come hell or high water. No one had ever read her so clearly, except Bert, which made her even more anxious. But she couldn't tell him all those things now. He had a life.

"Don't you ever crack?" she asked more calmly. "Stumble? Drink too much and wake up not knowing how you got in your bed?"

He sighed, his massive pecs rising and falling and making her stupid mouth water. He slid one hand casually into his pocket and rolled his shoulder back, looking at her with a careful gaze. "It must be hard trying to figure out who you are."

"What's that supposed to mean?"

He shrugged again. Of course he shrugged, goddamn him.

"Give me a call or shoot me a text if you want to go over the designs."

Christmas came through the door again, and Grayson crouched to let him slurp his entire face. She wished she didn't love that so much. And why did it make her a little jealous?

"See ya, buddy." He gave Christmas one final pet, then pinned Parker with another sinful look that made her lips tingle. "*I* carried you up to bed, right after you started to take your clothes off."

He disappeared into the garage, leaving her in another panic, wondering what else she'd done last night.

CHAPTER FIVE

GRAYSON LEANED OVER a drawing table at Grunter's studying the design for the Texas office of the Collins Children's Foundation. During the weeks of Parker's radio silence, he'd completed designs for the two remaining sites, but he needed her approval on both the site designs and the railing before he could begin work. He'd come to Grunter's to try to distract himself from thoughts of her, but here he sat, replaying every word they'd said, feeling her lush curves against him, seeing the look in her eyes when he'd finally found the strength to haul ass out of her house. He'd had a hell of a time leaving, but the fierceness that burned through them like an electric current every time they kissed made it nearly impossible to break the connection. If he'd stayed, he wouldn't have been able to keep from taking more, and as much as he wanted her, she was still his client and she was dealing with some heavy shit. He needed her to have a clear head before he allowed himself to get lost in her. Plagued by a full-on mental Parker Collins invasion, needing her approval to move forward professionally and wanting it to move forward personally, he was damn near worthless.

Hunter barreled out of the office in a fit of laughter, with Clark, their business manager, on his heels. He and Hunter had grown up with Clark, and after college they had hired him to run the business. Grayson counted himself lucky to do what he loved, with people who meant the most to him. They got into each other's faces sometimes, took each other for granted, gave each other shit. But that was part of any family. His mind traveled back to Parker, who had never known the love and loyalty that usually came with family. And yet she'd taken it upon herself to teach a bitter dying man the value of family. The knot in his gut tightened.

Clark hiked his thumb over his shoulder. "I'm heading out for the night. Got a date with my gorgeous wife." Last summer Clark and his wife, Nina, had gone through a rough patch. Thankfully, they'd found their way back into each other's arms.

Grayson forced himself from his sour mood long enough to say, "Enjoy, buddy."

Hunter peered over Grayson's shoulder. "That for the foundation or for Parker's house?"

"Foundation. Texas site." Hunter and Grayson had both been awarded the contract last summer, but Hunter had just fallen in love with his fiancée, Jana Garner, who had been opening her own dance studio at the time. Grayson had taken on traveling for the project so Hunter could remain on the

Cape with Jana. Parker had arranged for a smithy—a workshop—for Grayson to use near each of the sites, but there was nothing like working in the shop he and Hunter had renovated with the help of their eldest brother, Pete, and their good friend Blue Ryder, both skilled craftsmen.

"What are you going for?" Hunter asked. They were both stubborn, talented designers. Hunter was known for his ability to create intricately detailed sculptures, while Grayson made his mark with larger, bolder statements of architectural art, like railings, gazebos, furniture, and hibachis that were sold all over the Cape.

"I'm not sure. The Texas office is purely minimalist." Grayson ran a hand through his hair and looked up at his brother. He and each of his three brothers were tall, dark, and athletically built, but people often mistook Hunter for his twin. Hunter hated that, since he had a few years on Grayson, and Grayson had a hard time seeing the resemblance, given that Hunter wore his hair shaved military short, giving him a harder look than Grayson. Grayson had nothing but respect for his brother, so he chose to take the remark as a compliment.

"Minimalist? You need me in on this one. Shove over and let me in there." Hunter elbowed him out of his chair, which he gladly gave up. He was too restless to draw anyway. Plus, Hunter was better at finite details.

Grayson paced, thinking about the woman he was trying

so hard not to think about.

"How'd it go with Parker this morning? Did you nail down the designs for her railings?" When Grayson didn't respond, he said, "Bro?" a little louder.

"Huh?"

Hunter's face split into a knowing grin. "You want to nail Parker, don't you?"

"*Christ*, Hunt." He scrubbed his hand down his face, hoping to erase his confirmatory smile. Yeah, he wanted to get closer to Parker, but *nail* sounded wrong when connected with her. It was too cold, too harsh, and not at all indicative of the emotions he'd been feeling lately—or over the past few months.

Hunter crossed his arms over his chest, still grinning like an asshole. "That's it, isn't it? You're totally into her. Damn, Gray. All this time I thought you were frustrated because she was always changing her mind."

"She can be a pain in the ass when it comes to design decisions, but so are tons of clients," he said in her defense.

"And?"

"And she's going through a tough time." He told Hunter about Bert and the situation with Abe.

"So put the old bastard in his place. Make him be civil," Hunter said. "It's not like you to let a woman deal with that shit."

"Can't." Grayson leaned against one of the workbenches

and crossed his arms, mirroring his brother's posture—another Lacroux trait, tying down the arms that wanted to hit something. "She needs to do this. I'm going with her, and if it gets out of hand I'll step in. But I can tell this is something she needs to know she handled on her own."

"Does *she* know that? Because women send all sorts of silent messages we're supposed to pick up on."

"I see Jana's trained you well," Grayson teased. Jana was every bit as stubborn as his brother, and somehow they made the perfect couple. He'd never seen Hunter happier or more at ease than he'd been since he and Jana had come together. "I don't know if she realizes it yet, but she will."

Grayson and Hunter's phones vibrated at the same time. They whipped them out and said, "Pete," in unison, then read the group text. *The Beachcomber tonight? Seaside gang has babysitters.*

Pete and his wife, Jenna, owned a year-round bay-front home as well as a summer cottage in the Seaside cottage community where Jenna had spent summers since she was young. She and her friends from the community each had their own families now, and they still spent summers in Seaside. Over the years the Lacrouxs had all become enmeshed in their close-knit group.

"Hell, yeah. Jana's been wanting to go out." Hunter lifted his eyes to Grayson. "You in?"

The Beachcomber was a waterfront restaurant and bar, the

perfect place for Parker to chill out and let go of all the stress she was dealing with. Grayson wasn't about to let her hide away in that big house on the bay. Not when he wanted to help her get through her grief and come out on the other side just as whole as she'd been when Bert was alive. Knowing his warm, funny friends would take to her as quickly as he had only made him that much more determined. Parker needed him. She just didn't know it yet.

"Oh yeah," he said to Hunter. "*Plus one.*"

PARKER TRIED EVERYTHING to keep herself from thinking of Grayson, but she was beginning to think there was no distraction big enough for the job. It had been easier when she was on location filming for twelve hours a day, when she couldn't see his face, fall under the spell of his rich, sexy voice, or get lost in his eyes, which said he wanted to take her and take care of her in equal measure. She'd already gone for a walk on the beach with Christmas, which had been a good distraction for a while. Her curious dog had decided to chase a bird. He'd broken his leash and scared five families by barreling over their towels and knocking over their umbrellas. By the time he'd finally given up on the bird, Parker had apologized a dozen times, signed a few autographs, and sworn she was going to kill her dog. But when Christmas ambled back to her, his tongue lolling out the side of his smiling mouth, murder went out with the tide. She'd fallen to her knees and chided him as any good mom would, then loved him up, getting nice and sandy with him. Once the families he'd scared saw how sweet the big oaf was, they'd also wanted to give him love, which Christmas soaked up, and Parker did, too.

She'd showered and changed into a pair of old cutoffs and her comfiest black tank top with graffiti-style writing that read, MUSTACHE RIDES $5. A leftover from her teenage foster care days, it had been washed so many times it was soft as butter. She'd bought it for a buck at a consignment shop after being caught in a downpour, and together with her favorite shorts, she was wearing the perfect outfit for another night of horror movies and junk food.

She'd wandered through the house, sat on the deck, and looked over the designs Grayson had drawn up, which, as expected, were gorgeous. *Like him.* That thought had sent her reeling back to their mind-blowing kisses—and she'd been stuck there ever since.

Now she was camped out on the media-room floor, consuming mounds of candy and determined to get through at least four horror movies. She wasn't overly sad, but she was nursing a pretty strong bout of jealousy over Grayson and his very full life that didn't include her. Chicken dog was sleeping with his head beneath a pillow. She was halfway through *A*

Nightmare on Elm Street and three-quarters of the way through a giant bag of pretzel M&M's. She'd have to spend a month getting back into shape before her next film, which reminded her that she needed to call her agent, Phillipa Grace. She picked up her cell and scrolled through the messages. Phillipa had left more messages than an obsessive teen, and by the multitude of messages from Luce, it appeared Phillipa had pulled her public-relations rep into her obsessive loop.

She sent Luce a quick text. *Still alive. Missing Bert. Have my back for a while? I promise to behave.*

Luce texted her back immediately. *Always. Want to talk? Get loaded? Pretend you're normal for a while?*

She smiled at Luce's response. She always knew exactly what Parker needed. And now Parker felt guilty, because she'd told Grayson she didn't have anyone, and that wasn't really true. She'd just been too upset to think straight. If she had one true friend who would tell off someone or hold her while she ugly cried, it was Luce. They didn't see each other that often, since Luce split her time between California and New York, but Parker knew Luce would come running if she asked, just as she would for her.

She sent Luce a reply—*I'm in Wellfleet. Already got loaded. Knee-deep in pretending. Thank you. Will call when I'm sane.*

Scrolling through her contacts to Grayson's number, she hovered her thumb over the green phone icon. She'd looked over the designs and debated using them as an excuse to call.

Nearly everything he did threw her for a loop, from his caring nature to his unwillingness to let her go see Abe by herself. She'd felt his mounting tension as Abe became more and more disrespectful, and when Grayson had finally snapped on her behalf, her first reaction had been to stop him, which she'd acted on solely because she'd been groomed by the industry to nix anything that could tarnish her reputation. That had never been a problem before. The guys she knew had reputations to think about, images to protect, and they'd never put that at risk. Grayson didn't seem to worry about any of that. She wasn't used to selfless people, which made it a little harder to accept him at face value. But the more time she spent with him, the easier it became.

Grayson had already put her ahead of himself in so many ways it blew her mind. And she was surprised at not only how good it felt to be protected like that, but also by how much she enjoyed being with him. He was stubborn and defiant, but so casual about that defiance, she found it alluringly seductive. She wished he were there now, but apparently she was the only one without a busy social calendar. She'd been careful over the months they were emailing not to ask if he had a girlfriend, telling herself it was to keep from having to share the details of her nonexistent private life or her past, but she knew better. She hadn't wanted to think about him with any other woman. But after those kisses, how could she not? He said he kissed his special friends like he'd kissed her.

And he *had a life.*

If he has a girlfriend, then he shouldn't have kissed me at all.

She set the phone down, tapping a frustrated beat with her foot. He was probably out on a date right now, kissing some other *special friend.* She shoved her hand in the M&M bag and put a fistful of the crunchy treats into her mouth. Staring at the movie, she tried to get into it again, but all she saw was Grayson's dark eyes and his scrumptious lips as they came down over hers. She rested her head back against the couch and groaned. Christmas's head popped up from beneath the pillow with a whimper. He licked her arm and scooted closer.

"I can't bury everything in candy, can I?"

He cocked his head to the side.

"Yeah, I know. This new habit of mine is pretty sucky. Bert wouldn't want me to be this person for much longer." She knew Bert would understand her need to grieve, but she could picture him standing before her now, his hands perched on his hips, shaking his head. *This is no kind of life for you,* he'd probably say. He was forever trying to get her to go out with other people her age. But she had a hard time relating to most of them. So many were materialistic or only interested in gaining press—bad or good. She hated the paparazzi that seemed to be everywhere back home, which was probably one of the biggest reasons she liked staying in, or visiting with Bert, where she could be herself without worrying about what anyone else thought. Which, she realized, was something she really liked about Grayson, too. He was so real and so confident in who he was. It made her long to be Polly even more than she ever had.

Christmas *woofed* and darted out of the room, startling her from her thoughts. The dog must have selective supersonic hearing, because he hadn't heard Grayson last night until he'd appeared in the room. She turned off the movie, grabbed another handful of M&M's, and shoved them in her mouth for the walk upstairs. *Dinner of champions.*

She found Christmas standing on his hind legs looking out the sidelight window by the front door, whimpering.

"More birds?" She cupped her hands and peered out the other sidelight. She couldn't see anything in the dark yard, so she nudged past Christmas and peered out that window. Grayson smiled back at her. Her heart—and her dog—went a little crazy as she threw open the locks and the door. Christmas barreled headfirst into Grayson's crotch.

"Whoa, hey, buddy. Careful there." He redirected Christmas's snout, eyes on Parker. "Hey. Sorry I didn't call first."

"Seems like a habit." *One I'm beginning to like.*

Christmas's giant paws inched up Grayson's stomach to his chest, and he licked Grayson's face. She wanted to shove her pup out of the way and take a turn climbing—*and tasting*—Grayson. But she was frozen in place, watching Grayson's gaze drop to her mouth. Her lips tingled with anticipation. His gaze moved lower, lingering on her breasts and waking up *all* of her very best parts for the party.

Christmas ran into the yard, apparently having had his fill of Grayson. She was beginning to wonder how anyone could get their fill of him. Two tastes and he was almost all she could think about, which was perfect, because he provided a happy distraction to her grief.

He reached into his pocket and handed her a ten-dollar bill.

"What's that for?"

"Sweetheart, if you don't know, you probably shouldn't offer it up." He shoved the money into his pocket.

She followed his gaze to the words emblazoned across her chest and gasped.

"Ohmygod. I forgot I had this on."

"Were you expecting someone else? I can take off." He pointed to his truck in the driveway.

"No!"

He flashed a wicked grin and reached into his pocket again. "No?"

"No, don't leave. And no, don't...do *that* either."

His eyes darkened as he stepped closer. His thick, muscular arm circled her waist and tugged her against him. She. Couldn't. Breathe.

"Ah, a freebie. Nice." He nuzzled against her neck.

Oh, she liked that. Oh my...She halfheartedly tried to

push him away. He was an immovable wall of rock-hard abs and other lickable muscles she shouldn't think about. But she was. Constantly.

He brushed his thumb over her lower lip, sending delicious shivers of heat down her spine. Grayson held up his thumb, showing her the smudge of chocolate he'd wiped off, and made quite a show of sucking the sweetness from it. She wondered how many M&M's it would take to smear chocolate over her whole body.

"I see my chocolate girl is in full force tonight. It's a good thing I'm here to rescue you. Come on. We're going out."

Her mind was still a little fuzzy thinking about his mouth, and thumb, and just about everything else. "Out?" she said absently.

"Yes. Out. I can't let you sit around and eat junk food all night. The next thing I know, I'll be prying your mouth from a tequila bottle and carrying you up to bed."

Oh God, yes. Come right in. She gulped that thought down.

"And what kind of friend would I be if I made you sleep alone again? I'm not sure I could do that to a sweet girl like you."

Stumbling backward with the visuals *that* brought to mind, she pointed over her shoulder. "Let me get the bottle. Chocolate." *Ack! Shoot me now!* "I mean *change.*"

He laughed. "Don't change. You look gorgeous."

Her brain finally broke free from imagining him perched

above her, naked.

"I can't go out like this. I have to shower, put on makeup, do my hair. One cell phone picture will make someone a lot of money and make me seem like a skank."

"Where do you come up with this crap?" He whistled toward the yard, and Christmas bounded into the house.

Now she had another reason to admire him. "How'd you do that?"

"Don't change the subject. Come on, let's go."

Thinking of everything she'd have to do to prepare to be seen in public, and not in the mood for any of it, she said, "I really don't feel like going out. I'm watching *A Nightmare on Elm Street*. Come in and watch with me?"

"What is it with you and horror movies?"

She wasn't about to admit that she'd grown up using them to remind herself that she was brave and could get through anything—because sitting alone in the dark and watching bad things happen on television reminded her that there were worse things than not having a family.

Luckily, he didn't seem to expect an answer.

"Come on, Parker. You need to get out of your own head for a while."

"Maybe I do, but I don't want to spend the energy getting ready."

His tone turned serious. "Is that why you won't go out with me?"

"Wait. Are you asking me out on a date?" Maybe she'd reconsider. The time it took to shower and do her hair and makeup would definitely be worth a date with Grayson.

He was looking at her like he wanted it to be a date. "Do you want it to be?"

Yes. But I need time to get ready. Would he wait? Where did he want to go? How should she dress?

Suddenly his arm swooped around her waist and he hoisted her over his shoulder.

"Grayson! What are you doing?" She struggled as he closed and locked the door, holding her against his shoulder with one arm. Him and that damn key!

"You were overthinking," he said casually. "I told you it would hold you back. You need to stop doing that and cut loose a little."

"Put me down! I swear I'm going to kill you."

"No, you won't. That would *definitely* make the papers."

CHAPTER SIX

PARKER FELL SILENT halfway to the Beachcomber, arms crossed over her chest and an adorable pout on her lips, and she kept it up even as he parked. He knew she was worried about her image, and cell phone pictures, and whatever else went along with being a celebrity, but he wasn't going to let anything like that happen.

"Are you really going to make me go in there looking like this?"

"I wish you knew how beautiful you looked right now. I can honestly say that I've never seen you look prettier." He tucked a strand of hair behind her ear, wondering if she'd thought about him all afternoon, as he'd thought about her.

"Without all that makeup and your fancy clothes, you don't look like a famous movie star. You look like a gorgeous beach bunny who needs to have a little fun. I don't think anyone will recognize you."

She rolled her eyes and finally cracked a smile. "Beach bunny?"

He hadn't realized how much he wanted to see her smile

until this very second, and now he wanted to see her smile more often. "I'm better with my hands than words." He liked the spark of heat that brought to her eyes a hell of a lot, too.

"You're pretty great with words," she said softly. "Typed or spoken."

Her confession brought his own. "The truth is, the thought of you hiding out alone in that big house was killing me." He added the surprise in her eyes to the growing list of things he liked about her. "I'll be your bodyguard tonight, and I won't let anything happen. No pictures, no autographs. But I really don't think you have to worry. The bar's dark, and it'll be so crowded, you'll blend in. Trust me?"

"Trust a guy who hauled me over his shoulder and kidnapped me?" She looked toward the bar.

"Yeah, trust that guy."

"I do trust you." She poked him in his chest. "But if I end up on the front of some rag magazine, I'm hiding out in your basement. With Christmas, chocolate, and a boatload of horror movies that *you* have to watch with me."

"Sweetheart, if you move into my house, you won't be watching movies or hiding out in the basement. You'll be lucky if you make it out of the bedroom. In fact"—he slid his hand to the nape of her neck, causing her eyes to glaze over with desire—"maybe I should take a few of those pictures and *make* that happen." He'd taken a chance, saying something so brazen and holding her like this in the cab of his truck, but he couldn't hold back.

Her breathing hitched, and her lips parted, a whisper away from his, giving him the clue he'd been looking for. So tempting. Too tempting. He forced himself to step from the truck before he succumbed to the lust coiling deep inside him, and inhaled the brisk sea air. Focusing on the music coming from the building instead of the kiss he'd just given up, he helped Parker from the car and slid an arm around her waist. He wasn't about to take her out in public and not claim her as *his*. Confusion filled her eyes, and he couldn't be sure if it was from what he'd said, that he hadn't kissed her, or his arm around her waist, so he went with the lightest of the three as he found his way through his own tangled thoughts.

"Bodyguard, remember?"

Thankfully, she didn't fight him on it. They made their way to the rear deck of the Beachcomber, which was packed with scantily clad twenty- and thirtysomethings bumping and grinding to the beat of the band. Parker's movements were rigid, her eyes wide with worry.

He tugged her tighter against him. "I've got this."

She nodded and slipped her arm around his waist. *An added bonus.*

His eyes swept over the crowd, looking for signs of recognition, but while a handful of men were checking Parker out, there was no indication that they recognized her as *the* Parker Collins. He moved through the crowd with her safely against him, ignoring the women checking *him* out, and focused on keeping Parker comfortable.

"Gray!" Pete waved from a table across the room.

They made their way to the two large tables his friends had pushed together. His younger sister, Sky, leaped to her feet. Her fiancé, Sawyer, tugged her down for a kiss before releasing her to greet them.

"My fiancé is so needy." Sky hugged Grayson. "I'm so glad you guys came. Hi, Parker. I'm Sky, Grayson's sister, and the hot guy I was kissing is Sawyer."

"Nice to meet you. I've heard a lot about you." Parker waved to Sawyer.

Grayson arched a brow, wondering when she'd heard about Sky.

"In the emails," she reminded him. "You talked about her tattoo shop and a bonfire. Oh, and a birthday party for your niece, Bea."

While he tried to process the fact that she'd remembered those things from months ago, Sky pushed past him and hugged her.

"He's crazy for Bea," Sky said. "Where's your entourage?"

"She doesn't have one," Grayson said possessively. "Speaking of which"—he moved to the head of the table and motioned for his friends to lean in and listen—"Parker's going incognito tonight. Let's keep it that way."

Sky put her arm around Parker. "You're just one of the

girls tonight."

"Absolutely," Pete said with a nod. "Hey, Parker, I'm Pete, and this is my wife, Jenna. Bea's our little princess."

Jenna came around the table and squeezed her petite self between Grayson and Parker. "We know all about you, because Grayson's been working for CCF, and it's our job to be nosy. Let me introduce you to everyone or you'll be standing here all night." As the organizer of their close-knit group, Jenna loved to take control. "You know Hunter from the competition, and the woman hanging all over him is his fiancée, Jana." Jana waved. "The perky blonde and her surfer man across the table are Amy and Tony. The other blonde, currently kissing her husband, Caden, is Bella, our resident prankster."

"Prankster?" Parker asked.

"Don't worry," Leanna said. "She only pranks the property manager at our community, Theresa. Bella's scheming tonight, so you'll get a good dose of what it's like to live in her brilliant brain. I'm Leanna, by the way, and this is my husband, Kurt."

Kurt waved. "Nice to meet you, Parker."

"Leanna, you make jam, right? Grayson mentioned you had a new flavor out when I was filming. I had a few cases of Sweet Temptation delivered for the cast and crew. It was so good! It tasted like chocolate and strawberries," Parker said, stunning Grayson again with not only her recollection of his emails, but also that she'd bought Leanna's jams. "And, Kurt, I've read some of your books. You're an amazing writer. I hope they make *Bonds of Steel* into a movie."

"You and me both. Thank you," Kurt said.

"No shop talk tonight, remember?" Jenna said with a sweet but authoritative smile. "The two cuties whispering to each other at the end of the table are Jamie and Jessica Reed."

Jessica waved. "What's a mustache ride?"

Parker covered her shirt and glared at Grayson.

"Jessica, how about asking your man?" Grayson chuckled when Jamie flicked him the bird. In a more serious tone, he said, "I made her wear it. It's part of her disguise."

She could have thrown her arms around his neck and kissed him for that. Instead, she turned and mouthed, *Thank you.*

"Smart thinking," Bella said as everyone took their seats. "Heck, I'd wear that shirt."

"Not when I'm not around, you wouldn't," Caden said.

Grayson draped an arm over the back of Parker's chair, and she eyed the incredibly well-muscled limb.

He gave her shoulder a possessive squeeze. "Just go with it." He leaned closer and whispered, "Or I could start taking pictures and calling rag magazines."

Her eyes went wide, then filled with heat. *No pictures necessary.*

PARKER HAD BEEN nervous about all the wrong things when they'd arrived at the Beachcomber. She'd worried about having to deal with autographs and embarrassing attention in front of Grayson and his friends, when she should have been worried about not having any control over her emotions around *him*. Her pulse had been racing since he'd made the remark in the car about his bedroom, and every brush of his leg, every stroke of his hand, every heated innuendo, only made it worse.

She wasn't used to the rampant desires heating her up every time they were near each other. Between that and his innate understanding of exactly what she needed, like being out with his friends tonight, she felt even more connected to him than she had when they were emailing.

They'd been at the bar for a couple hours, but it hadn't taken long for Parker to realize that it was nothing like the clubs in Los Angeles and that Grayson's friends and family were polar opposites of most of the people she knew. They didn't dress to the nines or wear formfitting clothes that showed off their figures. The girls wore pretty summer dresses, skirts, or shorts, and the guys were wearing either jeans or shorts and T-shirts, save for Kurt, who wore a short-sleeved collared shirt. Parker didn't even feel out of place with her raunchy T-shirt and old shorts. But it wasn't just their warm welcome or casual attire that struck her. The thing that made the biggest impression was that they weren't hanging on to their cell phones like they were their lifeblood, or looking in mirrors every few minutes to make sure their hair and makeup was perfect. They were holding their significant others and gazing into their eyes, the way she'd always dreamed life should be.

"Hey," Grayson said. "You okay?"

"I'm better than okay. Thank you for kidnapping me. I needed this."

He leaned forward and pressed his lips to hers in a quick, unexpected, *and welcome*, kiss. "I know you did. No thanks necessary."

The quick kiss left her hoping for more. She was getting used to the way he took what he wanted and gave her exactly what she needed. Her eyes skirted around the table, and she was relieved to see the approving looks from his friends. They were all so close. It was no wonder he'd missed them when he was working on site for CCF. She recalled the day Grayson had accepted the contract, when he'd explained that he would be traveling and Hunter would be staying on the Cape for the sake of his new relationship. Parker had thought Hunter's decision to remain on the Cape with Jana was about the most meaningful gesture a man could make. She'd been so focused on Hunter's chivalric decision, she'd failed to realize just how big of a sacrifice it had been for Grayson to be away from the people he loved for so long. Seeing him with them tonight drove that point home, and she knew she'd had it all wrong. It wasn't Hunter who had made the most meaningful gesture. It was Grayson, and he'd done it for a different kind of love. He'd done it for his brother.

That realization opened her heart to him even more.

The girls broke out in laughter, and she realized she'd missed whatever had been said.

"Remember the summer we pulled a Thong Thursday prank at the pool?" Amy's blue eyes widened.

"Theresa got Bella good with that one." Leanna laughed and elbowed Bella, who rolled her eyes.

The girls had told Parker all about how they'd grown up together over the summers and how Amy and Tony had been a secret couple when they were teenagers. They'd gushed about their weddings and shared pictures of their babies, who were so cute they made her ovaries ache. They were so blessed, living the lives she'd always dreamed of.

Grayson's leg pressed against hers, drawing her attention back to him as his watchful eyes scanned their surroundings. He was taking his bodyguard duties quite seriously. He'd had his arm around her all night, and she'd let herself fall into the comfort of his touch and his attention. He'd leaned in a dozen times to ask her if she was having fun, offer her a drink, or make a comment.

She knew they existed in a bit of a bubble here on the

dunes with his friends and family, a world away from her real life. But she liked this bubble. She felt more like Polly tonight than she had in a very long time. Even more than when she was holed up in her house. Maybe even more than when she was with Bert, because Bert would have had serious issues with her leaving the house in the shape she had tonight, and Grayson had encouraged it. She wondered what Bert would have thought of the way Grayson had kidnapped her. She happened to love it, despite worrying about being spotted without her Parker face on.

The girls laughed again, and Parker realized she'd had Grayson on her brain again. He was talking with the guys, paying close attention to everything Jamie and Pete were saying. She liked seeing him in his world, with his friends. It was easy to see how important they all were to each other.

"How long are you in town?" Sky asked.

"I'm not sure yet, probably a couple of weeks." She wasn't in a hurry to rush back to California, which was surprising to her, given her tendency to keep herself too busy to think. She knew Luce would have contacted Phillipa to let her know she was okay, but she made a mental note to touch base with her agent after wrapping up her visit with Abe.

"Oh, good! Maybe you can visit me at my tattoo shop in Provincetown," Sky said excitedly. "I'd love to introduce you to my friend Lizzie. She owns the flower shop next door."

"That sounds like fun." Parker wondered if Sky sensed

how much it meant to her that she wanted to introduce her to her friend.

"Will Grayson be here that long, too?" Jana asked.

I hope so. She looked at Grayson, and the seductive look in his eyes told her he did, too, but she didn't want to appear possessive over a man who wasn't really hers. "I guess that's up to Grayson," she finally answered.

"Well," Bella said with a smirk. "Based on the smoke rising from that side of the table, I'd say he's staying however long you are."

Parker's pulse raced at the thought of Grayson's friends recognizing what she'd felt all along.

"Maybe he and the guys can get together and we can have a girls' day or something," Jana suggested.

"Yes!" Jenna said, and immediately launched into a discussion about potential outings.

"Careful," Leanna said to Parker. "Bella will have you married off before you even leave the Cape."

"Hey, I just call it like I see it," Bella said. "I can't help it if I'm always right."

Grayson squeezed Parker's shoulder, and in that moment she realized she'd made a mistake. She'd thought she was the only one who could read the interest in his eyes, but his gaze held all the confirmation *anyone* needed.

"Dance with me?" Grayson didn't wait for an answer as he rose to his feet, bringing her up with him, and sliding an arm around her waist.

There was barely room to move on the dance floor, but she didn't mind. She wound her arms around his neck, her fingers playing over his skin as they gazed into each other's eyes. She felt like she'd been waiting for this moment all her life. To be looked at the way Grayson looked at her, like he saw more than just a pretty celebrity. He made her feel special, precious, and cared for, when he checked in with her so often.

"Are you as okay as you appear, or is this an act?" His eyes held a tease, but she heard the seriousness of his concern in his tone.

"I'm not a good enough actress to fake how happy I feel," she admitted. "I needed this." *I needed you.*

"My friends can be a little intrusive. By the time we leave, they'll all have your phone number and will bug you the whole time you're in town."

His hand moved to the base of her spine, bringing their bodies together. He didn't move his body in an overtly sexual way, or leer like other guys often did. This didn't feel like a prelude to an expectation of more. Grayson moved sensually but carefully, as if he was enjoying their connection as much as she was and was in no hurry for it to end.

"They're wonderful. So that would be okay with me. And your brothers and sister are really great."

"They're pretty cool," he said casually, but she'd witnessed the way he lit up when he was teasing Pete and Hunter and how serious he became when their conversation turned to their father and worries of him working too hard. He'd gone just as serious when he'd asked Sky about her tattoo business, as if he were analyzing her answers, making sure she'd made good decisions.

She wondered if he'd kept tabs on Sky with calls, texts, or emails when he was traveling for CCF, reminding her again of all he'd given up for his brother's relationship.

"You'd like my other brother, Matt," he said. "He teaches at Princeton."

"You mentioned him in an email over the holidays. You're lucky to have so many people who love you. I don't really have that type of group to fall back on. I have Luce, my PR rep who also happens to be a good friend, but she has so many clients and she lives half the time in New York, so we don't see each other that often."

"I think you've got *them* now, too." He searched her eyes, and she wondered if he could see her holding on to that offer with hope that it was true, or if her burgeoning emotions for him were blocking sight of it.

"I can only imagine how hard it's been going through this alone," he said, holding her a little tighter. "When I lost my mom, I was terrified that I'd forget things about her. So I closed myself off, thinking I needed to focus all my energy on remembering her. Eventually I realized I could never forget her. She'd been too big a part of my life. I see traces of her in everything I do and say and feel."

"You really do get it." Her voice cracked with emotion. She couldn't imagine Grayson being afraid of anything, but the fear he described was so real for her, she knew he must have experienced it firsthand. "It's hard knowing Bert's no longer a phone call away." They were barely dancing now, lost in a world where only they existed.

"I really like you, Parker. You're funny, and smart, and trying so hard to be brave in the face of losing the person you loved most. We spent months getting to know each other, and I wish I'd known about Bert so I could have been there for you sooner. But I'm here now, and I want to get to know you better and be here for you. If you'll let me."

She struggled against the lump in her throat. She'd thought about being with him for so many months, wondering, hoping what she'd felt wasn't fabricated from loneliness. But she hadn't imagined she'd be dealing with losing Bert, or finding Abe and trying to find herself again at the same time. She couldn't believe he still wanted to be with her, given all that she was dealing with, when he could have any woman he wanted. She wasn't blind to the looks pretty girls had cast his way all evening, though he acted as though he was. He could have a life unencumbered by film sets and unwanted photographers. Her life was across the country, and she spent it moving from one film set to the next. She knew emails would never again be enough. She had been falling for him for months, and in just the last two days she'd fallen even harder. What would happen if she allowed herself to really get close to him? Tell him all her secrets, follow her desires and her heart?

"I can see you overthinking this," he said with a knowing smile. "If you're worried about us not knowing each other very well, we're getting to know each other better. That's what people do."

"This feels very far away from my real life," she said honestly. "I know that's a strange thing to say, but what you have here with your family and friends is beautiful and special, and it's very different from the world I live in." *But it's the life I've always wanted.* "My schedule is never mine, the way it has been here. I'm usually bogged down with meetings, films, or public-relations events."

"I realize this isn't what you're used to. But you're here now. You're living your life. For tonight, for now, this *is* your real life."

He moved his hands up to her neck, and his thumbs grazed her jaw like they had right before he'd kissed her in the elevator. Her body remembered, heating, melting, aching for his glorious mouth to claim her.

"You mean you want this for *tonight*? *Us* for tonight?" She didn't do one-night stands, and she didn't want to start. Not even for Grayson.

His eyes warmed. "I mean I want to spend time with you. Tonight. Tomorrow. A week from now. We can see what happens, let time decide what real life is for both of us."

"Grayson…?" She sounded as breathless as she felt.

"Let's not overthink this."

His mouth came coaxingly down over hers, and for a second panic stole through her. *Cell phone pictures! Rag magazines!* But those thoughts were no match for Grayson's kisses. She wanted this. His kiss, his touch, his caring, intense affection. For the first time since she'd lost Bert, she felt safe enough to let it all go and gave herself over to the sweet tenderness of their kiss.

CHAPTER SEVEN

LATER THAT EVENING Grayson pulled into Parker's driveway and cut the engine. "Why don't we let Christmas out and sit outside for a while? Unless you're too tired and would rather I went home?"

"Stay. That sounds great." She wasn't ready for the evening to end either. After they'd danced—and shared more magical kisses—they'd spent time with Grayson's family and friends. Parker was delighted when, as Grayson had anticipated, the girls wanted to exchange numbers. She was starting to think Grayson had some type of weird cosmic connection to her. How did he know they'd want to bring her into their circle?

Christmas smothered them with kisses before running off into the yard. Parker grabbed a blanket from the house, and they went out back and spread it over the grass by the edge of the bluff. Grayson put his arm around her and tucked her against his side.

"I heard Sky say we make a cute couple," he said casually. They hadn't been a couple when they'd arrived, but somehow, in the space of a few short hours, they'd become one. "Are you okay with that?"

She wondered how she could be sending vibes that told him she might *not* be okay with any part of this. "Are *you* okay with it?"

"What do you think?" He lifted her chin and pressed his lips to hers. "But you're pretty image conscious, and I don't want to screw anything up for you."

"Grayson, it's not that *I'm* image conscious. I'm conscious of my public image because I have to be. It's my career."

"So I'm learning. But that doesn't negate the fact that I don't want to screw things up for you."

"Well, that's really nice of you, but dating you can't screw things up for me, unless you have a torrid past you're not telling me about."

"No torrid past. I've never been a saint, but I wasn't a scoundrel."

"Then what's not to be okay with?"

He shrugged. "Just making sure. How about you? Anything in your past that might tarnish my reputation?"

"No. Embarrassingly, I've always been a good girl."

"I bet you have." He kissed her again, a little longer this time. "I'll never make fun of your goodness, but I might bring out your naughty side."

"How do you know I have a naughty side?" *Do I have a naughty side?*

"Just a sense I get, that there's a lot more to you than you let on."

There he went again, seeing her more clearly than anyone else ever had. Could he also see that she was nervous about what was happening between them?

"I haven't been in a relationship for so long," she admitted. "I don't know if I remember how." The sea air swept up the bluff, serenaded by the sounds of the bay. She soaked up the peacefulness of the evening and the pulse-quickening waves of anticipation for what was yet to come.

"I guess that makes two of us. We'll figure it out." He laced their fingers together and gazed out at the water. "Tell me about your relationship with Polly."

"Polly?" She couldn't hide the surprise in her voice.

"You mentioned her last night. You said, 'Parker can't do things like cry, or curse, or eat an entire jumbo bag of M&M's and watch horror movies until her eyes nearly bleed without being judged. Only Polly can do that.' I thought she might be your sister, but you said you had no family."

"I...She's..." She looked up at the starry sky, wanting not only to share her past with him, but also to climb out from under the weight of it. Before she could talk herself out of it, she said, "I'm Polly."

"Oh. Is Parker your stage name? Is that what they call it?"

She was shocked and relieved by his unfazed reaction to what felt to her like a *huge* reveal. "Yes. My real name is Polly

Collins. My agent said Polly was too 'Pollyanna.' 'Being Polly' means being a normal person without worries about paparazzi or bad press, being able to go out with friends like we did tonight, without constantly looking over my shoulder. Which, by the way, you were right about that place. It was dark, loud, crowded, and I totally blended in with everyone. But it's not like that where I live. Paparazzi come out of the woodwork back home, in the grocery store, restaurants, beaches. They're everywhere. I want to be Polly so badly sometimes I can't see straight."

She pressed her hand to her chest, breathing deeply. "Wow, it feels *so* good to say that out loud. I've spent my entire adult life pretending to be Parker and, for much of that time, wishing I could be Polly in public, even for a day."

"I really like this side of you, whoever you are right now. Polly, Parker, *Parky*. Yeah, maybe that's a better name for you."

"Do *not* call me Parky." They both laughed at that.

"Thanks for trusting me enough to tell me. I won't out you to the press."

She playfully nudged him with her shoulder. "You joke, but you have no idea what this feels like. Do you know how many people I've kept that from? Directors, producers, actors."

"And a lowly steelworker got it out of you," he teased.

"Lowly nothing. You're more talented at what you do than

half the actors I know are at acting."

He shrugged, a humble smile curving his lips.

"I'm telling you the truth. I created that two-year contract because you and Hunter are so talented. Your work is striking. When I saw the model of your gazebo, I wanted to climb inside it with a good book, a comfy blanket, and some chocolate and hunker down for a month."

"Then I'll have to build you one for the yard so you can do just that. And I'm pretty sure Christmas would be upset if you didn't hunker down with him." He put his cheek beside hers and said in a low whisper, "I might want to do some hunkering myself."

Yes, please. "Build me a gazebo and I might let you. Did you always know you wanted to work with metal?"

"I never wanted to do anything else, so I guess you could say that. My father owns a hardware store, and he didn't have much free time when we were growing up, but he made time to help us find hobbies we enjoyed. Probably to keep the chaos level down. I'm sure we were a handful. He built Sky a small shed that they made into an art studio. Bought Matt every book under the sun and taught Pete to refinish boats. It's a little embarrassing to admit, and if you ever tell this to Hunter I'll deny it, but I always thought Hunter was so cool, you know? He's always been a bit surly, rougher around the edges than Pete and Matt. He wanted to forge metal, and I pushed my way into the lessons."

"You're so confident. I can't imagine you thinking anyone is cooler than you. You were probably competitive and wanted to do it better than him."

He laughed under his breath. "That's probably what I should have said, but it wouldn't be true. He's my older brother. I looked up to him. Wanna know a secret?"

"Who doesn't love a juicy secret?" She loved these intimate glimpses into his youth.

"I still think he's pretty cool."

Hearing such a virile man admit something like that, she found him even more attractive. "And I had you nailed as such a tough guy."

Christmas ambled over and stretched out on the blanket by their feet. Grayson slipped off his shoes and rubbed his foot along the pup's fur. "I am tough."

"Yeah, I can see that," she teased.

"What? How can you resist him?" He leaned forward and petted Christmas's head.

"I can't." *Just like I can't resist you.*

GRAYSON DIDN'T KNOW what it was about Parker that made him feel like he wanted to tell her all his secrets, but the caring look in her eyes drew the truth right out of him.

"I've always played my cards pretty close to my chest, but

that's impossible when I'm with you. With you, I'm more like my mother was. She couldn't hide her emotions if her life depended on it, and you bring that out in me. No one has ever done that before."

"I think your mom would be happy that you're taking after her," she said sweetly. "You must miss her."

"I do. I miss a lot of things about her, like the way she'd hum when she was hiding something. She was terrible at keeping secrets, even about birthday presents. She'd nearly burst, wanting to tell us what they were." He smiled with the memory. "And her homemade steak pie, which sounds really bad, was delicious. But what I miss most is that feeling of walking in the door and seeing her face light up, even when I was a teenager and a pain in the ass. Or when I'd call her on the phone and hear a smile in her voice, you know? Like she could push aside the annoying things we did and see the good in us all the time."

Parker dropped her gaze. "I don't really know those feelings."

His chest tightened. "Were you very young when you lost your parents?"

"I never knew my father, and my mom was killed when I was a year old." She drew in a shaky breath. "We were driving across the San Francisco-Oakland Bay Bridge when that big earthquake hit. I don't remember it, of course, although I wish I could remember something about her. Anything, really."

"Oh, baby. I'm so sorry." He gathered her in his arms, the soothing sounds of the bay playing in the distance, conflicting with the rampant beating of her heart. "Was Bert a relative? Did he raise you?"

She shook her head and sat back, finally meeting his gaze. "They weren't able to track down any relatives, so I grew up in the foster care system. When I was sixteen I started working part-time as a bus girl in a diner, and that's where I met Bert. He came in every Sunday. When I graduated from high school, I went full-time. We had become pretty friendly by then, and I knew he was a photographer, and when he asked if he could take a few pictures of me, I agreed."

"You know how dangerous that was, right?"

She smiled, nodded. "Yeah. But Bert was in his seventies, and he was gay, so I was pretty sure he wasn't interested in getting me naked. We met at a park one afternoon, and he took some pictures. After that we talked more often, and a few weeks later he asked if I'd ever considered modeling, which was a world away from anything I'd ever thought about. I was thankful to have a job that paid enough to rent a room. Anyway, a few weeks after that he told me he'd shown the pictures he'd taken to his friend who was a modeling agent and asked if I'd meet him. I agreed, and a month later I was earning three times what I'd been making at the diner, but I hated modeling. I wasn't used to that kind of attention. It made me uncomfortable, being the sole object of the camera and having people touch me, position my body. I don't know…It was just not my thing."

Grayson tried to imagine her at eighteen, putting all her trust in Bert and jumping into an industry that carried rumors of trading sex for jobs. "You're really lucky Bert was an honest guy. I hope he took your discomfort to heart."

"I'm lucky he was honest *and* caring. He was a good man, and he treated me like a daughter. When I told him I didn't like modeling, he arranged for me to meet Phillipa Grace, another agent, and when I decided to give acting a shot, he paid for private acting lessons. He went with me to auditions, helped me run lines, and watched out for me. Phillipa is still my agent, and she's always been very good to me."

Grayson was beginning to understand her need to do for Bert what he never could. He'd been there for her in the most important ways a person could be. "Do you like acting?"

"The work? Yes. I grew up living with one foot out the door at all times, even though the families I stayed with treated me well. Stability was the unattainable dream. The brass ring. I was with my first family for three years, and for whatever reason, I went back into the system. A year later they found me another home, but that lasted less than a year, and the one after that wasn't much longer. You get the picture."

"I can't imagine what that was like." He pulled her closer again, needing the contact.

"When it's your life and it's all you know, you figure out

coping mechanisms without even realizing you're doing it. Like not getting too attached. But that's what's so great about acting. I get to slip into a life and pretend to be a cherished daughter, sister, or mother. It's like living out a fantasy. But I don't like all the stuff that comes with acting. There's no privacy back home, and despite the tequila I drank the other night, I'm not a party girl and I don't really *fit* into that world."

"Which is why Polly's the fantasy for you." He saw her so much clearer now. "And for most people, you're living their fantasy."

She nodded, and her eyes went serious. "Please don't think I'm not grateful for everything I have and every opportunity I've been given, because I am. I know how fortunate I am. My career allowed me to create the children's foundation and to give other kids whose lives feel unstable a chance to have something to hang on to, to look forward to amid the chaos of moving, of trying to fit in and make new friends."

Her voice rose with excitement and purpose. "I know it's not much in the grand scheme of things," she said. "But when you grow up in foster care, your next move is determined *for* you. You're moved away from kids you've gotten close to, who you care about. It's not a choice; it's a given. Through CCF we're giving those kids a chance to come back together with the kids they've spent time with, they've lived with, they've bonded with. Coming back to the same place with the same kids each year allows those early bonds to become stronger. It's a way to maintain the relationship with the scared girl who slept in the bed next to you for a year, or a month, or whatever. It's keeping those friendships alive instead of trying to forget them because some other kid will be in that bed tomorrow. And, of course, it takes all sorts of approvals, red tape, and money, and—"

"Parker." He was momentarily speechless, in awe of her strength and courage with all she'd gone through. And shocked that she was still able to trust so easily after such a rocky start to her life. She was not only unveiling her past, but she was revealing her generous heart, her hopes, and her dreams, trying to give others what she never had. He'd undervalued the foundation's mission, and he realized, not for the first time that day, how much he took for granted in his own life. She was giving him renewed appreciation for his loving family, and she increased his desire to help her find the stability she craved, and all the things she wished for others, for herself.

"Sorry. I'm rambling again," she said shyly.

"No, sweetheart." He held her gaze, scrounging for the right words. "You're passionate and inspiring and so incredibly strong you make me look weak. Jesus, Parker, how do you survive in Hollywood? How has some guy not fallen head over heels in love with you and swept you off your feet yet?"

He didn't wait for her answer, couldn't wait. He had too

many things he wanted to say. "I wish…I wish for so much it's hard to put into words. I wish you hadn't lost your mom and that you'd known your father. I wish Bert were still here for you, and for me, so I could thank him. I was pretty mad at him for leaving you the letters that led you to Abe, but he really was your *everything*. How can I be anything but thankful for a man like that?"

"He was the kindest man I'd ever met, until you. You're right up there with him."

He slid his hand beneath her hair, to the nape of her neck. "Knowing what Bert meant to you, that's the highest compliment I could ever hope for. I didn't understand CCF's mission before, but it all makes sense now. I get it, and I am so proud to be part of it."

"You don't have to say that just for me."

"Not for you. *Because* of you. You've opened my eyes. I want to be involved, Parker. With the foundation, and with you."

Heat pulsed in the space between them.

"Grayson…?" She reached for him as he leaned forward. Her eyes held the same wonder about what was happening between them as he felt.

"I feel it, too, sweetheart. I don't have the answers." This was new territory, combining want and need with a heart that never wanted to let her go. "But I don't want to fight what we feel."

Her breath whispered over his skin as he pressed a soft kiss to the swell of her upper lip, then the lower. Her eyes fluttered closed on a sigh of surrender, and he sucked her plump lower lip into his mouth. She tasted so sweet he went back for more, kissing her tenderly, again and again. *Slow, slow, slow,* he told himself, fighting the urge to take it deeper, to make her his in every way and wanting to savor every anticipatory breath, every touch, every breathy plea as it fell from her mouth.

Slow, slow, slow.

Tracing her lips with his tongue, riding the sweet curves to the corner, he kissed her there.

"Grayson," she whispered in a shaky breath.

The desire in her voice slithered under his skin and blazed straight to his core. He gathered her hair over one shoulder and dragged his tongue along her sensitive skin, pausing to press a series of kisses to the curve of her neck. She was breathing hard, her nails digging into his chest, as he placed openmouthed kisses along the base of her neck. He continued the tantalizing assault, savoring the rampant beat of her pulse against his tongue. She tasted of summer and sex and sweet goodness he never knew existed. In one swift move, he swept her body beneath him, cradling her head as he came down over her, reveling in the passion in her eyes, the feel of her soft curves beneath him for the very first time. She rocked against his arousal. Torture didn't begin to describe the torment of holding back, but it was exquisite torture. *Slow, slow, slow.*

"We're going to be so good together," he promised. "When we're ready."

A whimper escaped her, and he pressed his mouth to hers, holding back from deepening the kiss, because if he did, *slow* would turn *fierce*. He wanted fierce, but first…

"Tonight I'm going to kiss you until you can't feel your lips." His lips brushed over hers. "Until your body is weak with wanting and your mind is so full of us that you taste us tomorrow." He kissed her cheek, her neck, her jaw, and the air left Parker's lungs in another dreamy sigh. "Until kissing me is the only thing you can think about." He sealed his lips over her neck and sucked, earning a wanton moan. She arched against him, fisting her hands in his hair, testing his control.

"And then I'm going to kiss you some more." He slanted his mouth over hers and made good on that promise.

CHAPTER EIGHT

THE NEXT MORNING Parker awoke without the weight of grief making it hard to breathe. This she was sure of, because the tightness in her chest had begun much farther south. It had begun between her thighs, where she was damp and aching after dreaming of Grayson's mouth on her, and had traveled north until her whole body was strung tight with need. In her dream, his talented tongue had her at the edge of ecstasy, holding her there in tortured bliss—and that's when she'd woken up, hot and bothered and needing release. She slid her hand beneath the sheets, remembering her erotic dream, badly wanting to feel his mouth on her. She was slick with need just thinking of the way he'd kissed her last night. Hours of exquisite, languid kisses, on her neck, her face, her shoulders, her ears. He'd licked and sucked and kissed every inch of her skin from her shoulders up, never once going lower, and by the time he left she was boneless and numb and on the verge of an orgasm. And through it all he'd said the sweetest things, making her feel special and cared for. Even more so—she'd felt treasured and cherished, like she'd pretended to feel in some of her roles. She closed her eyes, remembering how it felt to have his weight bearing down on her, his hot, wet mouth sucking her skin, his words floating around her. She wanted to feel his strength and passion with nothing between them. She'd felt the girth of his erection last night, and now, as she remembered just how good his hard cock felt rocking against her center, she pushed her other hand beneath the sheets. One hand stroked the secret spot inside her, and the other teased the bundle of nerves she knew would send her over the edge. Oh, it had been a very long time since she'd pleasured herself, and even longer since she'd been with a man. It only took a minute before she felt the tease of an orgasm just out of reach. Gritting her teeth and arching against her hand, she was almost th—

Woof!

Her eyes flew open. Christmas was sitting on the floor with his snout on the bed, watching her. *Really?* She closed her eyes, trying to get back into the game, but now all she could hear was Christmas breathing instead of the sound of Grayson kissing her. She opened one eye.

"Go lie down," she coaxed.

He whimpered. She closed her eyes, hoping he'd go lie down. He whimpered again, and she reluctantly opened her eyes. *Ugh!* She righted her panties and threw off her covers, no match for his sad puppy eyes.

"I haven't had an orgasm in months, and you pick this

second to ask to go out?" She went downstairs and let him outside, and by the time she returned to the bedroom, the moment had passed. She needed a very cold shower. Ice cold.

Arctic.

She might need to take two.

She showered and dressed and put on her Parker Collins face, thinking more clearly than she had in weeks—and sexier than she had in...*ever*. She hadn't realized how consumed she'd become in wallowing and holing up. Bert wouldn't have wanted that. *She* didn't want it, and she was ready to finally take a step forward. With the plans Grayson had drawn for the railing, she went out to the yard where Christmas was chasing birds from one end of the bluff to the other. *Glad you're happy. Orgasm killer.*

The sun shone brightly, warming the early-morning air. Parker spread the plans out on the patio table and marveled at Grayson's talent. The railings he'd designed were bold and unique, like him. He went with an oceanic theme of sea grass and fish and twisted metals that gave the effect of waves carrying the fish up the stairs. She never would have thought to have living creatures on a railing. He had such sharp vision, and he wasn't afraid to speak his mind or challenge her thoughts. *Or kiss me until I'm numb and boneless and make me feel so very cherished it scares me.*

She lifted her eyes from the designs, unable to focus on anything more than how he'd made her feel last night. She walked to the edge of the yard and watched a young family playing on the beach below. These feelings couldn't be real, not after just a few days. Could they? She knew those months of emailing counted, too, but it was still fast, wasn't it? Or was she in such a state of grief from losing Bert that she was misplacing her emotions? She'd never been one to have fleeting emotions, but she knew how fleeting emotions could be for others, and she didn't want to read more into Grayson than she should. She worked in an industry where nothing was valued beyond what it could do to further a person's career. Where things and people were equally replaceable. She'd seen it in her professional dealings and in her personal life. The guys who asked her out fell into three categories. Those looking for eye candy. *But pretty isn't special. Pretty is genetic.* Men who wanted a quick lay. *Wrong girl for that.* And then there were the guys who wanted to use her as a stepping-stone for their careers. Having their pictures taken with her made them the daily dish, and hot gossip brought exposure. She could usually spot those guys a mile away. The few guys she'd actually dated had been what she called the Great Pretenders. They'd slipped through her radar, eventually showing their true colors.

And then there was Grayson.

Grayson obviously thought she was pretty. She saw it in his eyes, heard it in his voice, but he didn't seem to give a hoot about her celebrity status, and that made him even more appealing. Sex had never been on her priority list, but Grayson's kisses were as hot as sex. And he practically oozed sexual prowess. *Yup,* she was definitely thinking about sex. A lot. He was right; other thoughts were going to have to battle for her brainpower today. But it was more than their kisses that made her feel so deeply connected to him. It was everything he did and said. It was ten months of falling for his thoughts, building a foundation, without the distraction of jealousy, or materialism, or press.

Her eyes drifted over the inky water, a feeling of bliss settling around her. She watched the children playing along the shore, their parents smiling and holding hands. Her thoughts returned to Grayson and how happy he'd been last night with his family and friends, reminding her again of how much he'd given up to take the assignment with the foundation.

Christmas *woofed* and darted toward the driveway, where Grayson was pulling in. She had to stop herself from sprinting over, too. The Grunter's Ironworks logo on the side of his truck brought back his remark about being a lowly steelworker and tripped up her heart. He was obviously kidding, but the truth was, a lot of people in the entertainment business dismissed those who weren't in the industry. It had always infuriated her, but she knew there was no changing people like that. That was the heartrending reality of the industry.

Grayson stepped from the truck and knelt to love up her

boy, smiling as Christmas lavished him with slobbery kisses. She'd hated leaving Christmas behind when she was on location. But film sets didn't always make for pet-friendly environments. Especially big attention-loving dogs like hers. Watching Grayson shower him with attention without a care about his dog breath, slobbery kisses, or getting fur on his clothes made her heart swell. She didn't care what anyone else might think about his profession. She liked Grayson's world, and boy, did she ever like him.

I'm here now. This is my real life, and I'm going to live it.

Christmas trotted happily beside him with an enormous bone hanging from his mouth, making her feel even fuller.

"You brought my boy a present?" She wound her arms around Grayson's neck and kissed him.

"Mm, I brought you something, too." He leaned in for another smoldering kiss, leaving a trail of goose bumps in his wake.

"You sure did," she said dreamily.

Christmas pushed his head between them, obviously not done with Grayson yet. Grayson laughed, framed the dog's face with his big hands, and kissed his snout. "I need a minute with your mom, buddy. Go eat that treat." He held up a scroll of design paper. "More ideas."

"But I love the fish. They go perfectly with the property."

He unrolled the new designs over the old. "I thought they went perfectly, too. Although"—he cocked a brow—"it's not like you not to ask for a dozen changes."

"I haven't looked at them *that* closely yet."

His arms circled her waist. "Why *do* you always insist on making so many changes?"

"I don't know," she fibbed. "I guess I tweak them until they feel right." *Or until I got to read so many of your emails I felt sated.*

His eyes narrowed. "And here I was hoping you'd say you were doing it so we had more time to interact."

"You were not." Her confession was on the tip of her tongue, but she worried he wouldn't believe it after he'd nailed her so perfectly.

"I'd hoped." Before she could respond, he said, "I had many long, lonely hours last night to think about you."

"Same." Her cheeks flamed with the memory of fantasizing about him this morning. "You definitely fulfilled your promise."

He leaned in for another kiss. "Wonder what tonight's promise will be?"

She could think of about a dozen promises she'd like to hear—all involving nakedness.

"Better get that look off your face before someone snaps a photo and posts it with a caption that says, 'Sexy Actress Drools Over Hot Artist.'"

"That's why I like you. You're so modest."

"It's embarrassing sometimes," he said seriously. "How

much you gawk at me."

She swatted him, earning a deep, sexy laugh.

He pointed to the designs. "Focus." Eyeing her with a heated look, he mumbled, "Damn. You're killing me."

"Sorry. Wait. *You* kissed me."

"Right. Sorry." He ran a hand through his hair and blew out a breath.

She loved seeing her in-control man flustered, the way he continually flustered her.

"I was thinking about our talk last night."

"And you decided a woman stuck between two worlds isn't really what you were looking for?" She said it lightly, though the worry was real.

"Not even close." He kissed the tip of her nose. "I realized you need roots. Thick, stable, unbreakable roots." He turned to the designs, tracing the lines as he spoke. "I'm thinking about tree trunks, like these, as balusters, with roots curling under the edge of each riser. See the twisted limbs winding up the staircase? We'd use those as railings, with thinner branch-es, a few leaves, and if you want, a bird or two thrown in for Christmas between the risers and the railings. It would be free-form, not uniform."

Roots. He'd really heard everything she'd said last night, and she was deeply touched that he'd thought of her boy when he was designing such a focal point of the house.

"I really love this idea."

"I thought you might." He pointed to the drawings again. "I thought you could carry the same theme along the railing that spans the walkway overlooking the living room. I envision a mix of metals, with roots hanging over the edge of the wood, and maybe we create one large tree between each span, framed with decorative wooden posts to match the floors upstairs. We might have to get my buddy Blue to handle the woodwork; he's an excellent craftsman. Or you can keep the traditional railings you have upstairs, of course."

"No, this is so much better and more meaningful."

"You sure? I know you'll have plenty of changes, and that's okay."

"This house feels lonely inside. I hoped that would change when the foundation took over and kids started using it. But now I can see what's missing. It was built with all the highest-quality products, but it wasn't built with *heart*. It's not a home. It's a house. How did I miss that?"

"You were thinking of giving the kids the best."

"But this..." Her eyes moved over the gorgeous drawings. "*This* is the best. These designs are perfect just as you've drawn them. With a bird or two for Christmas."

"Ah, a tweak." He leaned in for another kiss. "I'm glad you love them, but I've been working with you for long enough to know that tomorrow you'll change your mind. So why don't we set them aside for a day or two and then revisit them?"

She slid her finger into his belt loop and tugged him closer, realizing for the first time that he'd worn a polo shirt instead of a T-shirt. She wondered if that was for the sake of her image, since they were visiting Abe at the resort again today, which seemed like a very Grayson thing to do. With that in mind, she decided to change out of her expensive slacks and blouse before they left and into something more casual. He'd put in so much effort already. Now it was her turn.

ON THE WAY to Brewster, Parker and Grayson talked about their impending visit with Abe. Parker was determined to try to get through to Abe, and Grayson was equally determined to make sure she left Abe's room just as confident as she was when she arrived. He wasn't about to let the old man make her feel bad. Not now. Not after last night.

Not ever again.

She reached for his hand as they walked into the resort and flashed a smile that wasn't practiced or fake. He knew the difference now, which surprised him. When had he started noticing those things? By simply reaching for his hand and publicly claiming their relationship, she eased a worry he hadn't even realized he'd been harboring. It was one thing to kiss in a dark bar, and a whole different ball game to hold hands in the light of day at a posh resort where everyone dressed to the nines and acted like they were made of money—and he stood out like a sore thumb. Grayson had debated wearing slacks and a button-down shirt, but he wasn't into pretending he was something he wasn't. He'd worn a collared shirt, a step up from his normal T-shirts, but that was for Parker, not for these hoity-toity people.

As they crossed the lobby, Grayson had no way of knowing if the men ogling Parker recognized her, or if they were simply admiring the beautiful blonde in the sexy little sundress. The dress that stopped a few inches above her knees and made him want to run his hands up her luscious thighs— and follow them with his mouth. He'd been pleasantly surprised when she'd gone inside in her fancy slacks and blouse and returned in the dress, acting a little less rigid, even more flirtatious and, it seemed, more comfortable in her own skin.

"Love you in this dress," he said as they waited for the elevator.

She blinked a few times before answering, as if she were weighing her answer.

"Thanks. I wore it for you."

Damn, that made him feel good. They stepped into the elevator, and when the doors closed, he folded her into his arms. "Your heart is beating so fast. Nervous?"

"Yes, but I think it has more to do with you than Abe."

"Sweetheart, that's the best kind of nervous." Conscious of

her lipstick this time, he kissed her cheek, and when she made a sound of appreciation, he kissed her again, kissing his way over her jaw to the sensitive skin just below her ear. She rubbed against him like a cat, purring as he devoured her sweet, tantalizing nape. The sexy sound vibrated through her chest to his.

"More," she whispered.

He sealed his teeth over her neck and gave it a little suck, remembering how it had driven her out of her mind last night. She clutched the sides of his head, forcefully holding him in place as he kissed and sucked and took his fill. Her feminine scent beckoned him, and he quickly lost himself in the murmurs she made with every slick of his tongue.

"More," she said again, rocking against his hard length.

He glanced at the elevator. *Six more floors.* He had to have more of her. He dropped his hands to her thighs, squeezing as they slid up her trembling legs beneath her dress.

"Grayson," she whispered.

"Hm?" He eyed the control panel, acutely aware of how little time they had, and ran his tongue from her shoulder up the smooth column of her neck.

"Nothing," she said hurriedly. "Don't stop."

No chance in hell he was stopping now. He grabbed her— *Bare ass? Hot damn*—and pushed his hand between her legs, moving her skimpy thong to the side as she spread her legs wider. He'd been dying to touch her last night but had known she needed a different type of intimacy and tenderness. He'd had to take things into his own hands after he'd gotten home and again this morning just to get himself under control, but now she clung to his head, whispering, "Yes, yes, yes," as his fingers slicked over her wetness. Now she needed this as much as he did.

"I want to drop to my knees and bury my mouth in your sweetness," he said against her nape.

The sound she made fell somewhere between a whimper and a plea, making him wish they had all day to themselves.

He stroked her swollen sex, earning another erotic vibration, and dipped his fingers into her velvety heat. "Jesus, baby."

He touched his forehead to hers, trying to regain control and knowing there wasn't a chance in hell he'd leave her without hearing her cry out in pleasure. They were both breathing hard as he stroked his thumb over her swollen clit, earning another lustful moan, and buried his fingers deeper, furtively seeking—and finding—the pleasure point that brought her up on her toes. Her nails dug into his biceps as he sucked her neck and she rode his hand. Her thighs tightened around his wrist, and her breathing shallowed seconds before his name flew from her lips.

"Grayson, Grayson, Grayson." Her sex pulsed, hot and tight, as the climax coursed through her trembling body—and he took her higher.

"You're so beautiful when you come for me, baby." He kept her at the peak until her head tipped back, eyes closed. "So hot, baby, so sexy," he whispered as she panted through the last of her climax.

"More," she pleaded.

Eyeing the control panel, he debated hitting the stop button. She was ready, and he was so fucking horny he could barely keep his throbbing erection in his pants, but their visit with Abe was too important to Parker to blow off for self-gratification.

Two more floors.

"Later," he reluctantly choked out. He withdrew his hand from between her legs and brought his slick fingers to her mouth. "Open." Her eyes widened and just as quickly flamed with heat as her lips parted. He rubbed his fingers over her tongue, in and out of her mouth, as if it were his cock—and damn how he wished it were. Her lips closed around his fingers, and he nearly came at the sight of her sucking her juices from them. *What I'd like to do with your mouth, your tongue…*

One more floor.

He withdrew his fingers from her mouth and sucked them into his own, holding her surprised, and clearly intrigued, stare. *Oh yeah, let's take this further.*

"I don't want to mess up your pretty lipstick, but I want that sexy mouth of yours." He framed her face with his hands, holding their mouths a breath apart as his tongue dipped into her mouth and swept over hers. She jumped right into the seductive game, meeting every stroke of his tongue with a slick of her own and driving him out of his fucking mind.

When the elevator stopped, he pressed his lips to her forehead and said, "Oh yeah, baby. You've got a naughty side."

CHAPTER NINE

I HAVE A naughty side? I have a naughty side. Ohmygod! I have a naughty side! Parker's body was humming from head to toe. That probably shouldn't have thrilled her so much, considering her thong was drenched and she'd just done something she'd never imagined doing in an elevator, but it did! She must have a naughty side, because when Grayson had said, *Open,* in that deep, erotic growl, she'd wanted to follow his every command.

Grayson's hand came around her waist as they stepped from the elevator. *The hand that was just between my legs—and in my mouth. Holy cow. How am I going to think in there?*

"Mind if we stop at the restroom before going to see Abe?" he asked, calm and casual as ever.

Damn him. Her entire body felt like a bundle of exposed nerves.

He leaned close to her ear and said, "You've got me wired so tight I'm going to explode if I don't get some seriously cold water on my face in about ten seconds."

She followed his gaze to the impressive bulge behind his

zipper. The smile lifting her cheeks must have made her look like she was gloating, which she most definitely was.

"Sorry," she said lightly before popping into the ladies' room.

Ten minutes later they were standing beside Abe's bed. Parker's heart was beating so hard she wanted to hook herself up to one of his blinking machines to make sure she wasn't having some sort of attack. But it wasn't because of what she'd done with Mr. Naughty in the elevator. Seeing Abe, who looked as though he'd aged ten years overnight, had shocked her back to reality. His skin was ashen, and his breathing sounded rough, like he had rocks in his throat. Parker's heart ached for him. She wanted to climb into his bed and hold him so he wouldn't suffer alone, despite how mean he'd been to her and Bert.

"It's nice to see you again, Abe. How are you feeling?" She reached for Grayson's hand, needing his support to steady her nerves.

"I'm still here," he grumbled.

Would he rather be dead? Grayson cocked a brow, and she knew he was wondering the same thing.

"I'm glad you're still here. My friend Grayson is with me again today."

"I figured." Abe sounded bored. "Lacroux?"

"Yes, sir," Grayson said. "How do you know my name?"

"You think I let just anyone into my room? *A friend*, you

said," he scoffed. "A little money goes a long way. I knew who you were before you came into the room yesterday. Ironworker. Pretty damn good one, from what I'm told."

"Thank you," Grayson said, giving Parker a *what the hell* look.

Given Abe's wealth, Parker wasn't surprised he'd had them checked out. That was practically a no-brainer in her industry. Although she was surprised at how quickly he'd done so.

"Talk to me," Abe snapped, and launched into a coughing fit. His frail chest rose off the mattress, his neck muscles straining with each gravelly hack.

Parker grabbed tissues from the bedside table and placed them in his hand. "Are you okay?"

The doors opened, and the nurse hurried toward the bed. "Sir?"

He waved his hand dismissively, clearing his throat with a long, low sound before lying back on the mattress again. The nurse ran an assessing eye over him, then left the room without a sound.

"We can come back another time," Parker offered.

He waved his hand again. "Talk."

Parker squeezed Grayson's hand. She'd practiced what she was going to say in her head on the way over, but nothing she'd practiced felt real. It felt *practiced*, like a role, and that wasn't what she wanted, so she let her heart speak for her.

"I'm sure you don't want to talk about the past, but—"

"Don't tell me what I want to talk about." Abe curled his fingers around the sheet. "Didn't anyone ever teach you how to take control of a situation?"

"I'm sorry. I'm nervous." She swallowed hard at the unexpected confession.

"Nervous is good. It means you're alive," Abe said with a nod. "Spit it out or your boyfriend's going to explode."

She looked up at Grayson, who did in fact look as though he was still tightly wound. He cracked a smile, and a hint of seduction from their secret tryst passed between them, helping to put her at ease.

"This isn't easy for me to explain," she said, "but I'm going to try."

"Quickly," Abe said.

"Yes, sir. Quickly." She drew in a swift breath. "I loved Bert. Regardless of what happened between you two, he was a good, kind, talented man, and I wasn't there for him when he passed away. I was on location, filming." She felt Grayson's eyes hone in on her, and she realized this was new information for him, too.

"I never had a chance to say goodbye, and he never told me why he left me the letters you returned. But I know you were important to him, and Bert was important to me. And I hate that you both lost out on all those years when you could have been close. You were family!" No amount of acting lessons could have prepared her for the anger and sadness spewing from some deep emotional well she didn't know existed. "There are people who would kill to have family. I would kill for a family. I grew up in foster care, dreaming about the very thing you threw away. Pushing him out of your life was selfish and mean, and I want to understand it. To, I don't know, mend the fence before, before…"

"Before I die," Abe said flatly, his unseeing eyes pointing away from her.

"Yes," she admitted sadly. Grayson pressed a kiss to the top of her head.

Uncomfortable silence fell over the room. Parker looked for signs of emotions in Abe, but he hadn't flinched or sighed, huffed or fisted his hands. When he finally turned his gray-blue eyes toward them, he looked markedly older than he had only moments earlier. His sunken cheeks hung loosely from his angular cheekbones and jaw. The hollow crescents beneath his eyes seemed darker, more pronounced, and his colorless lips were unmoving. Had he looked this way all along, or was this new?

He finally inhaled a labored breath. "That was a mouthful."

"Yes. Sorry," she said softly.

"Honest." His eyes widened. "And *mean* for America's sweetheart."

"Sorry." *Shit.*

"It's okay," Grayson whispered to her.

"Is it?" Abe asked in a stronger voice.

"Yes," Grayson said confidently. "She needed to say it, and you probably needed to hear it. Only you can decide that, but she definitely needed to say it."

Abe nodded, new lines mapping his deeply etched forehead. "The Bert you knew, was he focused? Driven? Smart?"

"Yes. All of those things." Parker's heart was racing. Her inability to read him was more unsettling than his anger.

"He wasn't, you know," Abe said. "When we were growing up, when I was going to college, then working night and day in the chain of convenience stores our father owned in order to learn the business from the ground up, he was playing the part of a starving artist. Sleeping God knows where, *painting.*" He cringed, as if the word tasted acidic. "He couldn't have run the family business. He didn't have the wherewithal to manage a chain of thirty stores, to work fourteen-hour days, to manage the financials and legal divisions. We would have lost it all. He was too soft, like our *father.*" Another word he didn't seem to care for.

Something inside Parker snapped at the demeaning things he'd said about Bert. "I don't want to argue about if Bert could or couldn't have run the business, and I don't really care what you thought of his lifestyle as he was finding his way to being the incredible photographer he was. I just want to…" *What? What do I really want? Why am I here?* She stumbled over the thought. She'd wanted to fix their past, but she realized she couldn't, and it wasn't her place to try. Still, she felt a need to soothe Abe's bitter heart, even if he didn't know it needed soothing.

"I just want you to know that Bert loved you," she finally said. "And I know he would have liked to reconcile. He was hurt when you returned his letters, but I know he would have forgiven you if he'd been given the chance."

"I read his first letter," Abe snapped, anger returned to his narrowed eyes. "He wanted to fight it out, to defend himself."

"Wouldn't you?" Grayson threw back at him. "If the tables were turned, wouldn't you have wanted to defend yourself? To fight it out until you could see clearly again? Until you and your brother, your own flesh and blood, were on solid ground?"

She looked at him, but Grayson's eyes were trained on Abe. His jaw was tight, his tone firm, but his eyes were full of compassion.

Abe stared straight ahead, giving Grayson his profile. "Didn't take much to convince our father not to trust him. *Tsk.* So easy. So pathetic, the two of them."

Grayson's hand left her waist and fisted by his side. Compassion *gone.* "You *pushed* your brother out of the business?"

Tension rose in the room like a fever spike, threatening the powder keg standing beside Parker and the one in the bed. She held her hands up. "Enough. I don't want to do this. I made a mistake." She choked back tears. "I can't. It's too upsetting."

Abe turned toward her. "You came here to tell me my brother loved me, because you grew up in a crappy system with some fairy tale in your head about what life should be. I listened to you. Now you listen to me." He wagged a shaky finger at them.

Parker pressed her lips together to ward off the anger and hurt vying for release. Grayson gripped her hand so tightly she knew he was barely holding it together, too.

"You think you're telling me something I don't know? Something that'll change who I am?" Abe scoffed. "Nice is for the weak. I'm not a *nice* man. That's my cross to bear, not yours. My daughter ran off to join a rock band, or some such nonsense, and never looked back. Good riddance. My wife left me for another man." He smacked his hand to his chest. "Nothing breaks me. Pride kept me going. Strength and pride. That's what makes a man."

Grayson released Parker's hand, the muscles in his arms twitching, the veins in his neck plumped up like thick snakes beneath his skin. "Pride is earned when you've done something well." His tone was as icy as his stare. "Strength is the power to move through anything. And where family is concerned, strength takes stepping back, making room for those you love, putting yourself second or fifth or last, even when you deserve to be first."

Parker couldn't take her eyes off of the man who was claiming pieces of her heart by the minute. Conflicting emotions warred inside her. She hadn't come here to fight or make Abe feel bad. But every word Grayson spoke was powerful and true, and she didn't want him to stop.

"I'm afraid you've fooled yourself, Mr. Stein." Grayson rolled his shoulders back, and his tone softened. "You cheated your brother and father, disgraced your family, and you moved past that disgrace by hiding behind a bitter, condescending demeanor. You've driven away people who loved you because you didn't like the man looking back at you in the mirror. That's not pride. I'd call that a coward."

GRAYSON PULLED PARKER toward the door, fed up with Abe's nasty, bitter attitude. The comment he made about Parker's notion of a fairy tale was bullshit, and he wasn't about to let her listen to any more of the old man's hatred.

"Walk out that door, and *you're* the coward," Abe challenged.

Grayson spun around. Parker's eyes pleaded for him to let it go, but he was well past letting it go. He pulled free from her grip and stalked back to the bed. "You got something to say, old man?" he seethed. "Because I'm about a second away from losing my shit."

Abe grumbled something indiscernible. Parker opened her mouth to say something, but Grayson silenced her with one look, unwilling to allow her to fall into any more of this man's head games.

Abe turned to him, chin up, unseeing eyes holding a steady path. "Your speech was as lame as hers."

"Only to deaf ears," Grayson replied through clenched teeth.

"Touché." Abe coughed once, twice, then settled back against the pillow again. "Neither of you told me anything new. I *know* who I am." He paused, gathering the sheet in his fists, and when he spoke again, his tone was defensive rather than accusatory. "I *chased* after my daughter. Paid thousands to track her down, but she didn't want to be found. Gone, without a trace. My wife? *Pfft.* Left for another man, told you that. What kind of man fights for a woman like that?"

"I get that," Parker said softly, surprising Grayson. She stepped closer to the bed and reached for Abe's hand. Abe went rigid, but she softened. Her stance, her eyes, even the tension around her mouth. That sweet, lovely mouth curved into a small smile that made Grayson's heart soften, too. "I didn't know about your wife leaving for another man, but I understand why you didn't fight for her. And your daughter? I didn't know she left for that reason, or that you'd looked for her, but if you did—"

"For *years*," he mumbled.

"Then you did what you could," Parker said. "But Bert? Why, Abe? If he was willing to let the past go, to forgive, why couldn't you?"

Grayson had seen Parker morph into her actress persona, and he'd seen her climbing out from under too much tequila. He'd witnessed the real Parker, *Polly*, at the bar, and enough times since to recognize that transition, too. The person he was watching now, the empathetic, confident woman, was a beautiful mix of both. He had given the old man hell. Parker held her head up high, compassion practically dripping from her pores, her determination to get to the truth still driving her on, only this time she did it with a natural grace no one could fake. If anyone deserved to feel proud, it was the woman standing beside him.

"You've got guts, little lady," Abe said. "My Miriam had guts, too. Had to, to leave like she did. Maybe you deserve the fairy tale."

Parker placed her other hand over Abe's, unfurling his fingers and pressing them gently into her palm. "I know all about the arguments, the pissing and moaning and goading each other on that siblings and parents do. I've heard about loud, obnoxious holidays where they can barely stand to be in the same room. I want it all—the jealousies that come with family, the anger that feels like it'll break you, and the underlying love that lets you know you'll never really break, because your family's got your back no matter what. So, if that's a fairy tale, yes, I want it." Tears streamed down her cheeks. "And I'm not ashamed of my past or of wanting that fairy tale. Your brother gave me all I really ever wanted, a *sense* of family. And believe me, Abe, Bert wasn't always easy. He had his less-than-stellar moments, too."

Abe's eyes widened with a glint of interest. "Tell me."

His interest sent a jolt of surprise through her. "Gosh, okay. Well, for one thing, he chewed like a cow."

"Always did," Abe said with a hint of a smile.

"And sometimes he didn't think before he spoke, so he'd say something crass that he didn't really mean."

"He meant it, the bastard," Abe said with another small smile. "He was just smart enough to know he shouldn't." He must have noticed he'd gone soft, and grumbled, "What else did the pain in the ass do?"

"He refused to celebrate Christmas with me. Ever." Parker listed a litany of memories that seemed to pour straight from her heart, and Grayson found himself, like Abe, hanging on to every word she spoke. Even if Abe left things as they were, distant and cold, he knew she'd be okay, because the memories she was sharing were pushing her grief to the side and filling the spaces it left behind.

After she'd exhausted her lungs, she blinked her tears and inhaled a long breath, then blew it out slowly. Her lips curved up as her eyes rolled over Abe's face. "And he missed you, Abe."

Abe slid his hand from between hers and laid it over Parker's. "I've given you my answer," he said quietly.

Parker's brows knitted. "I don't understand."

Grayson put his arm around her. He'd been too angry before to hear the truth. "Pride kept him from reconciling with Bert, baby. It's a powerful thing."

Tears spilled from her eyes. Parker leaned over the bed and wrapped her arms around the frail old man. "Thank you."

Abe's arms lay rigid beside him. When Parker kissed his cheek, he lifted one hand to her back, holding her there for a long moment. When she broke the embrace, he gripped her forearm, keeping her near as he whispered so quietly Grayson barely heard him, "Thank *you*."

CHAPTER TEN

THE SECOND THEY walked out of Abe's suite, Parker pressed her hand to her chest.

"I can hardly breathe! One second we were leaving and I thought he was the biggest jerk on earth, and the next—" She threw her arms around Grayson's neck and kissed him, overwhelmed by the moment, the day, the week. Overwhelmed by his support. "Thank you."

"I didn't do anything. You got through to him in a way even his own brother never could. You were incredible."

"You supported me and made me go in there when I wanted to run away and forget the whole thing. You did a lot more, too," she said as they walked to the elevator. "You stood up for me *and* you backed down for me. You somehow knew how much I needed to do this, and last night you knew how much I needed to feel okay about being me. The real me."

"And here I thought you might fall apart after we left the room," he said with a warm smile.

"Fall apart? Maybe if we had walked out the door when we started to, but I'm so glad we didn't. This is what I wanted, for him to know how much Bert loved him and for him to remember how much he loved Bert. I want to come back in a few days. He shouldn't be alone."

"I thought you might."

"I do. I know I said too much about my own feelings, and he didn't deserve to have that dumped on him. It was obviously misdirected, which he totally picked up on with the whole fairy-tale thing. I thought I had dealt with all that stuff years ago. But maybe it'll always be there in the back of my mind. Maybe I should apologize next time I see him."

"Next time *we* see him again." The elevator arrived and they stepped inside. "That is, if you don't mind me going along. Just until we know he's not going to snap at you again."

"How could I mind? I love being with you."

He touched her cheeks and gazed into her eyes as the elevator doors closed. Her heart was beating fast, and her emotions were all over the place. She was on a high from what happened with Abe and pushed even higher by her feelings for Grayson *and* the fact that they were back in the elevator. Their kissing place. So high she couldn't hold them back.

"This," she said. "The way you're holding me right now, with your thumbs against my jaw, holding my head up so you can look into my eyes. This position right here has become my favorite."

"Careful, sweetheart," he said with a serious slant of his brows. "For ten months I thought we were building a friendship that we both hoped might lead to more. I thought I'd kept all that anticipation under wraps, but the moment I saw you, liquored up and full of sweets and sorrow, I knew I didn't stand a chance. I've come undone. What I feel for you is too big, and comments like that make it hard to reel back in."

Her emotions whirled even higher. "Then don't."

His mouth covered hers hungrily, demanding a response, which she was all too happy to give—*and take*. The kiss seared through her veins with fierce possession, and boy did she ever want to be possessed by Grayson. He took the kiss deeper, held her tighter. She was disappearing into the kiss, into him, letting their passion consume her.

Someone cleared their throat, surprising both of them, and they reluctantly parted, turning to the small group of people apparently waiting for them to step out of the elevator. Embarrassment heated Parker's cheeks as she took in the scene in two seconds flat: Two teenagers fiddled with their phones. A couple looked at her and Grayson with amusement in their eyes. An elderly man was shaking his head, and three teenage girls stood behind the group, whispering and giggling.

Grayson placed a possessive arm around her waist and held his head up high. "Excuse us," he said, and guided a stunned Parker toward the exit.

It was the longest two seconds of Parker's life, and only one thought registered—Thank God Grayson's brain was functioning, because hers was still lost in the kiss.

Once outside the resort, he brushed his thumb beneath her lip and smiled so wide it made her laugh.

"Sorry about your lipstick. I think I got most of it off."

"Yeah, you did." She rubbed a smear of lipstick from his lips with a laugh. "What is it with us and elevators?"

"I don't know, but I think you should add one to your house. And maybe I should, too."

"I FEEL DIFFERENT," Parker said as they pulled into her driveway. "More alive."

"There's definitely new light in your eyes and a spark in your voice that was probably tempered by worry before." She'd talked about their visit with Abe the whole way back. They were both pleased with how things had turned around with Abe, but Grayson also felt relieved. He'd been worried about the toll these visits might take on her if things had continued the way they'd started.

"I hadn't realized how much this was weighing on me, but I think Bert would be happy with how things turned out. I don't want to sit around the house hiding anymore. Do you have time to hang out?"

"Do I have time? Baby, you're my priority."

She seemed to melt a little at that, even though he thought

he'd already shown she was his priority through his actions.

"Why don't you go inside and do whatever you have to, fix your makeup, do your hair, or whatever else is required before you can go out for an afternoon, and we'll head up to Provincetown. We can bring Christmas. He'd probably like a change of scenery."

She dug a mirror out of her purse. "Do I look *that* bad?"

"Hell no. You need a warning label you look so sexy." He leaned across the car and kissed her. "I prefer you without lipstick so I can kiss you whenever I damn please, but I know you have to be photo and fan ready. I'm just trying to be supportive."

He came around the car and opened her door. She snapped the mirror closed, and he pulled her into his arms again, taking her in another long kiss. When they finally parted, it took a few seconds for her eyes to flutter open and clear themselves of their hazy look of lust.

"I'm definitely not wearing lipstick today."

"You sure?"

She nodded vehemently.

"You totally dig me," he teased, and kissed her again. "Just don't blame me for whatever not wearing lipstick does to your reputation. I don't know how many of the celebrity-lifestyle rules we're breaking. You might want to clue me in so I don't screw something up."

They loved up Christmas and let him out to do his business.

"You don't strike me as a rule follower." Parker dug through her purse and pulled out her cell phone.

Grayson realized it was the first time he'd even seen her look at a phone. "For you, I'll try." He eyed the phone. "Getting back into real life? That's a good sign." And another reminder that her real life was across the country. A reminder he still wasn't ready to think about.

"I promised myself I'd start returning calls after I dealt with Abe. I need to call my agent and a few foundation members before they send out a search party."

"I'll give you some privacy." He took a step away, and she reached for his hand.

"I don't need privacy. I'll call on the way into Provincetown, unless it'll bother you?"

"Nothing you do bothers me."

"That's because I've been hiding out. Once I get back into the swing of things, you might feel differently."

"Maybe," he said. "But we won't know until that happens."

Her brows knitted, as if she hadn't expected him to agree. "Oh?"

He gazed into her worried eyes and knew no matter how much it sucked to hear or say, he couldn't hide from his thoughts forever. "This is new for both of us, and you have a full life thousands of miles away from my life here. I've got another fourteen months of working on site for the foundation, but my life is here, on the Cape. If we really make a go of this, which I hope we will, then we'll have plenty of things to deal with."

"I know," she said quietly.

"Do you want to try to talk it out now? Figure out what those things are and how we'll handle them? I'm happy to do that. Or we can deal with issues as they arise, which I'm also okay with. Waiting gives our relationship time to grow legs even stronger than the ones we have now."

"What if we wait and we get really close and then we can't make it work?" She began pacing.

Grayson pulled her to him again. "First things first. When something comes up, please don't pull away. Issues seem bigger when you're alone." He tightened his grip around her, and a smile lifted her cheeks, the worry in her eyes softening. "If we can't make it work, it means we don't want it to work."

"Okay. I like when you're right."

"So do I." He gave her a chaste kiss, because if he kissed her the way he ached to, he'd end up scooping her into his arms and carrying her up to the bedroom—and her calls, and their outing, would be forgotten.

CHAPTER ELEVEN

GRAYSON HELD CHRISTMAS'S leash in one hand and Parker's hand in the other as they meandered through the shops in Provincetown. It had taken a great deal of mental reassurance for Parker to quiet the voices in her head telling her to primp and paint before going out—no matter how much she hated doing it. But she was glad she'd resisted the urge, because kissing Grayson was bordering on an obsession. And she didn't want lipstick or anything else to stop them from a single kiss.

She'd returned a dozen messages on the drive up, accepted sincere condolences, and agreed to read a script for an upcoming romantic comedy, which Phillipa was going to have delivered tomorrow. The thought of jumping back into her crazy schedule was exhausting, but it was her life, and she was grateful to have one to be exhausted over.

They explored the shops along the pier, stopped to watch a pantomime on a street corner, and picked up a few small things for the house. Provincetown was a colorful, artsy world unto itself, which was one reason she liked it so much. The other reason was because it was where Bert had gotten his start as a photographer, and that made her feel closer to him. Provincetown was also dog friendly, and Christmas was in his heyday, taking in the crowded sidewalks, sniffing other dogs, and being lavished with attention by strangers. She was happy that Grayson had suggested bringing him. He'd been loving up her boy all day, telling him he was a *good buddy* when they stopped in a store or allowed someone to pet him. He seemed as attached to Christmas as she was, and that etched his name into another piece of her heart. It was getting pretty full of Grayson, and the fuller it got, the happier she became.

They had lunch at Café Heaven, where one of Bert's photographs hung behind the counter. They sat out front, people watching as they ate, and talked about Bert. Parker noticed a few whispers of recognition throughout the afternoon, but thankfully, other than two teenage girls asking for a photograph with her, which she was happy to oblige, they had a fairly uneventful day in that regard.

"I'd forgotten what it was like to be *away* from the paparazzi," she said on the way to Sky's tattoo shop. She remembered Bert's comment about Provincetown being the only place he could really be himself when he was younger. She knew he had been referring to being a gay man in the fifties, but she couldn't help thinking the feelings she experienced as she moved through crowds without any fanfare were probably similar.

"And I'm not used *to* them at all, which is why when you mentioned pictures and gossip magazines, I wasn't too worried. I've seen lots of celebrities around the Cape, but I've never seen anyone making a fuss. I'm sure they do, but I think going over the top is a West Coast thing. Here, you're just a beautiful blonde who happens to make movies." He leaned in for a kiss, and Christmas shoved his nose between their legs.

They both laughed, and Grayson leaned down to kiss Christmas's head. "You are one jealous dog. But I don't blame you. If someone else were kissing your mom, I'd do a lot more than shove my nose between them."

Parker rolled her eyes. "Like you have to worry about that? I'm as loyal as…I was going to say Christmas, but he's already jilted me for you. So I'll say I'm as loyal as…*me.*"

He tugged her in for another kiss. "I'll take you all day long, baby."

Promise?

Grayson leaned closer and whispered, "When you look at me like that, you make me all sorts of crazy."

"Shh." She clutched his shirt. "When you use that voice, and…" Her brain was scrambling. *Nonono. Not now.* She didn't want to be a swooning mess when she saw Sky, but she needed him to know what he did to her and how good he made her feel. "The way you're looking at me right now? I've never been looked at like that. You look like you want to devour me, like you see all of *me*, not the actress. So, yeah.

You're hot, built like you were put on this earth to be touched and licked and ogled." She couldn't stop talking! "And if that's not enough, you're the best kisser on the planet and you love my dog to pieces." She had Grayson—and Christmas's—rapt attention. "How do you *expect* me to look at you?"

A wicked smile spread across his face, and his gaze smoldered. "Just. Like. That." He hitched an arm around her waist and began walking toward Sky's shop again. Quickly.

"Why are you hurrying? I think I left my legs back there. These rubber ones aren't working so well."

He laughed. "The quicker we say hello, the quicker we get back home. I have some touching and licking to collect on."

"Ohmygod." *Yes, yes, yes!*

He cocked a brow. "Infuriatingly male?"

"Right. Unfortunately, it turns out that I am totally into infuriating males."

"Plural?" His eyes slanted to possessive slits.

"Would you have it any other way?" She patted Christmas on the head, then kissed Grayson's scruffy chin. "One favorite man, one favorite boy."

He made a cute little growling sound as they came to Sky's shop. "Is that Sky's friend Lizzie's shop?" She pointed to P-town Petals, the flower shop next door.

"Yes. She's Blue's fiancée," Grayson said.

"Blue the woodworking guy? Gosh, everyone knows everyone around here."

"We like it that way." He took her hand, and they headed inside.

Christmas lifted his nose and sniffed. The scent of lavender flowed in a stream of dancing smoke from incense burning on the counter.

"Grayson!" A girl with jet-black hair jumped off a stool behind the counter and hugged him. Grayson kissed her cheek with a loud *mwah!* She had a beautiful smile and an arm covered in tattoos. "I wasn't expecting you. You must be Parker! I'm Cree. Sky told me you guys were going out."

"Hi," Parker said, surprised and delighted that Sky had already spoken of them as a couple.

Cree dropped to her knees and let Christmas lick her cheeks.

"This is my boy, Christmas," Parker said.

"Love his name!" Cree hugged Christmas around his neck, then popped back up to her feet. Her sunny disposition contrasted with her head-to-toe black attire and her heavy military-style boots.

Sky was leaning over a customer just beyond the counter. Her long dark hair was tied back, revealing the top of a tattoo on her left shoulder blade. The buzzing of the tattoo gun stopped, and Sky looked over her shoulder. "Come on back. I'm going to be a while."

Cree pushed open the knee-high iron gate that separated the waiting area from the work area. "She's got a few hours to go on his tat."

"Is it okay to take Christmas back?" Parker asked.

"Sure. Sky loves dogs." Cree laughed and returned to the counter.

"Hey, guys." Sky glanced at Christmas. "Aww. He's so cute!"

"You see me all the time, and now you notice?" Grayson leaned down and kissed her cheek. "How's it going, sis?"

"Awesome, like every day," Sky said. "You just missed Sawyer. He'll be so bummed. He had to do a training session down in Eastham."

"He was a professional boxer, but too many noggin knocks took him out of the ring," Grayson explained. "Now he trains other boxers in Jana's brother's club."

"And writes," Sky said, turning back to her customer, who seemed so relaxed he could have been sleeping. The buzz of the tattoo gun hummed again as she worked. "Sawyer writes poetry, and he and his dad published two books together."

"I'll give you one before you leave," Cree called to them, holding up a book.

"Wow, thanks. I love poetry," Parker said.

"Good to know." Grayson kissed her again.

"You just missed Lizzie, too. She got swamped about ten minutes ago. But you'll meet her at some point, Parker. Are you guys going to make it over to Seaside for breakfast sometime? Maybe next weekend?" Sky wiped blood from the area she was tattooing, then set the needle right back to work.

"I've got a bear of a client breathing down my neck to get her railings done. You'll have to ask my boss." He winked at Parker.

I'd like to do a lot more than breathe down your neck.

"A gorgeous blonde breathing down your neck?" Sky laughed. "You poor thing. Parker?"

"Oh, I think he'll deserve a morning off by then."

"Good! The girls and I were hoping to see you again soon."

She and Grayson hadn't talked about what they were doing tomorrow, much less what they were doing a week from now. In fact, she realized, they hadn't been making plans at all. They, as a couple, had been a given, and that gave her a solid sense of where they stood.

"So you guys are working while you're in town?" Sky asked.

"We're not getting much work done yet, but we will be." Grayson drew Parker into his arms and lowered his voice. "My famous girlfriend has a new script arriving tomorrow."

Her heart turned over in her chest at how casually he said *girlfriend,* and she was glad he'd thought to lower his voice when he'd said *famous.* Both were such *Grayson* things to do.

"How exciting!" Sky wiped more ink and blood from her customer's arm.

Christmas brushed against Grayson's leg. He petted him as

he whispered to Parker, "I can think of a few exciting things I'd like to do to you right now."

"Grayson." She hoped Sky hadn't heard him. Grayson kissed her again and stepped to her side, bringing Sky, who was watching them with *aww* in her eyes, into view.

"You guys are so cute," Sky said with an approving smile. "It's kind of sickening."

"It's awesome!" Cree called out. "Sky and Sawyer are the same way, which leaves me out in the cold. Don't you two have another brother?"

They all laughed. After talking for a few more minutes, Parker and Grayson headed back to the car. As they drove back toward Wellfleet, Parker realized she hadn't teared up with thoughts of Bert today. Not when she'd seen his photograph in Café Heaven, not when they'd talked about him, and not when thoughts of him had simply floated into her mind. Her talk with Abe had helped her through one of the most troubling parts of her grief, which helped alleviate the guilt she'd carried from being away when Bert died.

She looked at Grayson as he drove down the highway. Without him, she may never have gotten through to Abe. And it was Grayson who was right here by her side, reminding her how wonderful life could be if she slowed down enough to enjoy it instead of racing from film to film. As the sun began to set and Christmas yawned in the backseat, happier than she'd ever seen him, Parker knew that just as she'd been the only one to get through to Abe, only Grayson, with his patience, confidence, and innate understanding of what she needed, could have gotten through to her.

CHAPTER TWELVE

PARKER LEANED ON the railing of her deck, gazing out at the ocean while absently brushing her bare foot along Christmas's back. The tuckered-out pup lay fast asleep from their busy afternoon. They'd picked up dinner at the Bookstore Restaurant on their way home and had shared a bottle of wine while they ate beneath the evening sky. Parker's long hair was gathered over her right shoulder, her skin shimmering under the moon's glow. A gentle breeze brushed her dress against her thighs.

If ever there was a perfect moment, this is it. Right here, right now. They were too far above the beach to be seen, making the whole star-filled sky and beautiful bay seem like their own private paradise. Grayson slid his arms around Parker's waist from behind and kissed her cheek. She rested her head back against his shoulder and sighed with pleasure.

"I think you were put on this earth just for me," he whispered against her cheek.

"Oh yeah? Why's that?"

"Because you were all I thought about when you were

thousands of miles away, and when we're together, everything feels good and right." He licked the shell of her ear and pressed a kiss to her delicate skin just below.

"What else?" Her eyes were closed, a sweet smile on her lips.

He kissed his way back down her neck and over her shoulder, loving the shivers that trembled through her. "I love seeing you smile and hearing your laugh. Being with you makes me happy."

She leaned in to him, her ass brushing over his arousal. "Mm. I can feel how happy it makes you."

"And?" he teased with a press of his hips.

"And tell me more, but keep kissing me."

"Oh, yes. You're definitely put on this earth just for me." He kissed her shoulder again and grazed his teeth over her freshly kissed skin, repeating the sensual rhythm and reveling in the hitching of her breaths.

She reached behind her and gripped his hips, craning her neck, pushing it toward his mouth. "Grays—" The end of his name was drowned out by a moan as he sealed his mouth over her neck and sucked.

Splaying his hands over her belly, he pressed his hips tighter against her ass. Her fingers tightened on his hips, holding him firmly in place.

"Don't worry, baby. I'm not going anywhere until you're fully satisfied." He gathered her silky hair and draped it over her other shoulder, giving the newly revealed shoulder the same loving attention as the other.

"Tell me how," she whispered.

Her hands moved up and down his hips in time to every kiss. He tangled one hand in her hair and moved his other arm up her body, between her breasts, and curled his fingers around the nape of her neck.

"First I'm going to kiss your mouth."

With a not-so-gentle tug, he angled her head just so and captured her mouth in a greedy kiss. Her mouth was hot and sweet, but the kiss was urgent and messy. There was no room for finesse as their tongues tangled and their bodies rocked to an erotic beat. She moaned and whimpered and dug her nails into his flesh just above his waist. He told himself to slow down as he ground his throbbing erection against her ass, but the torrent swelling inside him was too powerful. He turned her in his arms, never breaking their connection. He groaned at the sensation of her supple curves conforming to his. His hands moved over her ass, groping her firm cheeks.

"So sexy, baby."

Their mouths crashed together, and he hiked her leg up to his waist, caressing her outer thighs, then traveling over her silken skin to her ass again. She moaned into his mouth, clawing at his back. There was no slowing this runaway train. He was lost in the feel of her hot skin, the erratic pounding of her heart against his, and the erotic pleas spilling from her lungs. His hands pushed beneath her dress and curled around the sliver of material riding over her hips. She lowered her leg from his waist, and in one hard yank he tore the seam free, dropping the shredded material to the ground.

He tore his mouth from hers, both of them panting for air. Her blue eyes stormed with need as he ran his hand down her taut belly, pressing his palm flat as it moved over her belly button. When his fingertip grazed the damp cleft of her sex, she closed her eyes and her head tipped back again.

"Look at me, sweetheart." Keeping his hand still was killing him. He wanted to feel her desire, to see her shatter at his will, but she'd asked for him to tell her *more*, and nothing was going to stop him from fulfilling her every fantasy.

Her eyes fluttered open, and he kissed her softly.

"Tell me," she urged. "While you touch me."

"You have no idea what it does to me to hear my good girl being naughty." He claimed her in another punishingly intense kiss as he pushed his fingers inside her tight heat. Her sex clenched around his fingers, and he groaned with the immense pleasure.

He moved his fingers right where he knew she needed it most. She sucked in air, and her eyes fluttered closed again. He teased over that spot again and again, causing the same scintillating reaction.

"You're going to come for me, like this, while I'm kissing you."

SEASIDE LOVERS

"Yes," she said in a heady voice.

"And then you're going to come on my mouth." He took her in another plundering kiss, searching, taking, with both fingers and mouth. He felt her body tense and tremble as she rose on to her toes. He pressed a series of softer kisses over her lips, wanting to drag out her anticipation and her pleasure.

"Please," she begged.

He took the kiss deeper, stroking over her swollen clit with his thumb. Her hips jerked forward.

"You like that, baby?"

"Yes. God, yes."

He kissed along her collarbone as he teased and taunted and loved his way up to her mouth again. Fisting his hand in her hair, he held her just where he wanted her and kissed her again, deeper, rougher, more possessive, following the same thrusting rhythm with his fingers as his tongue. She went up on her toes again, trembling, barely breathing as he teased her to the edge, then higher still, keeping her there, knowing it would bring the most intense orgasm yet.

"Ready to come for me, sweetheart?" he asked against her lips.

She whimpered as he brought their mouths together again, taking her in a slow, sensual kiss while moving his fingers faster, harder. Her nails dug into his arms as his name sailed from her lips like a plea.

"Grayson—" Her inner muscles clamped down tight,

153

pulsing against his fingers.

He claimed her mouth again, breathing air into her lungs and keeping her at the peak of her orgasm. Her hips bucked and he kissed her harder, slowing the speed of his fingers as they moved in and out between her legs, prolonging her pleasure.

Just as her climax began to ebb, he said, "Again," and dropped to his knees.

Christmas's head popped up.

"It's okay, buddy," Grayson said with more control than he felt. Christmas settled his chin between his paws and closed his eyes.

Grayson nudged Parker's legs farther apart, thanking the heavens above that they were too high above the beach to worry about being seen. She ran her fingers through his hair as he rolled her dress to her hips and held it there, exposing her glistening sex to the cool breeze.

"Baby," was all he could manage before taking his first taste of her. He slicked his tongue between her swollen lips, and she fisted her hands in his hair. "So sweet." He brought his tongue to her again and again, nudging her legs open wider with his knees, until he could fit his entire mouth over her entrance. She rocked against him as he ate at her, thrusting his tongue into her heat until she cried out.

"So good, baby. So fucking good." He reached up and guided her hand between her legs. "Touch yourself, baby, while I make you mine."

He felt her reluctance and drew her fingers into his mouth, swirling his tongue over their tips. Then he set them against her clit and held her gaze as he moved both of their hands.

"With me, baby. For me. Be my naughty girl."

He pressed a kiss to her fingers as she touched herself, then sank lower and covered her sex with his mouth, fucking her with his tongue as she stroked herself.

"Hold your dress with your other hand." He moved her hand from his hair to her dress. "So sexy, baby. Jesus, you're gonna make me come just watching you."

"You better not," she choked out.

He chuckled, knowing there wasn't a chance in hell he'd miss out on loving her properly. He gripped her ass with both hands, holding her to him as he stroked and sucked and teased and fucked her with his mouth until her entire body was shaking. Her fingers moved fast and determined, matching his fervor. He masterfully thrust his tongue over the spot that shattered her control.

"Yes. So good. Ohgod. Grayson. More. Ohgod—"

He stayed right there, drinking in her desire, until the very last shudder rippled through her. Then he drew her glistening fingers into his mouth and sucked them clean. He licked her overly sensitive flesh one last time, causing her entire body to shudder, and rose to his full height.

He framed her face with his hands, the intoxicating scent

of her sex surrounding them, and kissed her—*hard.*

"Taste that?" He kissed her again. "So sweet. So perfect." He kissed her again and brushed his thumb over her glistening lower lip. "So *mine.*"

CHAPTER THIRTEEN

PARKER TRIED TO form a response, but she was floating in post-orgasmic bliss. If not for the railing she was leaning against and Grayson's arms around her, she'd melt into a puddle on the deck. Grayson lifted her into his arms, and he must have seen the confusion in her eyes. She was enjoying being outside. It brought an element of danger and made her feel sexy. He kissed her again—oh, how she loved his kisses. *Mine,* he'd said. *You have no idea how very yours I am. Take me. Love me. Keep me.*

"Bedroom," he said, and let out a short whistle. Christmas stretched lazily and lumbered inside. Grayson closed the door behind them and carried her upstairs.

"Why?" she managed.

"Because there is no way I'm laying your beautiful body on that hard deck. I want to feel you writhing beneath me, and I want to see you arching your back when you're riding me, and I don't want my girl's pretty little knees or sexy back to get scuffed up."

She pressed her finger over his lips. Every time he talked

dirty her body responded in ways she had never known before. His words made her hot, and wet, and aching for him. "No more promises. I'm not sure I'll survive them."

"Okay, baby. You let me know when you're ready to hear more."

He carried her into the bedroom. Christmas plopped down on the floor, somehow knowing Grayson had become the alpha of the house. Her big, strong alpha set her down on wobbly legs, still holding her around her waist, and unzipped her dress. He slid the thin material off one shoulder, pressing a kiss to her skin, then repeating the sensual move on the other side as her summery dress fell to the floor, leaving her bare, save for her sheer bra. She reached for his shirt, though her movements were slow. She was still recovering from her intense orgasms. He pulled his shirt off, dropping it to the floor, and took her face in his hands, kissing her again, sweet and tender this time.

She reached behind her to unhook her bra and he shook his head. "That's my job, baby." He brought her fingers to his mouth and licked the tips, making her sex clench with need. "I'm not in a rush. You haven't come nearly enough."

Lord. She'd fallen for an orgasm machine. *Lucky me.*

He unzipped his jeans, easing them down his powerful thighs and stepping out of them, revealing his formidable erection beneath his black boxer briefs. Watching him watch her made his striptease even more erotic.

He took her hand and spread it over his girth. His cock pulsed against her palm. "Yours, baby."

Two words. *Two.* And her heart stopped cold.

He brought her hand back to his mouth and kissed it. Taking her by the shoulders, he turned her away from him, pressing his erection between her cheeks, and kissed her beside her ear. "No rush," he whispered.

She closed her eyes as he kissed the nape of her neck. Her head tipped forward with the thrilling pleasure of giving herself over to him, of trusting him completely. He kissed a trail down her spine, stopping to run his tongue just above her bra before unhooking it, leaving it loose while he pressed his mouth to each vertebrae, all the way to the base of her spine. Goose bumps rose on her flesh.

He held tightly to her hips as he kissed the curve at the top of her ass. Then he kissed one rounded cheek from the top all the way to the crease where it met her thigh. He ran his tongue up the back of her thigh. She was shivering with need, drenched between her legs, and he was taking his sweet damn time. He spread his hands over the backs of her thighs, opening them wider. Her heart thundered with anticipation, and when he slid one hand between her legs and teased her sex while simultaneously licking and sucking the back of her thigh, it took only seconds before she was coming again— hard. Her body shook and thrust as he rose to his feet and stripped off his boxers, positioning his hard length between her legs, parallel to the floor. Every rock of her hips slid along his length, from root to tip. He wrapped his other arm around her waist, holding her against his chest.

"Ride me, soak me, make me yours," he said in a guttural tone that sent her right over the edge again. "That's it, baby. Come for me."

He let her guide their pace, and as she came down from her orgasm, he thrust again, dragging his cock along her swollen lips, drenching his shaft, never trying to enter her. She thought what he'd done outside was the most erotic thing she'd ever seen, but this? The teasing, the friction, the commands. This was addicting. *He* was addicting.

He slid his hands beneath her bra, brushing his thumbs over her sensitive nipples.

"Oh God, Grayson." The neediness in her voice could not be missed, not even by her. She moaned, and when he squeezed her nipples between his finger and thumb, it sent sparks to her core, and her hips bucked, on the verge of another climax.

"Again, Parker. I want you to come until it's all you can think about. *Us. This. More.*"

He sucked the back of her neck, and fireworks burst behind closed lids as she shattered again, heat and ice tearing through her chest and limbs.

"Ohgodgodgod. More. More," she begged. He'd turned her into some sort of nymph.

His hand rose from her breast, and he thrust his fingers into her mouth.

"Suck it, baby," he growled.

God help her, she did. Like her life depended on it. She sucked and licked and bit. Her hips thrust and bucked as she rode his length and he fucked her mouth with his hand. His other hand tweaked her nipple with mind-blowing precision, and she came again. She melted against his hard chest, weak and sweating and still wanting more.

He gathered her in his arms, set her on the edge of the bed, and slid her bra off her shoulders. She'd forgotten she had it on. He knelt before her, his eyes full of love as he took her face in his hands and kissed her. His tongue was like silk, moving sensually, hot, slow, hungry.

"Still with me?" he asked.

"So very with you." She'd never felt this feminine or sexual in all her life, and he made her feel whole and special with every touch and every word.

His lips curved up in a sinful smile. She wanted to be *his* sin tonight. He cupped her breasts, still looking her in the eye.

"Tell me." The desperate plea came unbidden, but she didn't care.

"I'm going to kiss you, and suck you, and love you until you come again."

"Ohgodyes."

"But I'm only going to touch your beautiful breasts."

"Grayson, I won't. I can't." What was he thinking? She'd never be able to come without some sort of friction where she needed it most.

He covered her mouth with his, kissing her into silence. "You can, baby. You will."

He lowered his mouth to her right breast, teasing her nipple with his tongue as he squeezed the left one. She arched against his mouth, but he refused to give her more. His tongue flicked over the sensitive bud and dragged over her entire breast, miles away from where she wanted it. He moved to the other side and repeated the torture. Every squeeze of her nipple made her sex clench until her nipples pulsed and ached. She never knew nipples could ache.

"Grayson, please," she begged.

He sucked her nipple into his mouth and slid his index finger into hers. Her lips closed automatically around it. Jesus, she wanted him in her everywhere. She'd take a finger, a thumb, his tempting cock. She'd take them all. She closed her eyes, zeroing in on the sensations burning her nipples and pretending his finger was his hard length. Her hips moved to the same rhythm as his finger while he sucked her breast, grazing his teeth over the sensitive tip to the point of pain— exquisite pain. She lost herself in the eroticness of what they were doing.

"Christ, baby, you're so close." He sucked her nipple again. "Let go, baby. Come for me." He clamped down hard on her nipple, sending darts of pleasure and pain like lightning between her legs.

Her head fell back and her hips thrust off the bed as she lost all control, coming and screaming she had no idea what as Grayson sucked the life out of her breast.

She grabbed his head, holding him there, panting as she came down from the peak.

"More," she demanded.

He rose to his feet, and she grabbed hold of his thick, eager erection. She was salivating for him, and the look in his eyes told her he was right there with her. He stepped forward as she opened her mouth. He wrapped his hand around the base of his cock and squeezed.

"I'm clean," he said.

She hadn't even been thinking about *that*. Thank goodness he was. She nodded, hoping he'd understand she was, too, because she wasn't about to try to speak.

She leaned forward and licked the bead at the tip, tasting his essence and earning a groan that sent even more heat between her legs. His eyes turned fierce. She swirled her tongue around his swollen glans and took him in her mouth. He gathered her hair in his hand, holding it back. She realized he was watching her, and she closed her eyes, sucking, licking, and loving the feel of his thick shaft against her lips. Knowing he was watching her made it even more exciting.

"Open your eyes, baby." She met his intense gaze, and his

lips curved up seductively. "I'm going to come in about twenty seconds, and I'd rather do it inside you."

She shivered all over, thinking about his thick shaft inside her. She stroked him with her hand as he withdrew from her mouth, and then his hands were around her ribs, and he lifted her to the center of the bed. Perched between her legs, he squeezed the base of his cock again. His muscles were corded with restraint, running over his broad shoulders, up his neck, his powerful thighs flexed and ready. The sight of him took her breath away.

"Condom?" he asked.

She shook her head. "I'm on birth control."

As he came down over her, awareness consumed her. The feel of his thighs pressing against hers, the moment his arousal touched her entrance, the weight of his muscular chest touching her breasts. *Perfection. Exquisite and luxurious.*

He pushed the tip of his erection into her, and she closed her eyes. He stroked her cheek with his thumb. "Open your eyes, baby. Let me see what you feel."

She did, and the emotions looking back at her swamped her. "Grayson."

"I know, baby. It's almost too much, this thing between us. I feel it, too."

"It's…" She blinked several times, on the verge of tears she didn't understand.

"Real. It's ours." He kissed her softly as he pushed in deep.

She felt him stretching her, filling her in the most delicious way. He cradled her head in his hands and kissed her again, drawing her deeper into him, into them.

"I'm so lost in you," he confessed, every word laden with emotion. "So lost."

She was right there with him, losing herself in them, giving herself over to him, and as they fell into a sensual, heavenly rhythm, she surrendered the last of her heart.

CHAPTER FOURTEEN

GRAYSON HAD ALWAYS been an early riser. Like his brothers, he enjoyed morning runs to clear his mind. He'd been doing it so long that the habit had become as much of an addiction for him as coffee was to others. But this morning, going running—and getting out of Parker's bed—had been the last thing on his mind. Of course Christmas had other ideas, so Grayson had gotten up long enough to feed him and put him out before returning to Parker—and loving her thoroughly. *Several times.* In the bed, the shower, and later, on the couch. She made him want in ways he'd never wanted before, and crave so much more than sex. He wanted today, tomorrow, and even though it might be crazy, he wanted every day thereafter.

He looked up from the railing designs he was working on and admired her as she read her script, which had been delivered when he'd gone home to pick up clean clothes and toiletries. She'd had a bout of sadness over missing Bert when they were eating lunch. She'd shared a few memories of their visits to the Cape. Talking about him had helped her feel better, and they made plans to visit Abe again Saturday morning. He thought that visit would help, too. Grayson knew grief was like a cloud, appearing unexpectedly and stealing your light. A person could try to outrun it, but grief was a very patient competitor, and eventually it always caught up. Dealing with it, accepting the pain and anguish and figuring out how to survive with a different kind of light was the only way to truly move past it. Parker was walking down a rocky road, but she wasn't running from her grief, and Grayson welcomed the chance to help her find her way.

Now she sat sideways on the couch, her bare feet tucked beneath the cushion. She vacillated between scribbling notes, twisting the pen between her finger and thumb, and holding the pen between her teeth. Everything she did was enticingly adorable, but he especially liked when the pen was in her mouth and she twisted her hair around her finger as she read. Her brows knitted, and every once in a while she'd laugh, gasp, or smile. He could see that no matter how much she disliked the media attention that came with her job, acting was as much a part of her as metalwork was to him. If he wanted Parker in his life, he had to get over his dislike of the lifestyle her career demanded.

"I can feel you staring," she said with a mischievous smile. Her eyes were still trained on the script.

"You're distracting, sitting over there with your tank top slipping off your shoulder. You know how much I love kissing that particular body part." He could still feel her silky skin against his tongue—among other delicious parts.

She met his gaze. "You like kissing all of me."

"Fishing for more?" He cocked a brow, loving when she fished for more.

Her cheeks flushed.

He rose from the chair and took the script from her hands.

"Hey, I'm working." A smile accompanied her complaint as he parted her knees and lay between them, resting his chest on her belly so they were eye to eye.

"Grayson…"

Breathless. I love that. "How can I work with you looking so cute and sexy?"

She ran her fingers through his hair. He loved that, too. There wasn't anything about Parker he didn't love, and that was the other thing making it hard for him to concentrate. He'd fallen for her, overnight it seemed. He was completely and utterly taken with her, and as he gazed into her beautiful eyes, fear tiptoed in and her words came back to him. *This feels very far away from my real life.*

He'd spent time working in the foundation's Beverly Hills site, and he'd gotten his fill of the elitist personalities and materialistic lifestyles that seemed to go hand in hand with the wealthy in that part of the world.

"Are you even listening to me?" She tugged his ear.

He pushed his thoughts aside and focused on Parker. "I

was thinking. Sorry. What did you say?"

She rolled her eyes. "You came over here and then ignored me? Hm? Honeymoon's over, huh?"

He pressed his lips to hers. "Never, sweetheart. I was thinking about *you*. I'm sorry. Tell me again. You've got my full attention."

"I have a confession to make, and I should have told you a few days ago, but it's embarrassing." She twisted her hair around her finger.

"After last night, how can anything possibly embarrass you?" He'd loved her body so thoroughly he could still recall the scent of her desire.

"Not that kind of embarrassing." She paused, as if she was remembering their intimacy, too. "You know how I always asked you to make changes to your designs?"

"Do I remember?" He laughed. "Baby, I spent more hours on your designs, and the emails explaining why I chose to take the avenues I did, than I would have spent with six other clients over the same time period."

Her lips curved up in a gratified smile. "Yeah, I know. That's kind of why I did it."

"Huh?"

"I *loved* reading the whys and hows of your design process. I'd get back to my trailer after hours of acting, exhausted, with more hours of studying ahead of me, and totally unmotivated to dive back in. And your emails were like rejuvenating treats.

I'd stare at my laptop, wondering if you'd sent an email. My heart would go crazy, and then I'd be afraid to look. Because if you didn't send one, it made me sad, and if you did, I sometimes felt guilty knowing I'd made more work for you just to fill my empty spots."

"So, your changes weren't because you were overthinking every little detail?"

She shrugged. "Isn't that overthinking? Only it wasn't the designs I was overthinking. It was you."

He rose onto his palms and pressed his lips to hers again.

"Then by all means, overthink me, baby. Overthink me all you want. That's the very best news you could give me."

"Why?"

"Because I thought I'd misinterpreted the tone of your emails, that you hadn't meant them to feel as personal as I took them. The only thing that held me back from asking you to video chat with me, like I would have done with any other client who requested a million changes, was the feeling that if we did, we'd have a hard time keeping our relationship professional. And I'm not sure why I worried about keeping our relationship professional, but I did."

Wonder filled her eyes. "All that time, you were feeling something for me?"

"Feeling the possibility of something and wanting there to be something more. Yes."

"I was feeling that way, too. But you were stronger than

me. I gave in to my feelings when I sent you the email about building the railing. I had planned to see Bert, then come here for a few weeks after filming. I wanted to see if...to spend time getting to know you in person. I didn't expect to lose Bert, or to go into radio silence for two weeks. I'm sorry about that."

"Don't be sorry, baby. I just wish I had done something sooner, asked you to video chat, or told you what I was feeling, because I could have been there with you when you found out about Bert. I could have gone to the funeral with you, been there when you went to the bank, when you needed someone to hold you and tell you everything would be okay."

"Grayson," she whispered.

She did that a lot, said his name like it contained all her thoughts. And he had a feeling that in those moments, it did.

"I know, baby. We've got a lot of time to make up for." He sat up and pulled her into his arms, where she belonged. "You're an incredibly capable and strong person, and you were blessed with Bert for a long time, but in a sense, you've been on your own your whole life, finding your way to a great career and hoping for more. I'm here now, and I want to be your *more*."

GRAYSON'S EYES WERE so full of emotions Parker thought he'd named them perfectly. *More.*

"You already are," she said, leaning in for a kiss. Her phone rang beneath Grayson's leg.

"Oh, baby, you make my whole body sing."

She laughed and shoved her hand beneath his leg to retrieve her phone. "It's Luce." She moved from his lap and answered. "Hi, Luce."

"I thought you were lying low?"

"I am," Parker said, confused by her comment. Grayson blew her a kiss and went back to the drawings. "I'm at the beach house reading the script Phillipa sent."

"And who is the stunning creature kissing you in the elevator?"

Parker's jaw gaped. "What?" *Ohmygod, the elevator!* Her mind whizzed through the possibility of hidden cameras, and panic spread through her chest.

Grayson launched to his feet at her shriek and came to her side, eyes narrowed, worried. *Possessive.* She loved that.

"Seriously, woman," Luce said. "We're *friends.* If you've got that artist, or any other hot and hard man for that matter, holing up with you, the least you can do is give me the juicy details so I don't have to see it on the front of *Us Weekly* first."

Parker covered her face with her hand. "Oh God, Luce. How bad is it?"

"Bad?" Luce scoffed. "Are you kidding? It's smokin' hot. I'm surprised you didn't short-circuit the elevator."

"Are we...? Where are his hands?" She closed her eyes

against the fierceness of Grayson's stare, hoping Luce didn't say, *Beneath your dress.*

"Where *were* they is a better question," Luce asked.

"Luce! Hands! Where are they in the picture?" She held up a finger to Grayson, who was practically breathing down her neck. She wanted to know what she was dealing with before saying anything. He sank down on the couch a few inches away, giving her a little more space to breathe. She needed to stand in the middle of a deserted island to have enough air right now.

Luce sighed the universal dreamy sigh that women used when something was overtly cute or romantic, and Parker breathed a little easier. She wouldn't have sighed if his hand was between her legs. Her public-relations damage-control claws would have sprung out.

"His hands, which are absolutely enormous, by the way, and which we're definitely going to revisit, are on your neck. His thumbs are resting on your jaw, and the kiss is…intense. It's perfect. It's the kind of kiss that will have women yelling at their husbands for *not* kissing them like that."

Parker reached for Grayson's hand. "I know that kiss well. So, give me the bad news. The caption?"

"How could they write anything bad? You look like a couple in love. The caption reads, 'Parker Collins Comes Out of Hiding with Hot New Man,' and then it goes on to talk about Grayson winning the award for the foundation, and they speculate about this and that."

Parker was still stuck on looking like a couple in love, and Grayson was still watching her like a hawk. "Hold on, Luce." She lowered the phone and said to Grayson, "Someone took a picture of us kissing in the elevator. It's in *Us Weekly*."

"Christ. I already screwed things up for you?" He scrubbed a hand down his face.

"No. Not at all. Let me find out more from Luce, but don't worry. It's fine." She was surprisingly not as worried as she had been initially. It *was* a perfect kiss, and she could kiss anyone she wanted to. It wasn't like they'd caught her with her Mustache Rides shirt, her butt hanging out of her shorts, and looking like she'd just crawled out from under a night of boozing it up.

Grayson didn't move. He stared straight ahead, a rigid statue of concern. *Over me.* An unfamiliar, safe feeling moved through her. Where had he been all her life?

She lifted the phone to her ear, smiling as she hashed out the situation with Luce.

"This is *not* a situation, Parker. This makes you *normal*." Luce paused long enough for Parker to agree. "Now, let's talk about where you thought his hands were. And is it true, the bigger the hands—"

"Luce!" Parker laughed, and Grayson lifted his eyes. She mouthed, *It's fine. I promise.* He rested his head on the back of the couch and sighed, like she'd just told him he didn't have cancer. And she fell even harder because of it.

She watched as he went back to the table and leaned over the drawings. A moment later she realized Luce was still talking.

She'd completely lost track of their conversation and caught up as Luce warned her to expect more pictures to pop up. Not that Luce thought she'd be hounded there on the Cape. Luce said it was too far from the real gossip and not controversial enough of a story to warrant the paparazzi's travel expenses. But now that they had the scent of something, they'd want to blow it up to sell magazines. She told Parker to expect random photos of her with other guys to pop up, claiming to threaten her relationship with Grayson.

After the call, she joined Grayson at the table. He set his pencil down and opened his arms, and she settled onto his lap.

"I'm sorry, sweetheart. I never would have kissed you in the elevator if I'd thought it would cause trouble for you."

She touched her forehead to his shoulder. "Yes, you would have."

He smiled and framed her face with his hands. *Oh yeah, Luce, it's true. Big hands, big everything. Heart, mind, and body.*

"Yeah, you're probably right." He pressed his warm lips to hers. "So what happens now?"

"Nothing. All they did was speculate that you were my new man, which is true. I mean, it puts us in the spotlight, and Luce said the photogs will probably try to take pictures of me with other guys to stir up trouble—and sales. But you know I'm not like that, so I'm not worried."

"That's a relief. We'll be more careful from now on." His eyes shifted away, the muscles in his jaw suddenly tense.

"I don't want to be more careful, Grayson." His expression remained tense. "What is it?"

"Who was your *old* man?" he asked in a low voice.

"You're jealous." She poked his chest. "You! The most confident guy I have ever met is jealous? Over me?" She laughed, and he cracked a smile.

"I'm not jealous. I'm curious."

Oh, this was going to be too much fun. "Well, there was Bradley Cooper, but we only dated for a few weeks because he sucked in bed and, well, who wants to deal with that? And Liam Hemsworth, but he was on the rebound from Miley, so I don't count him."

Grayson ground his teeth together, and she couldn't resist saying, "I guess you could call Christian Bale my *old* man, because he was the last one I slept with, but only to bide my time as I waited for—"

"Christ, Parker. What the hell are you doing with *me*?"

Taken aback, she pressed her hands to his cheeks and, in her most serious voice, she said, "You didn't let me finish."

"Do I really need to hear who you were waiting for? I'm not anything like those Hollywood guys, Parker. This is me. This is my life. Going out to shabby bars with friends who don't give a shit about what they wear, not caring who sees me because I'm happy as me, and…" He shook his head, and her stomach sank.

"I was teasing, Grayson. I haven't dated any of those guys, and I was going to say that I was waiting for *you*, but you're really worried about this, aren't you?" He'd knocked her completely off-balance, and she didn't know how to right herself again. "What happened to all that stuff about this is our reality and dealing with things as they come up? I thought we were growing legs? I want legs!"

Great, now she was on the verge of tears. She snapped her mouth closed and fought against the torrent. Grayson's lips split into a wide grin, and understanding dawned on her, bringing with it a flash of anger.

"You jerk!" She smacked his chest, and he laughed, which only made her angrier. "You scared the bejeezus out of me! Stop laughing!"

He grabbed her face and kissed her right through her mini tantrum, until she was moaning and laughing intermittently right along with him.

"Your pretty-boy actors have nothing on me, baby."

"I hate you a little right now," she said. "And I'm concerned that you really *are* worried about those things."

His eyes turned serious again. "Not the men, baby. Never the men. But the other stuff? I think we both are, but as you said, we're growing legs. And boy do I love these legs." He slid his hand up her thigh.

"But maybe we should figure it out," she said. He kissed her again. "You're really good at distracting us," she said.

"We'll figure it out," he promised, and brought his mouth to her neck—he knew just how to make her brain stop working.

"I want...Oh, that feels good." She struggled for focus. "I want you to come spend time with me next month in LA, after you're done with the railing and before you go to Texas, and..." *Ohmygod that feels so good.*

"Whatever you want." His breath slid over her skin.

Eyes closed, reveling in the feel of his lips on her neck, a memory of something he'd said in one of his emails came back to her. "But you hate LA."

"But I would do anything for you." His tongue slicked over her bottom lip.

"Me too," she said breathlessly.

He took her face in his hands and his eyes turned coal black. "Good, baby. Now stop overthinking. There's nothing we can't handle. We've got this."

He kissed her again, and she closed her eyes, trusting his promise and soaking up his confidence—and his glorious kisses—as the next one extinguished her worries, replacing them with something much sweeter.

178

CHAPTER FIFTEEN

OTHER THAN DEALING with a week of ribbing from his family and friends about the photograph of him and Parker kissing on the cover of *Us Weekly*, Grayson had had a damn good week. And it passed at a perfect pace, each day beginning and ending with Parker in his arms. Christmas adjusted well to Parker's new bedmate. The smart dog waited until they were done with their evening lovemaking to crawl not so stealthily to the foot of the bed, where he slept until morning. They definitely needed a bigger bed, but Grayson didn't mind the company. After all, Christmas had been there before him, and the big dog needed love, too.

By Saturday the three of them had fallen into sync with other aspects of their lives as easily as they'd fallen into each other's hearts. Grayson spent his days at Grunter's working on the railing, which Parker had made only one change to—adding two birds for Christmas. Christmas had jumped into his truck and gone to work with him twice this week, and he had to admit he liked the company. He liked the railings even more as each piece was forged and the roots came to life, just as he'd noticed Parker coming into her own as time passed and she healed from her grief. She'd gone out with Sky and the girls twice this week, and now they were texting one another like old friends, which thrilled him to no end.

Parker had loved the script she'd been given, and it seemed like that had started a flurry of activity, including a barrage of emails and phone calls, texts, and scheduling of future meetings. When her calls ran late, Grayson used that time to fit in a run. But he didn't crave those runs the way he had before Parker came into his life. Now he craved their intimate mornings and shared evenings, when they walked on the beach with Christmas and watched the sunset, met friends for dinner, or talked into the wee hours, sharing their hopes and dreams. Lately Grayson found himself imagining a future with Parker. He had no trouble picturing the life they'd share or even the family they'd raise, as long as he didn't try to figure out the logistics. He got hung up there every time.

He pushed those thoughts away now, as sunshine and a cool bay breeze streamed through the open French doors, filling the living room with the promise of a beautiful Saturday. Grayson reached for Parker's hand and sat down beside her at the table, where she'd spread out the contents of Bert's safe-deposit box. He took in the numerous unopened envelopes, yellowing with age and dating back to the early seventies. He picked up a photograph of a man, Bert, he assumed, and a much younger Parker, getting his first glimpse of the girl she'd been and the man who had been her *every-thing*. Her hair was longer and all one length, not layered or styled, like she wore it now. She was smiling, but her eyes told of her worries—wariness, fatigue, hope, and beneath it all was the confidence she must have been honing her whole life. Bert was soft around the middle, his eyes the same gray-blue as Abe's, though filled with welcoming kindness. No wonder Parker trusted him. If Grayson had met this man, he had no doubt he'd have trusted him, too.

"That was taken the day he took me to meet the first modeling agent. Bert asked her to take it so we would always remember the day. I told him he could keep it. I think I knew even then that modeling wasn't my thing."

She picked up another picture and smiled as she ran her fingers over her image, then handed it to him. "This was the first picture Bert ever took of me, at the park."

He felt like he was looking at a different girl than the one in the previous picture. She was laughing, and she must have just turned around, because her hair was blurry, swinging across her face and chest. Sunlight reflected in her eyes, accentuating the moment with a youthful, carefree exuberance. He didn't recognize that carefree look, and he wondered if she'd been acting even then, or if in that moment she'd felt that way. He hoped for the latter, and even more, he hoped one day to see that carefree side of her firsthand.

"That's the picture he gave to the modeling agent. It's one

of my favorites." She leaned closer. "He got all excited and told me to turn around and look at the balloons. I remember looking so hard, wanting to see the balloons. Not because they were balloons, but because his excitement was contagious. So I've got my back to him, and I'm scanning the park and squinting up at the sky, trying to find them, but of course there was nothing there. He knew just how to trick me into getting the shot he wanted." She laughed softly. "I loved that about him. Anyway, suddenly he yells *Puppies!* and, well, you know how I am with Christmas. I love puppies, and I spun around to see the nonexistent puppies. That's why I look so excited. Bert was good, wasn't he?"

Grayson's chest warmed with emotions for the man who'd had her figured out and had used that knowledge to help her. He hugged Parker, loving them both a little more, and kissed her temple.

"He sounds wonderful. Are you okay? Are you sure you still want to go see Abe this morning?" They'd also planned to stop by his father's hardware store afterward. He was excited to introduce Parker to his father, and he wanted to check on him. He'd sounded tired the last few times they'd spoken.

"Mm-hm. I'm just deciding if I should bring the letters and the pictures, or if it would upset Abe to see the letters again."

She showed him more pictures of her and Bert from recent years, and a picture of Bert and Abe when they were boys.

Someone had scribbled their names and ages on the back of the black-and-white photos, along with *Mom, Dad, and boys* on a family photo. She picked up another picture, of Bert and an older man arm in arm. The look of love in their eyes was undeniable.

"This was Bert's lover, Alan. They were together for forty-five years. Alan passed away two years before Bert and I met, but Bert didn't tell me about him until months after the day he took that first picture at the park. He said he knew we needed each other. That he recognized the loneliness in my eyes." She paused, and he knew she was probably remembering their conversation. "I'm glad they had each other for so long, and I'm glad Bert and I had each other for so long."

He thought of Abe, whose beliefs about what made a man strong were so off, and thought it would make sense that his ideas of what made a man weak were also misconstrued. "I wonder if Bert being gay had anything to do with Abe's feelings toward him."

"I don't know. I wondered about that, too, but that's not a battle I want to fight, and I don't think Bert would want me to, either. He told me stories of what it was like to be a gay man when he was young, and how things had changed over the years. From what he said, Alan hated keeping their relationship a secret. He was eleven years older than Bert and had been dealing with hiding his sexuality that much longer. One day Alan said he was done hiding, and they came out together. Bert said it was the most freeing—and the scariest—thing he'd ever done, but that Alan was his rock."

She set down the picture. "Bert was my rock, and I hate that I wasn't there when he needed me most. He did so much for me, and I didn't—"

Christmas lumbered in from the deck and stood beside them, his big head cocked to the side, as if he wanted to know what had made his mom so upset.

Grayson gathered Parker into his lap and pressed one hand to the back of her head, and when Christmas whimpered, he petted his head.

"He knew, baby," he reassured her. "He knew how much you loved him, and it sounds like what you gave him was exactly what he needed. You were there to share his life. You loved him, and he loved you back."

She nodded against his chest. "I know, but..."

Grayson took her face in his hands and wiped her tears.

"But it hurts, and you feel like you let him down. I know. I felt the same way about my mom when we lost her so unexpectedly. But they knew, baby. I'm sure of it." He kissed her softly. "It's okay to feel sad and even to feel like you let him down, but know in your heart that you couldn't have done anything differently. We're all going to die someday, which is why we live for now and we love the people we care for with all we have so they know it after we're gone."

"How do you do that? You always make me feel better."

"I just tell you the truth. I wish I could make it so you'd never feel this type of pain again, but even Herculean efforts can't do that. But I can promise you, if we're not physically in the same place when you're sad, or lonely, or just need me, one call is all it'll take, and I'll be there as fast as I can."

"I promise you the same."

Christmas pushed his head between them, lightening the mood and earning a few extra promises to be there for him, too.

PARKER FELT MUCH better after her brief cry, but she was pretty sure it had more to do with Grayson than the actual release of her tears. She decided to bring Abe the photographs and the letters, because they were rightfully his, and if they upset him, she'd simply take them back home. The normally stoic nurse was a little less rigid today, and flashed a brief, seemingly relieved, smile when they arrived.

"He's very tired today, but I know he'd like to see you," she said. "Please keep it brief. He hasn't had much energy lately."

"You go ahead," Grayson said. "I'm going to hit the men's room, and then I'll be right in."

Parker pushed the door to Abe's room open, feeling the absence of her boyfriend's bigger-than-life presence beside her.

She looked over her shoulder and saw him speaking with the nurse, then stepped into the room. Abe's eyes were closed, and she wondered if he was asleep, but as she came to his bedside, his eyes opened.

"She returns," he said quietly, with a hint of his grumpy self. It was just a hint, and it made her smile, because that grumpy self was *Abe*.

"Hi, Abe. How are you?" She leaned in and hugged him. His skin was still ashen, and his breathing was even more labored.

"You sure do hug a lot," he grumbled.

She could tell he was forcing the grumpiness and decided to tease him a little. "I only hug grumpy old men."

"I think Lacroux might refute that."

She smiled. "Yes, you're probably right."

"Where is he?"

"He's in the bathroom. He'll be in shortly." She slid her bag from her arm to retrieve the pictures and letters. She hadn't considered his lack of sight until now, and wondered if he could see anything at all. "I brought you a few things."

His fingers curled around the sheets. "Why?"

"Because I'm a nice person. And because I thought you might want them. Abe, please excuse me for asking, but—"

He held up a shaky hand. "Confidence. Control. Didn't Bert teach you anything? Don't say excuse me for asking and then proceed to ask a question. Just ask the damn thing. Or don't. But be confident in whatever you do."

She was strangely pleased with the life lesson he doled out so adamantly. That had to mean he cared, at least a little. Otherwise why bother? She heard Grayson come into the room.

"Right, sorry. Abe, can you see anything at all?" She cringed inwardly at the directness of the question.

"No. And don't get all sappy," he said sharply. "Macular degeneration happens to old people, and it's a blessing. I don't have to see myself wither away."

"Okay, no sappiness," she said as Grayson came to her side and placed his hand on her lower back.

"Lacroux." Abe gave a single, curt nod.

"How are you, Abe?"

"How do I *look?*" He waved a gnarled hand. "Don't answer that. Tell me how Parker looks."

Grayson's eyes widened, and Parker was sure hers were just as big at the unexpected request.

"My pleasure." Grayson's eyes rolled over her face and moved slowly down her body, making the room feel a hell of a lot hotter. "Let's see. I'm sure you don't want to hear that she's beautiful, because that's too easy of an answer. Or that her blue eyes are a soft Carolina blue and her hair is the color of corn silk, fresh off the cob. You know that stringy stuff? My mother used to make us kids strip it away, but I digress."

He paused, and she knew he was enjoying the way each

description hit her square in the center of her chest, which she didn't even try to hide.

"I'll skip all that," Grayson said with a grin, "and go right to the slightly embarrassed look on her face, which is quite obviously warring with the smile she can't even begin to contain."

"Christ," Abe mumbled. "Carolina blue?" He shook his head. "Parker, what'd you bring me? Give me something to get the sappy taste out of my mouth."

She and Grayson both laughed, but her heart was still racing from the things Grayson had said. The bit about his mother felt special, and when he'd said it, his eyes had warmed like it felt special to him, too.

"I brought a picture of you and Bert when you were boys. And one of the two of you with your parents."

Abe's eyes narrowed, but he remained silent, which Parker took as a good sign. She described the picture of Abe, Bert, and their parents.

"I remember," he said under his breath. "Go on."

She described what he and Bert were wearing in the picture of the two of them, and the house behind them. Abe held a shaky hand out, palm up. She and Grayson exchanged another surprised glance as she set the photograph in his palm. He held it tightly between his finger and thumb and lowered his hand back to the bed.

"We *were* friends, once," he grumbled. "What else?"

She was more nervous about the letters than the pictures. "I brought Bert's letters that you returned. I wasn't sure if you would want them, or want me to read them to you, but they're yours. They belong with you."

He waved toward the bedside table. "Set them over there."

"Okay." She set them on the table. "Maybe I can read them to you the next time I visit."

Abe reached a hand up and Parker took it. His skin felt like tissue paper over sharp bones, making her ache down deep.

"I want you to listen to me, Parker, because I'm only going to say this once." His brow furrowed, and he squeezed her hand. Tears filled her eyes before he said another word, because his voice had a finality to it that cut like a knife. "Lacroux, you listening?"

"Yes, sir," Grayson said solemnly.

"Parker, you did what you set out to do. You should feel good about that, and I appreciate how difficult it must have been for you."

Emotions clogged her throat, causing tears to spill down her cheeks. Grayson tucked her beneath his arm.

"Tears. Just 'cause I can't see doesn't mean I don't hear. Give her a tissue, will you, Lacroux?" His sharp tone made Parker smile.

"Of course." Grayson handed her a few tissues from the table.

"Those better be tears of joy," Abe said with a stern voice. "You've got nothing to be sad about. You hear me?"

She nodded, realized he couldn't see her, and choked out, "Yes."

"Good, because this will be our last visit."

"But—"

He held tightly to her hand and cut her off. "No. I'm an old man, and these visits exhaust me. You've got a life to live, and thanks to you I've got some remembering to do before I kick off for good. I'd like to do that alone, knowing you're out there happy with your bodyguard slash boyfriend, who, I assume from his heartfelt, lovesick description, isn't going anywhere anytime soon."

A sob escaped her. Unable to hold back, she leaned in and clung to Abe. "But I'm here for a little while longer. Can't I come back?"

His frail arms came around her. "No, honey, you can't."

The endearment made her sob even harder.

"Lacroux?"

"Yes, sir?" Grayson's voice was also thick with emotion.

"You'll take care of her." It wasn't a question.

"Always."

Parker kissed Abe's cheek, unsure if the wetness she felt was from his tears or hers. "Thank you, Abe. I think I love you."

"You still haven't learned." He huffed, but his thin lips

curved up in a teasing smile that made her cry again.

She tried to square her shoulders, despite the gut-wrenching sadness of knowing this was their final goodbye, and wiped her eyes. "Confidence. Control." Drawing in a deep breath to steady her shaky voice, she said, "I love you, Abe."

He nodded and tightened his jaw against his trembling lower lip.

Grayson took Abe's frail hand into his big, strong one, and the sight brought more tears to Parker.

"It was a privilege to meet you," Grayson said tenderly. "You old bastard."

Parker gasped, and Abe coughed out a laugh.

"I knew I liked you," Abe said. "Now get her out of here. I've got things to do."

CHAPTER SIXTEEN

PARKER WAS QUIET after their visit with Abe. She'd stopped crying when they were in the elevator, and now, as they waited for the valet, her eyes were hidden beneath her sunglasses. As much as Grayson wanted to know what she was thinking, he knew the best thing he could do was hold her and give her time to process everything she'd just been through. He was still working through his own thoughts about it. Who knew the old man had a big heart under that bitter demeanor?

He tipped the valet and opened the passenger door for Parker. She started to get in and then turned and threw her arms around his neck. He held her as she cried.

"It's okay, baby. We'll get through this." Over her shoulder, he noticed a kid taking pictures of them with his cell phone. The same kid he'd seen standing outside the elevator when he and Parker were kissing.

"Get in the car, baby." He guided her into her seat. His eyes remained on the kid, who was furiously typing on his phone. "Stay here. I'll be right back." He closed the car door and headed for the kid. The last thing Parker needed was a picture of her grief.

Standing before the scrawny teenager, Grayson was breathing fire and working hard to douse the flames. He was just a kid after all, probably paid a hefty sum for the last photo and dreaming of all the video games he could buy with his loot. Grayson held out his hand.

The kid's thumbs stopped moving over his phone. He lifted his eyes to Grayson's hand and up his arm. Grayson took great pleasure in knowing his size alone should intimidate the kid into giving him what he wanted. The scruffy-haired kid shoved his phone in his pocket.

"How much?" Grayson had a hard time keeping his anger out of his voice.

"What?" His eyes darted away from Grayson.

Grayson stepped closer. He hated to intimidate the kid, and he'd never touch him, but a little fear went a long way. And for Parker, there was nothing he wouldn't do. "How much do you want for that picture?"

The kid swallowed so hard his eyes squinted.

"How much?" Grayson repeated.

The teen took a step back. "They gave me five hundred for the last picture. Said they'd give me more if I got her with another guy. I figured they'd pay the same for another of you two."

"Did you post this one anywhere yet?"

He shook his head.

"Fifteen hundred, here and now, to never take her picture again—but I get your SIM card."

"But—"

"Take the deal, or I track down your parents and you deal with the consequences." Grayson held out his hand, and the boy hesitated. His eyes shifted to the car, where Parker was watching, glasses still in place. He knew the boy was calculating how many more pictures he could take and sell—and probably also how fast he could run—so Grayson went for the kid's heart.

"She's a person, not just a celebrity, and every picture you sell makes her life ten times harder. Do you really want that on your conscience? Don't you have better things to do with your time?"

The kid looked up at him, then down at his phone.

"Didn't your parents ever tell you it's not how much money you have, but how you earn it that counts?" Grayson must have heard that a million times from his father, and he'd taken it to heart. Cheating, lying, scamming—none of that was in his repertoire.

The boy looked up and said with an attitude annoyingly fitting for his age, "My dad's a lawyer. Maybe *his* father never taught him." He took the SIM card out of his phone, smacked it into Grayson's hand, and looked at Parker again. "Keep your stupid money."

He took a step away, and Grayson grabbed his arm. The

kid's eyes widened with fear. Grayson pulled out his wallet and handed him five twenties. "For a new SIM card. Thank you. You've just made her life easier."

The kid snagged the cash. "Whatever," he said, and stalked away.

Grayson let out a heavy breath, feeling like he'd just helped Parker dodge a bullet, and returned to the car. How in the hell did she live like this?

"What was that about?" she asked.

He shook his head, reaching for her hand as he drove away from the resort. "Nothing. Are you okay?"

"Surprisingly, I think I am. Sad, you know, but I understand why Abe asked me not to come back. He's right. I came there to try to put the feud between him and Bert to rest, and I got so much more. He's cranky, and he's probably been a jerk to a lot of people. But I don't know. I guess I feel like he's paid his dues. As he said, it was his cross to bear, but I could tell he feels bad about how his life unfolded. And that makes me really glad that I had a chance to connect with him. I feel like he's in a better place emotionally than he was when we met him."

She took off her sunglasses, and in her eyes Grayson saw it all—sadness, acceptance, and satisfaction.

"I think I'm in a better place, too," she confessed. "Would you mind if we lived in your world for a while? Go see your dad as we'd planned and maybe stay at your place?"

"Whatever you'd like, sweetheart." Grayson knew his simple cottage on a small private pond would pale in comparison to Parker's bay-front home, but the thought of Parker there gave him a deep sense of pleasure. He wanted her in his life, and not just for a while.

LACROUX HARDWARE WAS located on a quiet side street, reminding Parker of a small-town film set. Trees sprouted up beside narrow sidewalks, their leafy branches reaching out like umbrellas, shading the glass storefronts from the hot sun. Planters overflowed with bright flowers, and wooden benches offered passersby a place to rest. A young family sat on one of those benches in front of a chocolate shop, dipping their hands into white bakery bags and popping goodies into their mouths. Across the street, a couple stood in front of a shoe store. The woman pointed inside while the man tried to pull her away. Parker had always loved spotting those types of shared moments. Moments that she imagined were forgettable for most but she'd always longed for.

"Ready to meet my old man?" Grayson leaned in for a kiss.

I have my own moments now.

"Yes." She reached for Grayson's hand. "Your dad's a smart marketer." She pointed to the storefront window display. "Putting plants in with the tools makes it feel less like a guys-only store."

"Sky ran the store while Dad was in rehab, and she added those and some other homey touches." He laughed under his breath and shook his head. "She even painted murals behind the shelves, because to Sky, everything is a canvas."

"Including people's bodies."

"Exactly. She really brightened the place up. Dad had always worked alone, which I think fed into his drinking after we lost our mom. He hired a part-timer last year. Mira's a single mother around Sky's age, and I think the company's been really good for him, too."

As Grayson reached for the door, she reached for him. "Before we go in—you said you weren't going to sit around and let me fall into a bottle, or something like that. I'm not a drinker, and I don't want you to worry about that with me. I almost never drink. And I've never been drunk like that before. I have a glass or two of wine sometimes if I'm having dinner with friends, or with you, but candy and chocolate are my drugs of choice. That night..." She fished for the right explanation. "That night I couldn't see a way out from under how much I missed Bert. It was definitely a rock-bottom moment. And that next day I couldn't believe how much of the bottle I drank. It wasn't like a three-day binge, or—"

"I know." He kissed her softly. "You might not remember, but you spilled a good bit of the tequila. If you were a drinker, you'd have gone for it the very next morning, but you didn't.

Stop overthinking. I see who you are, and I like who I see."

She craned to reach his lips, and he met her halfway in a long kiss that confirmed everything he said.

"Dude?" Pete came out of the store, a bell ringing behind him as the door swung closed. "I thought public displays were off the table?" He laughed as he reached for Parker and hugged her. "How're you doing?"

She knew he was kidding about their kiss, but she liked kissing Grayson, and she didn't want anyone to think otherwise. "I'm doing well, thanks. And public displays are *not* off the table." A fluffy golden retriever pushed past him. Parker crouched to pet him and let the excited pup drench her with kisses. "Aw, hello. Who are you?"

"That's Joey, Pete's other daughter." Grayson gave Pete a quick hug. "How's Pop doing?"

"Good. Seems a little tired, but he's on his feet a lot. Other than that, he's solid as a rock." Pete gave him a reassuring nod. "We're just heading out. Haven't seen you guys at Seaside. Come tomorrow for breakfast; we'll catch up."

Grayson looked at Parker. She loved that he checked with her before answering, though she wouldn't have minded if he'd just accepted for the both of them.

"We'd love to." The girls had been asking her to come over for breakfast, too. They'd had a great time on their outings. Earlier in the week they'd spent the day at the beach, and a few days ago they'd met for lunch and then gone to a library sale in Brewster. But she selfishly hadn't wanted to give up her mornings alone with Grayson.

"All right." Pete leashed Joey. "We'll see you then. Pop's in the office."

As Pete walked away, Grayson asked, "You sure you're up to going?"

"Yes. I love your friends, and you don't have to worry. I'm not going to hole up, scarfing down candy and watching horror movies twenty-four seven. Abe will always be special, but he's not Bert. I wish I could see him again, but I'm trying to respect his wishes." She laced their fingers together and added, "Now, take me to meet the man who raised my amazing man."

The bell above the door sounded as they walked into the store, and it suddenly hit her that she was meeting Grayson's father, which was a big deal. An especially big deal for her since she'd never been in this position of meeting a boyfriend's father before. Her first instinct was to slip into actress mode and make the best impression she could, but she stifled that urge.

"Hey, Grayson!" a pretty brunette called from behind the counter in the back of the store.

"How's it going?" Grayson said as they walked down an aisle lined with cans of paint and brushes of varying sizes and color. "Mira, this is my girlfriend, Parker. Parker, this is Mira."

"I think the whole town knows who you are. It's great to meet you." Mira had a wide, beautiful smile, olive skin, and a light spray of freckles across the bridge of her nose.

"You saw the picture?" She shouldn't be shocked that everyone had seen their front-page smooch. Grayson's siblings had teased them relentlessly, and the girls ended their jokes with, *Wait! Let me get my camera!*

"Saw it? Me and my friends drooled over it." Mira gasped and waved a dismissive hand. "Oh, not like that. Not over Grayson. No offense, Grayson. You're cute and all, but…"

"No offense taken," he said with an amused grin.

"*Whew!*" Mira laughed. "What I meant was the passion searing off the page between you two was super hot and super cute. Totally drool worthy."

She had an easy way about her that Parker instantly liked. "Thank you."

"Neil's been smiling about it for days." Mira lowered her voice. "You can thank Sky for that." The bell above the door sounded again. "Duty calls. Nice to meet you, Parker. Don't be a stranger." She hurried toward her customer.

"I *love* her," Parker whispered as they headed to the office.

"Maybe I should grow my hair longer and paint on a few freckles."

She laughed. When they came to his father's office and she saw the picture from *Us Weekly* framed in the center of his desk, she nearly swallowed her tongue.

Neil looked up from the ledger he was working on, and when his lips curved up, it was easy to see where Grayson got his good looks. His father's hair was lighter, and the strong angles of his face were softer but clearly similar. Her eyes returned to their front-page kiss, and her nerves came back to life. The frame sat beside a wedding picture of Grayson's parents, and another of Pete and Jenna. His love for his children was inescapable. Pinned to the wall above his desk were pictures of Grayson and his siblings, from toddler to man and woman. Parker's heart squeezed at how much love a few pictures could convey, and she felt honored to have her picture beside the others.

"Gray." Neil pushed from the chair and embraced his son. He was a big man, though not as broad as Grayson.

"Hi, Pop." Grayson reached for Parker with pride in his eyes, but before he could get a word out, his father's arms engulfed her in a warm hug.

"Parker, it's nice to meet you, sweetheart." When he drew back, his smile still in place, his eyes moved between her and Grayson.

Sweetheart. She wondered if that's what he'd called Grayson's mother, and the thought made her feel even more special.

"It's nice to meet you, too."

"Pop?" Grayson picked up the framed picture of them kissing. "Seriously?"

"Your sister gave one to each of us." He chuckled. "I guess she didn't tell you."

Parker stifled a giggle when she realized Sky and the girls hadn't said anything to *her* either. Maybe Bella wasn't the only prankster. Or maybe it wasn't a prank at all. She smiled at the thought.

"Pete and Hunter have them?" Grayson's eyes narrowed.

"Yup." Neil said. "Matty, too. Sky said if we waited for you to give us pictures, we might not ever get any 'cause you're too busy smooching."

"Christ." Grayson shook his head.

"Aw, son. Your sister loves ya. And apparently she and the boys are keen on Parker, too. Besides, I added in the 'smooching' part." Neil's eyes went serious, and he turned his attention to Parker. "Sky also told me that you don't want any hullabaloo about being an actress. It's nice that you've done so well for yourself, and I'm sure you're a fine actress. But whether you're an actress or selling newspapers on the street corner, what matters is who you are without all that other stuff mucking things up, like how you treat my boy. I hope you're not just dating him for his good looks and wealth." He winked. "Because neither one will get you very far."

"Darn," she teased. "I guess I'll have to rethink my plans."

Grayson smiled at that. "I was worried you weren't feeling well today, Pop. Good to see you're still as humorous as ever."

"I'm fine, Gray. Just a little tired is all." He sank back

down to his chair and reached for his wedding picture. "Real life is now, and we don't get to live these days again, so tired or not, I'm living it."

Real life is now. The apple didn't fall far from the tree, and that familial connection made her feel good all over.

Neil gazed compassionately at Parker. "Sky told me you lost your friend, and I'm sorry you had to go through that. Grayson knows what it's like to lose someone you love, so you're in good hands. But if you ever want to talk to an old man, my door's always open."

"Thank you," she managed, touched by his kindness and by Sky's thoughtfulness. She'd not only thought to tell her father not to make a big deal about her celebrity status, but also to tell him what Parker was going through. She imagined some people might find that intrusive, but to Parker, those were hallmarks of a caring friend.

"With the right people by your side"—Neil lifted his eyes to Grayson—"there's nothing you can't get through."

CHAPTER SEVENTEEN

LATER THAT EVENING, after picking up Christmas and all of his doggy paraphernalia, clothes, toiletries, the script Parker was working on, and a few other necessities, Parker and Grayson settled into his cottage. The three-bedroom home was nestled among a sparse forest of pitch pine trees, overlooking a private pond. Christmas sniffed every inch of each room, finally claiming the spot before the fireplace.

As Grayson went through the motions of opening up his private world to Parker, he waited for panic to trip him up. But the only thing tripping him up was how much he loved seeing Parker move from room to room as she put her things away.

"You have such great taste." She kissed him, her arms full of toiletries, then disappeared into the bathroom. "I love the pictures of your family in the living room and the sculptures in the yard."

Over the months they'd been emailing he'd dreamed of her being there with him, but seeing her things mingling with his—her clothes hanging beside his, her perfume and brush beside his cologne on the dresser—made his cottage feel even more like a home.

She returned to the bedroom and put her clothes in the drawer he'd emptied.

"And this bed? Oh my goodness. I've never seen anything like it, which means you must have made it."

She had no idea how big a deal it was for Grayson to *want* to share his bed with her. He'd never wanted to share his home, or his bed, with a woman before. The bed he'd designed and forged with his own two hands. But when it came to Parker, nowhere was off-limits.

Later that evening they ate dinner on the patio. After dinner he leaned against the doorframe of the master bedroom as Parker got ready for a walk around the pond.

"How did you stand staying at my house when yours is so wonderful?" she asked.

"What's to stand? You were there. We could stay in a palace or my truck and I would be fine with it as long as we're together. I was worried my place would be too rustic or too small for you."

"Too small? You have three bedrooms. How many more do you need?" She grabbed her sandals from the closet and set them in the room.

"Not too small for *me*. You're used to big, fancy places. This is anything but."

"You're right. It's not big and fancy. It's cozy and homey,

and I can't imagine loving anyplace more."

I can't imagine loving anything more than you. He'd been having those thoughts more often the last few days, and it was a struggle to keep them to himself.

She bent to slip on her sandals, giving him a clear view of her perfect ass. He pushed from the doorframe and gathered her in his arms.

"Bending over like that was very unfair. Taunting me, when I've had to watch you looking torturously sexy in my bedroom all day."

She wound her arms around his neck. "How did I look in the living room?"

He kissed her deeply.

She let out a long breath. "That good?"

"Mm-hm." He kissed her again.

"And in the bathroom?" She closed her eyes and tipped her head back, giving him access to her neck.

"Sinful, just like you do now. Like you needed to be stripped naked, bent over the sink, and loved hard." He slicked his tongue over her pulse point, and she whispered his name. "Mm. My girl likes that."

"What about…?" she said breathlessly. "In the kitchen?"

"The kitchen?" He pressed his hands to her cheeks and gazed into her heavily lidded eyes. "You should always be naked in the kitchen."

"Naked," she whispered, pressing her body to his. "Why?"

The way she fished for dirty talk always turned him on. "I want to make love to you on every counter, spread-eagle on the table, on the floor…" He tangled his hand in her hair and lowered his mouth to hers, kissing her with long, deep strokes of his tongue. She moaned with pleasure, and when he intensified the kiss, she pushed her hands into his hair and held on tight. Damn, he loved that. He grabbed her ass and crushed their bodies together, groaning at the feel of her against his hard, eager cock.

"Baby, I don't think we're going to make that walk." He sucked her earlobe into his mouth, grazing it with his teeth.

"There's always tomorrow."

With that green light, his hands traveled over her luscious curves, up her rib cage, over her breasts, and back down the way they'd come. They kissed and groped, nipping at each other's lips and tongues, their necks and shoulders, until they were both panting with need. He tugged her shirt off and tossed it across the room. In one snap her bra followed suit. Moonlight cut a path across her bare breasts, the sight of her taut nipples heightening his arousal. She unbuttoned her jeans as he stripped off his shirt, and he made quick work of ridding himself of his pants and briefs. She watched, licking her lips and slowly unzipping her jeans.

"Let me." He moved her hand and held her by the hips as he sat on the edge of the bed and guided her between his legs. Unzipping her jeans, he said, "I want you right here, where I can see and touch and taste."

Holding her hips again, he visually feasted on her. She was stunning, bare from the waist up, her breasts rising with each heavy breath. "You're so beautiful, sweetheart."

He pulled her closer and brought his mouth to her breast, teasing her nipple with his tongue and earning another greedy moan. She arched against his mouth, urging him to take more, but he continued teasing, licking circles around the tight, sensitive bud.

"Grayson, please," she begged. She fisted her hands in his hair, trying to direct him. But he was too strong, too determined to bring her pleasure.

He dragged his tongue in a horizontal path down the side of her breast, to the dip between the two, and over the swell of the other, seeking her nipple. His mouth hovered over the taut peak, licking, then breathing on her wet skin and repeating the tease until her nipple was so tight he knew she could feel it between her legs.

He grazed his teeth over the tip, and she cried out. "Please, please, please."

"Soon," he promised, and kissed the space between her breasts.

He hooked his fingers into the waist of her jeans and silky panties and kissed her belly, loving the way her skin jumped against his tongue. She clawed at his shoulders, sure to leave marks, but he didn't care. It was exquisite, feeling need in her touch, so tightly wound she was almost ready to come. He tugged her jeans and panties down her hip to her thighs, revealing her smooth, bare sex he couldn't wait to get his mouth on. He kissed her from hip to hip, pausing to thrust his tongue into her belly button as he would his cock into her sweet, hot center. She pushed his shoulders, urging him lower.

"I don't need guiding, baby. You need patience."

He brought his tongue to the cleft of her most sensitive lips and slid his tongue over it, tasting her desire. She fought against her jeans, trying to spread her legs, but they were trapped. Perfect for the titillating pleasures he had in mind.

"*Ohgod*, Grayson."

"I've got you, baby."

He slicked his tongue over her sensitive nerves. Her thighs flexed, her breathing went shallow, and her nails clawed into his flesh as he took her higher. Stroking, licking, teasing her until her entire body trembled with need. He pressed his hand flat on her lower back, bringing her flush against his mouth, and filled his other hand with her breast.

"Need you," she said, trying to push her jeans down.

"You'll get me, baby. I promise. Come for me." He slid his tongue from her clit to between her swollen, wet lips in a quick repetitive pattern.

"Ohgodohgod, Gray—"

She bucked against his mouth, but he didn't relent, stroking her faster, as her hips thrust and her sex pulsed against his tongue.

"Grayson, Grayson, Grayson." She panted, shaking from head to toe, as the orgasm eased.

He rose to help her out of her clothes and gathered her in his arms, needing a deeper connection.

"Dontstopdontstop."

"I'm not baby. I just want to hold you." *In my arms forever.* He captured her lips, warding off his confession, possessing every corner of her mouth. He'd crawl inside that sexy mouth of hers if he could. She was so fucking sexy, so sweet, so *his.* Love coursed through him, dragging him further into her depths. It was all too much, the wanting sounds she made, the passion in her eyes, the way she moved with him.

When their lips parted, she pleaded, "Tellmetellme."

Holding her in his arms, he sank down to the edge of the bed again. "You're going to come on my cock, and then you're going to come on my mouth." He lifted her easily and guided her legs around him as he lowered her onto his eager erection. They both groaned at the intense coupling.

"Oh God. So good." She touched her lips to his. "Love this."

Love coursed through his veins, rode the surface of his skin, and stole from his lips. "I love you, baby."

She opened her eyes and searched his.

"I do, sweetheart." It was too fast, too much for her. He knew she'd overthink this, just as he probably should, but his

SEASIDE LOVERS

emotions were too real to question.

"Don't think, Parker. Feel." He placed her hands on his shoulders. "Ride me, sweetheart. Make me yours."

"I..."

He kissed her to quiet her thoughts. "Shh. You don't have to say it. Just *know* it."

A worried look hovered in her eyes, bringing with it a new ache.

"What, baby? Tell me. Too much, too fast?" He'd barreled into her life, a life that had been tossing and turning for weeks. He wanted to settle her, make her feel safe and loved. To be her rock, her anchor, her *everything*. But he could wait a lifetime if that's what it took.

She shook her head, and a stream of emotions washed over her face—worry, love, lust. It was the lust that seemed to win. "If you come, we can't..."

He couldn't suppress his smile at her sweet seductive pleas and the love she wasn't ready to share with him but that he saw and felt in everything she did and said.

"I won't. Not yet." It was torture, being surrounded by her tight heat and not coming, but he wanted so much more of her. "Stop overthinking, sweetheart. I've got you. I've got us."

He sucked her nipple into his mouth, holding her hips, and they found their rhythm.

"Harder," she said. "Suck harder."

She arched against his mouth, riding him fast, her sex

211

tightening with every downward stroke. Her breasts bounced, sweet sexy noises escaped her lips, and just when he wasn't sure he could hold back another second, she cried out his name—"Grayson"—and spiraled over the edge.

PARKER WAS BONELESS again, floating in the post-lovemaking daze she'd come to know, to crave, with Grayson. He gathered her in his arms and laid her on the bed, following her down. *You love me, you love me, you love me.* She ached to tell him she'd been falling in love with him for months, but they were supposed to be taking their lives day by day, living for *now*, and the fear of laying her heart on the line without knowing what the future held was too much. What would happen when she went back to her life in California? And after his foundation work was completed? His life was here at the Cape, and hers was all over the place, depending on the roles she took on. She knew it didn't make a lick of sense to think it would hurt less if they broke up and she hadn't said she loved him, but she was learning that when it came to love, nothing made sense.

He brushed her hair from her face, a tender smile on his. "Had enough, baby?"

He hadn't come yet. He was a machine. That was the only explanation she could come up with after having so many orgasms she'd lost track. *Six-Million-Dollar Penis.* She smiled at the thought.

"No." *I love you.* "You promised me your mouth."

"I always keep my promises." He brushed his thumb over her lips. "I love your mouth, baby. And your eyes. And your cheeks. And most of all, your—"

"Heart?" *I love your heart.*

His eyes turned wicked. "That, too, but I was going to say your knockers."

She laughed, loving his sense of humor. "You were not."

"You're right. I was going to say your sweet, delicious…*kisses.*"

She rolled her eyes. *I love your kisses, your touch, that wicked love machine between your legs.*

"Yes, your *heart*, you dirty girl. I love that sweetness between your legs, too, in case you're wondering, but that's just an added bonus."

Her jaw gaped.

"And I love that, right there. That oh-my-God-you-filthy-pig look you give me. You love to hear me talk dirty, but you hate that I know you do."

Spot. On. Another reason I love you. She pushed his shoulders, urging him lower. "Stop teasing and keep your promise."

He framed her face with his hands and kissed her softly.

"Grayson?" *I love you.*

"Yes, dirty girl?"

"Stop." She playfully swatted his arm. It was hard to concentrate with his hard length pressing between her legs. "I'm being serious."

"So was I." He kissed her again and rocked his hips, pushing the head of his shaft into her.

"God, that feels good."

"Want it, baby?" His eyes grew impossibly darker.

"No. Your mouth. I want your mouth."

He thrust in deeper, and she gasped. *Yes, yes, yes* was on the tip of her tongue. Just as she opened her mouth to say she wanted all of him, he withdrew, and she heard herself whimper.

"Mouth," he said in a gravelly voice, and moved down her body, pressing her thighs open wider and hiking one leg over his shoulder. "Hold my hands."

His fingers curled around hers as his talented mouth came down over her center. *Oh God, I really love your mouth.* She squeezed his fingers as his tongue teased and thrust, furtively seeking her pleasure point—and nailing it, over and over again. He held her hands tight, pulling her toward him and keeping her sex flush against his mouth. *Smart man, this sex god of mine.*

"Grays—" Lights flashed behind her closed lids and heat flamed in her core as the orgasm tore through her. Before she came down from the peak, Grayson was over her again, the scent of her arousal on his breath. He captured her in another kiss at the same moment he thrust in deep. She moaned, lost in the fullness between her legs, the weight of his body, and the strong beat of his heart as he wrapped her in his arms.

"Love you, baby," he said between kisses.

His words wound around her. Her thoughts ebbed and flowed with each thrust of his powerful hips. *I love you. I'm scared. I love you. I love you.* His hands moved to her neck, holding her in the position she loved, as he filled her, inch by glorious inch, time and time again. *More, more, more.* He angled his hips, hitting the spot that detonated another explosion, and they both went wild. Panting, kissing, groping, pleading, thrusting as they rode the tide of their passion.

She lay in his arms afterward, their bodies spent and slick from their lovemaking, her heart bursting with love.

"Sleep, baby. I've got you," Grayson murmured.

You do, Grayson. You definitely do.

CHAPTER EIGHTEEN

"KURT HAD TO fly back to New York for a book signing."
Leanna bounced her little boy, Sloan, on her hip. At just over
a year old, he was the spitting image of her, with brown hair
and the prettiest hazel eyes Parker had ever seen.

Parker was glad she and Grayson had seen Kurt earlier in
the week, when they'd gotten together at Pete and Jenna's
beach house for dinner. She and Grayson had been spending
the early-morning hours consuming each other instead of
food. But they'd made a concerted effort today not to get
sidetracked by mind-numbing kisses and explosive orgasms
and spend time with their friends at Seaside. She was glad
they'd come—*both in the shower and to see their friends*. It was
fun seeing everyone working together, cooking, and taking
care of each other's babies.

"Too bad Blue and Lizzie and Hunter and Jana couldn't
come. They said they were busy." Sky picked up a sippy cup
from the deck and set it on the table. Grayson had given her a
hard time about giving everyone framed copies of their front-
page kiss—including, it turned out, each of their friends—but

Sky had taken his complaint in stride. *A kiss like that should be memorialized.*

"They're busy banging," Bella said.

The guys nodded in agreement. Parker wondered if they'd known that's why she and Grayson hadn't joined them for breakfast before today.

"You just have sex on the brain," Leanna said to Bella. "They're probably…"

"Banging," Sawyer said. "Which is where we'd be if I didn't have a training session in twenty minutes."

"Whatever," Leanna mumbled.

"Why do you always deny that people have sex?" Jenna asked. "We had to rig your bedroom window so we could close it from the outside. Remember?" She turned to Parker and said, "She and Kurt always forget to close the window. It was like listening to the porn channel." She waggled her brows, and Leanna turned bright pink.

Parker could only imagine how embarrassing it would be if she or Grayson had neighbors. She'd only slept with a few men, but she'd always been a silent lover. Grayson brought out sides of her she'd never known she had. Including the warm and squishy feeling moving through her now at the sight of her big, virile man bouncing his adorable year-and-a-half-old niece, Bea, on his knee. Bea's dark hair curled up at the ends, and her smile lit up her blue eyes as she giggled anew with every bump of Grayson's knee.

"*Your lover's calling. Your lover's calling. Your lover's calling.*" Everyone turned toward the automated voice coming from the other side of the road, where a short-haired woman was poking at her cell phone.

"What was that?" Jenna whipped her head around.

"*Your lover's calling. Your lover's calling. Your lover's calling,*" sounded again, and the woman poked at her phone again.

"*That* is Bella in action." Leanna pointed at Bella, whispering in a harsh tone, "You have got to stop this. Seriously. Theresa turned us *blue* last year as payback for your pranks. God knows what she'll do next time."

Parker realized this was another one of Bella's pranks.

Bella was busy breaking up little pieces of a muffin for her daughter, Summer. "What makes you think I did anything?"

"*Your lover's calling. Your lover's calling. Your lover's calling,*" sounded again, and Bella stifled a laugh. Theresa stormed inside her house and slammed the door.

"You changed Theresa's ringtone?" Jenna laughed. Then her face went serious. "You know she has no clue how to fix it, right?"

"You should probably fix it," Amy said. "Not that I don't love your pranks, but what if she's in a store and it rings?"

"Ugh." Bella pushed to her feet. "Fine, I'll go fix it, but you know what this means, don't you?"

"That you're lying and you won't really fix it?" Amy

teased.

Bella crossed her arms, shaking her head. "No, that this is it. The pranks were the last link to our carefree years. What's left? Getting old and gray and fat and boring?"

"You're only thirty-four," Amy reminded her.

"Down!" Summer demanded.

"You're not hungry?" Bella asked, holding up a piece of muffin. "Auntie Leanna made this especially for you."

Summer shook her head, sending her blond ringlets swinging against her cheeks. Bella reached for her, and Caden said, "I've got her. Why don't you go help Theresa? I promise, babe, I'll never let your life get boring."

Bella rolled her eyes. Caden whispered something to her that made her turn beet red.

"I'm going!" Bella bounced down the steps.

Caden lifted Summer from her high chair. "You guys know she adores Theresa. She wouldn't prank her if she didn't."

"We know," Jenna said. "And now she'll probably pull more pranks in hopes of getting even more sexual favors."

"Lucky me." Caden smiled and lowered Summer to the deck. The moment her feet touched down, she was off and running, which caused Amy and Tony's daughter, Hannah, to squeal with delight and fight for freedom, too.

"Of course you want out." Amy lifted Hannah from her high chair and kissed her cheek, setting her down to chase

Summer. Pepper, Leanna's dog, popped up and followed the girls. "Where Summer goes, Hannah follows."

"Which will be hell when they're teenagers," Tony added.

"Not this one," Grayson said, kissing Bea's cheek, then lifting her into the air. "Pete's going to lock her in a closet as soon as she discovers boys."

"Gway!" Bea shrieked.

Gway. You're too freaking cute.

"Bea!" he teased, and pulled the baby down to kiss her chubby cheeks, earning more sweet giggles and melting Parker's heart.

"He will," Jenna said to Grayson. "But I'll have the key."

"Keep dreaming, babe," Pete said. "She's not dating until she's thirty."

"Don't worry, Jenna," Sky said. "You can give Bea to me and Sawyer when she's a teenager. We'll raise her right."

Sawyer's dark eyes narrowed. "What makes you think I'd let her date? I'm right there with Pete. Thirty sounds about right."

Jenna rolled her eyes. "But Sky believes in experiencing love as it comes, and we all know we women eventually get our way." She jumped up as Jessica and Jamie came out of their cottage and headed toward them. "Hey, guys!"

Experiencing love as it comes. That was so similar to Grayson's thoughts on their real lives being right that moment, whatever that moment might be. It must have come from their father.

"Did we miss breakfast?" Jamie carried their son, Dustin, who had been born around the same time as Sloan. Dustin had hair as black as his father's and eyes as blue as Jessica's.

When Dustin saw the mayhem on the deck, he thrust his hands out and bounced up and down in Jamie's arms. "Pu, pu, pu!"

Jamie set him on his hands and knees, and he crawled over to Pepper, who slobbered his cheeks with puppy kisses.

"How can you stand it?" Parker loved babies, although she had little experience with them. "I'd spend all day making them giggle."

Grayson lowered Bea to his lap, his eyes honing in on Parker. "I'm not sure you'd get much acting done."

"Who cares?" Parker looked around the table at the high chairs, colorful plastic toys, wet wipes, sippy cups, and other baby paraphernalia. She was surrounded by the sounds of toddlers giggling and running along the deck and Pepper's nails tapping out his sentinel path.

"This is what life should be about. A gaggle of kids, surrounded by friends, and—" She realized everyone had gone silent, save for Hannah and Summer, who giggled as they snuck down the deck stairs backward. Tony stood watch at the bottom of the steps. "Anyway, acting is great, but this would be nice, too."

On that little reveal, all eyes shifted to Grayson, who was

still staring at Parker like she'd just revealed she was a long-lost princess. Thankfully, the others chose that moment to begin cleaning up from breakfast, causing a flurry of activity. She and Grayson pushed from their chairs, but he was still giving her that look.

"What?" she finally asked.

"Nothing. I just figured…" He shrugged. "I didn't expect to hear that."

Neither did I, but it's true.

Bea pulled his hair, breaking their connection, and Jenna lifted her from Grayson's arms.

He waited for Jenna to leave, then guided Parker away from the others. "So, you want a gaggle of children?"

"One day. But isn't it too soon to talk about this? We aren't even talking about what's real, like where we both live. Not that I want to jump into that, but…" She paused, not knowing where she was going with that thought, because part of her wanted to talk about everything, but a bigger part of her didn't want to think about the harsh reality of their lives being on opposite ends of the country.

He searched her eyes, his own serious—*and slightly annoyed?* "You're absolutely right. It's too soon."

A confusing wave of disappointment swamped her.

CHAPTER NINETEEN

GRAYSON WAS WORKING at Grunter's on the railings for Parker's house two days later, still thinking about what she'd said Sunday morning. *Isn't it too soon to talk about this? We aren't even talking about what's real, like where we both live.* He'd been the one to say they should take things as they came, and now he regretted ever saying it. Even though she hadn't confessed her love for him, he *knew* she loved him. Knew it with the same confidence he knew he loved her. Maybe it was time to get it all out on the table and deal with what they'd been trying to avoid.

He gripped the metal tongs and held a piece of metal over the brick forge, trying to lose himself in the sounds of the blowers, the heat thrown by the brick hearth, the scent of smoldering metal. But the things that normally calmed him weren't even scratching the surface. His gut churned with the need to clear the air with Parker.

Hunter came into the workshop with a big grin on his face as he texted, which told Grayson he was texting Jana. The two of them texted often, or rather, sexted, which Hunter loved to gloat about.

Hunter shoved his phone in his pocket. "Hey, bro. You look about ready to explode."

"I'm good," Grayson lied.

"Uh-huh." Hunter began sifting through a stack of iron rods. "How's the railing coming along?"

"Good. Couple more weeks." He shouldn't take out his bad mood on his brother, but he'd done him a favor by taking on the travel for their contract with CCF, and he wished there were someone in line to do the same for him. Only he didn't really wish he could move out to California. He just hated the idea of being away from Parker.

Last night, after they took a walk around the pond with Christmas, Parker had spent an hour on the phone with her agent. Grayson was looking forward to spending time with her in her world and sharing that part of her life, despite his distaste for the celebrity lifestyle. They had planned on traveling back to LA when he was done with the railing, but after her phone call she'd told him she had to leave next week to attend meetings for the role she hoped to get in the new film, and reality came rushing in. He had to stay here and get this railing done if he was ever going to get back to finishing the work for CCF. The designs for the last two sites, Texas and Georgia, loomed. The sooner he completed the work, the more settled he'd feel, making it easier to deal with their schedules and living arrangements.

He carried the red-hot metal to an anvil and picked up a hammer, thinking about what his future with Parker really looked like. Eventually Parker would be filming on location, even if she didn't get this role. Very soon their lives were going to be even farther apart.

Grayson focused on hammering the metal, forming it into the image he'd created in his mind. If only life were that easy.

"You wanna fess up about whatever's got your briefs in a knot?" Hunter asked. "Or are we going to pretend you're not chewing nails?"

He stopped the hammer midswing and met Hunter's gaze. "It's nothing anyone can fix."

"Try me." Hunter leaned against the drawing table and crossed his ankles, casual as could be. Cocky bastard. Probably where Grayson had learned it.

"Okay, sure." Why the hell not? Grayson clearly didn't have the answer. Maybe Hunter would. "I want to be with Parker. Her life is in LA, and traveling to film on location all over the world. Except for the travel for the foundation, my life is here. I can't see a way to make those two things come together."

Hunter shrugged. "Why not?"

"What the hell do you mean why not? She lives across the country. It's not a weekend drive."

"And…?"

Grayson clenched his teeth against the urge to throttle his

brother. "And I've got to work. She's got to work. What should we do? See each other once every few weeks?"

"No. You'd never last."

"No shit." Grayson went back to pounding the metal.

"Have you talked to her about it?"

Grayson shook his head. "Can't. There's no answer, so what good would it do?"

"I don't know. Maybe *she'll* have an answer."

He set the hammer down and moved the metal aside so he could pace. "She's been through so much already. The last thing she needs is to think I have any expectations of her changing her life for me. I'm the man. I need to make the sacrifice if I want to be with her, but, man, do I hate it out there. Something about that area rubs me the wrong way."

His cell phone vibrated, and Parker's name flashed on the screen. He opened and read the text. *Christmas misses you. But I don't. Nope. Not at all. And I didn't spray your cologne on my wrist so I could smell it all day, either. It attacked ME.*

He read it again, consumed by the intensity of his love for her and wondering how he'd manage to be away from her for a day, much less a few weeks.

He lifted his eyes to his brother. "I *love* her. She's it for me, Hunt. I think about her day and night. I want to give her everything she's ever wanted—family, stability, kids. Whatever it takes to fill her heart so full she never longs for a damn thing. I really believed we could take this day by day and the answers would come, but I'm so fucking lost in her, I can't even think rationally enough to figure it out."

"You know what Pop would say?" Hunter said. "Level-headed decisions have no place where women are concerned."

"So, what are you saying? I'm overthinking this?"

"What would you tell me if I came to you with this dilemma?"

"To figure it out and make it work." Grayson paced again. "Maybe I am overthinking, which is exactly what I told Parker *not* to do. But still, there's no clear answer."

"The answers are never clear. You know that, Gray. After we lost Mom, all of us reacted differently. The answers, the way we got through it, were also different. Look at Matt. Shit, he still hasn't really dealt with it. There's a reason he's never here." Hunter knelt by the iron rods again and began picking through them. "You never know what'll come up, so just deal with it the best way you know how as it comes." He lifted his eyes to Grayson. "Aren't you the one who taught *me* that?"

"Probably. I'm smart as shit." He smirked.

Hunter shook his head. "Apparently dumb as shit, too, if you need me to remind you of your own advice." He held up two different-length rods. "Help me get this under control, will ya?"

Grayson crouched beside him. "What are we looking for?"

"I saw your drawings of a gazebo with Parker's name on it. I'm assuming we need supplies if you're building her one. I thought I'd get started on the ordering, seeing as you're too busy being lovesick to think straight."

Grayson had sketched the gazebo for her yard. Now it looked like she might need two—one for Wellfleet and one for Los Angeles.

PARKER AND SKY talked while Christmas played along the pond's edge, hurling himself at birds and barking when they flew away. Sky had surprised Parker that morning when she'd dropped by to give her a framed copy of the *Us Weekly* kiss, and they'd ended up spending the day together. They'd gone shopping, and Parker had found a cute pair of pink panties that said *Taken* across the front, which she'd changed into to surprise Grayson later. After having lunch at a café, they'd gone back to Grayson's cottage, and they'd been sitting on the dock chatting ever since.

Parker told Sky about what happened with Abe and how wonderful Grayson was through the whole thing. Sky told her about how depressed she'd been after she'd lost her mother.

"If Pete hadn't come to stay with me, I'm not sure how long it would have taken for me to come up for air," Sky said.

"I think Grayson did for me what Pete did for you," Parker confided. "I don't think I realized it at the time, but during all those months we were emailing, he'd become as important to me as Bert was. And after I lost Bert, I cut myself off from everyone—including him. And then, there he was, in the middle of my sugar-infused, tequila-laced nightmare. Like a knight in shining armor." He'd become such a big part of her life. Regardless of what she was doing—studying the script, talking to her agent, discussing press with Luce, or hanging out with Sky and the girls—she felt like Grayson was right there with her.

At the sound of tires on gravel, Christmas took off for the cottage to greet one of his favorite humans. Parker's heartbeat quickened. It always did when Grayson was around. He knelt to love up Christmas and waved to them.

"Speak of the devil." Sky waved as she pushed to her feet. "He wasn't your knight in shining armor, because you didn't need to be rescued." Her colorful skirt swished around her legs as they headed up to greet Grayson. She lowered her voice as Grayson approached with his four-legged buddy trotting happily beside him and a beautiful bouquet of flowers in his hand. "You needed to be loved so you could heal, and he was *ready*."

Before Parker could ask what she meant, Grayson closed the remaining distance between them and slipped an arm around her waist, kissing her softly and handing her the pretty bouquet.

"Hey, sweetheart."

"They're so beautiful. Thank you."

"Told you he was ready," Sky said with a knowing smile.

"Ready for?" Grayson gave her a quizzical look.

"Oh, nothing." Sky pointed at them. "I love seeing you two like this. It's as if the universe knew exactly when to swoop in and bring you together."

"Because you believe nothing happens by coincidence," Grayson said as they headed for the cottage.

"You should listen to me. I know what I'm talking about." Sky hugged Parker and Grayson and petted Christmas. "I'll see you guys later. I've got a date with my fiancé." She walked backward toward her car and called out, "We're wedding planning!"

"About time," Grayson called, then to Parker, "Hey, be my date for the wedding?"

"You don't even know when it is," she said as he held the door open for her.

"It doesn't matter when. I know we'll be together."

Her mind skidded with the realization that she knew it, too. They'd been staying at his place for only a few days, but it already felt like home. She didn't miss her lonely house on the bay one bit. The railing Grayson was making would make it feel homier, which would be wonderful for the kids visiting through the foundation. But she knew it would never feel like home to her the way his cottage did. How could it, when the man she loved had built his life here, taking every day as it came?

They went inside, and Christmas plopped down in front of the fireplace. Grayson grabbed a vase from the floor by the hearth and filled it with water. "Sweetheart, the wedding? Would you rather I ask someone else?"

"Yes, that's exactly what I want. Some other woman's hands on you." She pushed between him and the sink. "You better not."

"Never." He pressed his lips to hers.

"Not even when we're apart for long spans of time? You're a guy. You have needs."

He lifted her in his arms, and her legs wound around his waist. "The only woman allowed to satisfy my needs is right here in my arms." His brows knitted. "What about you?"

"I don't need a woman to satisfy my needs, but thanks for asking."

He nipped at her lower lip, making her laugh.

He placed the flowers in the vase and set it on the counter, then carried her over to the couch.

"I know I said we'd figure out each day as it came, but not talking about the future is eating me alive." He laid her on her back and came down over her. "There are a few things we need to clarify."

"So you're trapping me beneath you like a prisoner?" she teased.

"What was it that Abe said? Control? Confidence?"

"You've got those down pat." *In more ways than one.*

231

"Good, then hear me out. The way I see it, all we know right now is that you're leaving next week to go back to California, and I'll join you a few weeks later, when I finish the railing. We'll spend a week together, and then I'll head out to Texas to work on the piece for the foundation." Grayson's calming voice soothed her nerves. "And beyond that, we have no idea about your schedule. Do I have that right?"

"Yes, I think so. When it was just me, having an ever-changing schedule was fine. But I hate it now, and I know it's not going to be easy. I'm sorry."

"Don't be sorry, and don't worry. We both have important careers. We'll figure this out. Maybe not today, or next week, but if we want this to work, we'll find a way."

"But what if we can't find a solution, and we miss each other too much?"

"Then we deal with it and make whatever changes need to be made. I spent today tied in knots about not having the answers, and it sucked. But I realized we don't need an answer today, baby, or tomorrow. All we need is the trust that we'll work together to figure it out. This is our real life. Now, here, us."

Christmas lifted his head.

"And your boy," he said, making her love him even more. "Parker, in all the months we were emailing, I was never once with anyone else."

Shocked at his confession, it was all she could do to remember to breathe. She blinked up at him, trying to process the new, heartwarming information.

"I wasn't either," she finally managed. "But I've never dated a lot, so that's not unusual for me. But you? I've seen women checking you out everywhere we go, and you're so sexual. I'm surprised that you would do that, when we weren't even a couple."

His eyes warmed. "I told you I felt like we had something special, and I'd hoped that once we saw each other we'd see we had more. Sweetheart, I'm the way I am with you because of what I feel for you. But before you, sex was just sex, totally different from what we have together. I don't want you to worry about me being faithful, no matter how long we're separated."

"Grayson, I'd never—"

He silenced her with a kiss.

"I never thought you would, but I wanted you to know I wouldn't. There's no one else for me, Parker. Just you."

"For me, too. There's only you, Grayson. I love you so much. I've been afraid to say it, because what if we can't figure out how to make it work? I thought it would hurt more if I'd said the words, which was really stupid. It would probably hurt more if I'd never told you how much I love you and that I think I was falling for you over all those months we were emailing. And now I'm rambling, and…" She drew in a deep breath. "I love you, Grayson. I love you so much."

"Trust me, baby, even if you'd never told me, I knew you loved me."

"I do trust you. I've trusted you since day one. Just look at our perfect kiss. That is a kiss of trust."

He wrinkled his brow and followed her gaze to the picture Sky had given her, which she'd proudly placed on the coffee table, and he shook his head.

"Oh, stop. Sky gave it to us. You know you love it as much as I do."

"Kissing you? Hell yes. At least all those Hollywood hot-shots will know you're taken." He ran his hand down her hip. "You look gorgeous in this sexy little dress. Maybe you shouldn't wear it when I'm not around."

"Mm. You look pretty hot yourself." She ran her hands over his shoulders. "Maybe you shouldn't wear *any* clothes when *I'm* around."

"Your wish is my command." He reached behind him and tugged his shirt off. Every time he did that it sent shivers from her head to her toes.

"I got you a surprise today."

"Yeah?" He kissed her collarbone.

"Mm-hm. It's on me. You'll have to find it."

"I do love a challenge." His mouth took a leisurely stroll along her shoulder, placing tantalizing kisses all the way down her arm to the tips of each of her fingers.

His eyes narrowed seductively. "I'm going to have to be excruciatingly thorough."

"I wouldn't want it any other way."

CHAPTER TWENTY

GRAYSON AWOKE TO the sound of his cell phone vibrating on the bedside table. A quick glance at the clock told his fuzzy brain they'd gone to sleep only two hours ago. Parker sighed in her sleep beside him. He grabbed the phone with two fears racing through his mind—*Dad, Abe*—and slipped silently from the room to answer it.

The relief he felt that the call wasn't about his father was short-lived. He returned to the bedroom with a heavy heart, hating the world for crashing down around Parker once again. He hadn't told Parker he'd kept in touch with Abe's nurse, because Parker was doing so well, and he knew her world would be shaken up again soon enough. There was no reason to upset her in the time between coming to grips with Abe's wishes and this difficult moment.

She looked so peaceful he didn't want to wake her. She still felt guilty for not being with Bert at the end of his life, and he wasn't going to let that happen again. He sat beside her on the bed and brushed her hair from her shoulder. She reached for him, and he kissed her cheek.

"Wake up, sweetheart." Damn, he hated this.

"Hm?" She looked up at him with a small smile. "Hey, is it morning already?" She glanced at the dark windows.

"No." He swallowed hard to force the lump from his throat. "It's Abe, baby."

Her eyes filled with tears. "Is he...?"

Grayson gathered her in his arms. "No. Not yet. I wanted you to have a chance to say goodbye."

She pushed from his arms, tears streaming down her cheeks. "He said I couldn't."

"I know, but I know you, baby, and I didn't want to take the chance that you'd feel like you let him, or yourself, down." He pulled her close again. "We need to hurry. His nurse, Helga, said he doesn't have long."

She clung to him as if she'd like to climb beneath his skin. He wished he could take away her sadness, but there was no time for futile wishes. And despite the heartache, he knew she needed this chance to say goodbye.

"I love you, baby. We're going to get through this."

"*He* won't," she choked out.

"No, he won't." He closed his eyes against his own sadness. "But now you'll have a chance to say goodbye, and you've already given him the gift of a lifetime." Acutely aware of how little time Helga said Abe had, he forced himself to gently draw her away from his body. "We have to go now, baby. I'm sorry to rush you, but it's time."

He wiped her tears and helped her from the bed.

"How did she get your number?" She pushed to her feet and into her jeans.

"I gave it to her on our last visit, and I've checked in with her a few times."

She pulled on her shirt at the same time he did. "Abe doesn't want me there."

"You want to be there, and I'm pretty sure he'll be glad you came." He went into the bathroom and put toothpaste on their toothbrushes, handing her one when she followed him in.

"What if he doesn't?"

"Then we'll leave. Baby, I was going with my gut on this. Is this what you want? We don't have to go if you'd rather not."

She nodded vehemently. "Yes. Yes, more than anything. I'd just given up." Fresh tears slid down her cheeks. "Thank you for not giving up."

"I'll never give up, baby. Not where you're concerned."

HELGA ANSWERED THE door with damp eyes. Her professional attire was replaced with a pair of slacks and a rumpled blouse. Her shoulders sagged, just like Parker's heart. Grayson held Parker close, whispering reassuring thoughts, kissing her temple, and anchoring her as the world around her spun.

"Parker, Grayson. Please, come in." Helga stepped aside, filling them in as they crossed the room. "It won't be long. I'm glad you came right over."

"Thank you for calling," Grayson said.

Helga looked thoughtfully at Parker. "The doctors said he should have passed months ago. But he's an ornery man. For weeks he told his doctor he 'wasn't done yet.' Your visits helped him, Parker. I've come to believe he was waiting for you."

"But how could he know I'd come?"

"He couldn't have known. But maybe someone more important did." Helga lifted solemn eyes toward the ceiling.

Parker didn't even try to hide her tears as Helga pushed the door open and led them into Abe's room. Abe lay so still she feared they were too late. *No, no, no.* Her heart climbed into her throat. An oxygen mask covered his mouth and nose. Helga lifted the mask.

"Stubborn girl," Abe said just above a whisper.

A garbled half laugh, half cry fell from Parker's lungs. She reached for Abe's hand.

"Last time I was here you said I didn't learn, but I did." Ignoring her heartache and focusing solely on making him proud, Parker said, "'Control.' I'm here against your wishes. 'Confidence.' I love you, Abe Stein. Your brother loved you.

And I'm so glad I had a chance to get to know you."

His fingers closed a little tighter around hers. "Good girl."

Helga replaced the mask, and the room went silent again. Abe's chin bobbed, and she removed the mask again.

"Lacroux." The softness of Abe's voice did nothing to lessen the force behind his words. This frail, bedridden man, hovering between life and death, possessed more authority per syllable than any man she knew.

Besides Grayson.

Grayson leaned closer, his eyes damp and his voice tender. "I'm here, sir."

"You done good." He inhaled a few jagged breaths. "You big bastard."

Parker laughed and cried, glad that what were sure to be some of Abe's last breaths were happy ones.

Helga lowered the railing on the side of the bed so Parker could give him one last, long hug.

When Abe's frail arms embraced her and he whispered, "I love you, too," Parker shed more tears and silently thanked Bert for leaving her the letters. She'd never know if Bert had meant for her to visit Abe, but she had to believe this was meant to be. She silently prayed that Abe would pass without pain and with a feeling of peace. As she held him, she sent another thanks to the heavens above, for Grayson—his strength, his support, and his insurmountable love. Without Bert, she wouldn't have come to Wellfleet, and without

Grayson, she wouldn't be holding Abe.

Maybe Sky was right and the universe really did know exactly what they needed.

CHAPTER TWENTY-ONE

PARKER PADDED INTO the living room late in the afternoon, looking sleepy and sad with her tousled hair and puffy eyes, but when she saw Grayson, her lips curved into a grateful smile. Christmas was right behind her. The lovable pup had remained by her side since the minute she'd climbed into bed when they'd arrived home after visiting Abe. Grayson had lain with them until Parker had fallen asleep. Too restless to lie still, he'd come into the living room and called to check on Abe—and Helga. Over the last few days of calling to check on Abe, he'd learned that Helga had been in love with Abe for years, and he worried about her. He'd also phoned Sky, since she and Parker had become so close, and she must have filled everyone else in, because he'd heard from his father, Hunter, and Pete. Pete said Jenna and Sky were reaching out to the other girls.

Grayson held his cell phone to his ear, listening to Matt, who had called a few minutes ago, and wrapped his arm around Parker. He whispered, "Hey, sweetheart." Into the phone he said, "Hey, Matt. I've got to go. Parker just got up. I appreciate the call."

"I'm here if you need me," Matt said. "Give Parker my condolences. Love you."

"Will do. Love you, too."

He set his phone on the counter beside the wooden box Helga had given them when they were leaving. She'd told Parker it contained Abe's most treasured things, and he wanted her to have them. Parker hadn't been up to looking inside it, but there was plenty of time for that.

"Matt sends his condolences."

"You told him?"

"I told Sky, and I guess Sky told everyone. I'm sorry, she's just—" He realized what Sky was doing and knew it would make her feel better. "She's treating you like family. She worries, so she thinks everyone should."

She tipped her chin up. "That's nice."

"Yeah, she's pretty thoughtful."

Christmas pushed between them, and Grayson petted him.

"Are you hungry?" Grayson asked, but Parker was moving from his arms, having spied the basket of goodies he'd prepared a few days earlier.

She sat on the couch rifling through the basket, fighting for space as Christmas nosed in beside her. "Peanut *and* pretzel M&M's? Snickers? Twizzlers? Laffy Taffy?" Her mouth and eyes widened when she got to the bottom and found the movies. "*Psycho, The Blair Witch Project, The Cabin in the Woods, The Ring.* Grayson…"

"I wasn't sure what flavor of horror you liked, but these seemed like your go-to remedies for sadness."

She set the basket aside and went to him. "They were."

"I didn't get tequila."

"I don't need tequila, and honestly, I don't need these things, either. I need you, Grayson. You're my go-to remedy now."

He hated to tell her the news about Abe, but Matt had reminded him that one of the hardest things for him to deal with when their mother passed was that he hadn't received the message until two hours after the rest of the family knew. He'd been teaching a class, and his cell phone had been turned off. With that in mind, he sat down on the couch and brought Parker down beside him, holding her hands in his.

"He's gone, isn't he?" she said softly.

"He is, baby. I'm sorry. Helga said he fell asleep right after we left, and he went peacefully. In his sleep."

She blinked away fresh tears and snuggled into his side. "It's good that he went in his sleep. Will they let us know about his funeral? I'd like to go."

"There won't be a funeral. Abe didn't want one."

"I guess that makes sense. He wasn't really the kind of guy who would want to be the center of attention."

"Helga said you were the only person who visited him."

"The *only* person? That's so sad, and it's probably why he left me whatever's in that box."

"Apparently he sold their family business years ago, and once the transition was complete, she said he preferred a solitary life."

"At least he had Helga." She eyed the box and sighed. "I'm going to wait to look at what he left me."

"Wait as long as you'd like. No rush."

He gazed into her eyes and was surprised to see light beyond the shadows of sadness. "You've had a rough few weeks."

"It's funny how the bad comes with the good. Losing Bert was awful. Losing Abe is sad but not as hard as losing Bert. I had no warning with Bert, but I knew from the first day I met Abe that he wasn't doing well. And while all that sad stuff was happening, you and I had all these wonderful moments. So I'm in this weird place where I feel okay instead of devastated. Does that make me a bad person?"

He gathered her against him. "No, baby. It makes you someone who knows she's loved. You felt alone when you lost Bert, but now you have me and our friends. You have family."

CONVINCING GRAYSON TO go to work Thursday morning was like pulling teeth. But as much as Parker wanted to spend time with him, which had become her favorite thing to do, she needed him to know she was okay. And the only way to do that was to push him out the door.

She'd taken a walk with Christmas and returned the calls and emails she'd missed. Phillipa had sent her two film pitches to consider. A few weeks ago she would have been chomping at the bit to get the most challenging roles. But her life had changed so much, the idea of filming ten to fifteen hours a day and being away from Grayson and Christmas for weeks on end didn't sound the least bit appealing. She was excited about the romantic comedy script she'd read, though, and she hoped to secure the lead role. But that was only *one* movie.

She no longer needed to fill empty hours with work to avoid a life she wasn't living. She liked the life she and Grayson were building together. She hadn't even realized that's what they were doing, *building a life together*, but that was exactly what had happened. And the life they were building was becoming *their* real life.

In the afternoon Parker armed herself with a bag of pretzel M&M's and took Abe's box down to the dock. She was doing well, but she wasn't a fool. There were going to be tears, and tears required hugs or chocolate. Since she'd sent Grayson away, what other choice did she have?

Christmas lay on the dock beside her, his tail slapping the wood in a pattern that seemed to say, *Hurry up! Hurry up!*

"You can go chase birds. I don't need a babysitter." She kissed his head. "Really, I'm good now." *Good. I'm so much better than good. I'm happy.*

Christmas *woofed* and bounded back toward the beach, leaving Parker alone with the box Abe had given her. She was happy that Abe had thought of her and sad that he'd had nobody else. Running her finger over the rough wooden edges of the box, she thought about Bert and the day she'd opened his safe-deposit box. She'd cried the whole way home from the bank. Now, thinking of what Helga had said when she'd given it to them, she wondered how a man's most treasured possessions could possibly fit in a box. Then she thought about the things she cared about, and she had the answer, and her heart ached anew. Her most treasured things weren't possessions at all. They were a man, a dog, a few close friends, cherished memories of Bert, and Grayson's emails and all the memories they'd created together recently. Abe didn't have anyone.

Drawing in a stabilizing breath, she opened the lid and saw the pictures she'd given Abe looking back at her. Her heart squeezed with the memory of his knobby fingers holding the picture of him and Bert. She lifted them from the box, enjoying the memories of both men they roused.

Setting those pictures aside, she withdrew an aged and worn envelope. The handwriting and date told her it was the first letter Bert had sent to Abe. The one he'd said he read. With shaky fingers she opened the letter, missing Bert anew at the sight of his familiar script. She smiled at the succinct note and wondered if he'd kept it short because confidence and control were so important to his brother.

Abe, you stubborn son of a bitch. Call me. Bert.

Abe was right. He had wanted to fight it out.

Quiet laughter slipped out, and she turned damp eyes up toward the sky.

"You two. I love you guys."

Christmas barked, and birds scattered. Parker watched them fly toward the clouds, thinking about the three people she'd lost. She'd been an infant when she'd lost her mother. She didn't have any memories of her, but she'd always felt she was missing a piece of herself. But she'd moved on. Bert had taken a bigger chunk of her heart, and Abe had taken another piece. She never knew a heart could take so much loss and still function, but Grayson had shown her that not only could her heart still function, but it could be strong and happy and feel full again.

Lifting out the stack of Bert's letters, she fingered the neatly spliced edges, imagining Helga's capable hands sliding a letter opener along the creases. Parker chose to believe Helga had read each of the letters to Abe. Pleased with that thought, she put them aside. Whatever the letters contained was between Abe and Bert. It was enough for her to know the letters had been among Abe's most treasured possessions.

She withdrew a book wrapped in red cloth from the box and unwrapped it. Turning the pink journal over in her hands, she saw the word *Diary* written across the front. The pages were frayed, as if they'd been read many times. A small golden lock hung crooked from the hinges, the tiny clasp broken. *Like the man who left it to me.*

She opened the cover, her pulse quickening at the scrawl of youth in the center of the page. *Miriam Stein.* Her heart stumbled as Abe's voice whispered to her, *My girl Miriam had guts.* With shaky hands, she flipped the page of his daughter's diary and read the date written in the top left, *December 3, 1980.*

It's Chanukah. All I wanted was a guitar. I got this stupid diary and a bunch of ugly jewelry and fancy clothes...

CHAPTER TWENTY-TWO

THE SOUND OF car doors closing and Christmas's barking pulled Parker from Abe's daughter's diary. She had no idea how long she'd been sitting on the dock reading, but she'd read every entry from December 3, 1980, through November 2, 1982, and was nearing the end. Christmas charged up to meet Sky, Bella, Amy, Leanna, Jenna, and Jessica, who were headed down to the dock. Parker waved, still in a bit of a fog from all she'd read. The girls looked like they'd come from the beach, each in a cute sundress, the tops of their bathing suits tied around their necks. Their flip-flops slapped against the dock as they made their way to Parker with Christmas bumping into their legs and excitedly licking their hands.

Parker smiled up at her new friends, traipsing toward her like the cavalry.

"There you are," Amy said. She set a bag down beside Parker. "We were worried about you."

"I've been calling you all day." Sky sat beside Parker, and the other girls sat, too, forming a circle around her. "Jana wanted to come, but she wasn't able to reach her dance students to cancel her class."

"My phone's inside. Sorry. I guess I've been out here longer than I thought."

Jenna reached into the bag and withdrew a jumbo package of snack-sized candy bars. "We brought grief food."

"Aw, you're so sweet. But Grayson beat you to it." She grabbed the unopened bag of chocolate from behind her. "Did he ask you to check on me?"

"Please, we don't need to be asked," Bella said. "We wanted to come earlier, but when you didn't answer your phone, Sky called Grayson, and he said you were probably sleeping. So we waited, and waited, and finally got sick of waiting."

"Um, full disclosure." Sky wiggled a finger in the air. "Grayson did call me this morning on his way to work and asked if it would make him a total overbearing a-hole if he turned around and refused to leave you alone today."

Parker melted. That was *so* Grayson.

"I told him it would, and that if you told him you were fine, you were and he should trust you." Sky leaned closer and said, "I hope that's what you wanted, but don't think for a minute that we girls think 'fine' means 'fine.' We know better."

Unexpected tears welled in Parker's eyes.

"Oh no," Leanna exclaimed. "We didn't mean to make you cry."

Parker shook her head, overwhelmed with affection for

these women who had so quickly become a part of her life, and for Grayson for calling Sky, and for…Well, hell. Couldn't a girl just cry? She swiped at her tears.

"You didn't make me cry. I mean, you did, but not in a bad way. I'm really okay. As okay as I can be. I just…" She tried to find the right words to express how much their friendship meant to her. "Grayson called you, and you're all here." She fanned her face to dry her tears. "I've never had this type of support before."

"Tissues," Jessica said.

"On it." Jenna dug in the bag again and tore open a big box of tissues. She handed a bunch to Parker.

"Thank you." Parker wiped her eyes and held up the diary. "I think I'm crying because of this. Abe left me his daughter's diary, among other things, but *his daughter's diary*! It's so full of teenage angst and heartache."

"Why did he leave it to you?" Amy asked.

Parker shrugged. "His nurse said he had no one else. Abe said his wife left him for another man, and he was so full of hate when he spoke of her, I'm not surprised they didn't keep in contact. And his daughter?" She ran her hand over the diary, remembering the frustrations it held. "Abe said she ran off to join a band and he spent thousands trying to find her but she left no trace."

"I wonder if she was abducted," Jenna said.

"You never know," Jessica added.

"She was *so* unhappy. I think she really did run away. She wrote a lot about wanting to play in a band." Parker flipped through the diary. "But I don't think it was just the band. Listen to this. 'Today Ass'—that's what she calls Abe." Her heart hurt thinking about Abe reading those words, and she wondered if he'd read them a million times, or only once, and tossed them aside with the rest of his emotions. She forced herself to continue reading. "'Today Ass actually spoke to me. He said to be dressed and ready by seven for dinner with the Paddingtons. That's eleven words in six days. A record.'" She lowered the diary.

"Can you imagine your own father never speaking to you? The whole thing is filled with this kind of stuff. He worked all the time. Her mother seemed nice, but listen to this." She flipped a few more pages. "'Two hours of straight fighting. Going on three now. I begged Mom to leave him again'— 'again' is underlined about ten times—'but she looks at me like I'm crazy and says he's a good man, he's just stressed, he doesn't mean it, and all the other crap adults say to kids like we're idiots.'"

"Wow," Sky said. "No wonder she left."

"Does it say where she was going?" Jenna asked.

"No. It doesn't even say she planned to run away in so many words, but there's this." She flipped to the last entry she'd read. "'I'm saving every penny Ass gives me. I was going to finally buy my guitar, but it would be too bulky to carry and too easy for people to remember.'"

"Sounds like she didn't want to be found. And she was smart," Sky said.

"She'd written about that guitar since the very first entry, and this one's dated two years later. It makes me so sad to think that's the thing she clung to with all the stuff she was dealing with. She wrote about having a ton of cash, and in all that time she never bought the guitar. I think she must have been saving up to run away all that time." Parker closed the diary. "I guess Abe was always giving her money."

"Instead of love," Jessica said. "It happens a lot in wealthy families. And the guitar? If she's anything like I am with my cello, it signifies something much bigger than just an instrument to her." Parker knew Jessica had played for the Boston Symphony Orchestra before having Dustin.

"Maybe it signified freedom," Parker said. "I have to find her mother and return this to her."

"Definitely." Leanna petted Christmas, who was snoozing between her and Jessica. "I can't imagine not knowing where Sloan was. That's a parent's worst nightmare."

Parker thought of her own mother and wished for the millionth time that she'd been a little older when she'd lost her, so she could remember her face, her voice. *Anything.*

"We can help you," Jenna said. "Do you know anything about her? Name? Where she lives? I guess if she's remarried, she'd have a different name."

"I bet Caden can do some kind of search at the police station," Bella offered.

"Jamie knows how to pull anything and everything off the Internet, and I know he'd help." Jessica smiled reassuringly.

Parker knew Jamie had developed OneClick, a search engine rivaling Google.

"Kurt's friend Treat Braden has connections with private investigators in and out of the country," Leanna said. "I'm sure he'd be willing to connect you with them."

"You guys are so awesome." Parker was overwhelmed by their support. "But I'm hoping Helga, Abe's nurse, might know where to start. She worked for him for several years, so maybe she has her new last name or an address or something."

"Okay, but if she doesn't, we're here to help," Amy reassured her.

"Then we have a plan. If Helga can't help, the Seaside girls are on the case!" Jenna took the diary from Parker, set it in the box, and carried the box to the far end of the dock. When she returned she pulled her sundress over her head. Christmas's head popped up to watch the pretty girl in the blue bikini that barely contained her enormous boobs. "But before we start this mission, we have to initiate Parker to our group."

Parker watched as each of the others pulled off their dresses and dropped them to the deck. "Initiate?"

"It's time for you to become a Seaside sister." Jenna stripped off her bikini—right there on the dock! She yelled,

"Chunky-dunking!" and leaped into the water, splashing them all.

Christmas barked, leaping around the dock as bikini tops flew in the air, bikini bottoms fell to the girls' feet, and naked women dove into the water, one after the other.

"I've never skinny-dipped!" Parker knew her cheeks were bright red, but as the girls laughed and splashed, urging her on, her embarrassment slipped away with every cajoling plea.

"Take it off!" Jenna hollered.

"Come on! It's totally fun!" Amy yelled.

"Don't be a chicken!" Bella called out.

She looked at her new friends who had come over despite the fact that she'd sent Grayson away, somehow knowing what Parker didn't, what she couldn't, having never had sisters— they knew she needed them, regardless of how well she thought she was doing.

GRAYSON PULLED DOWN the driveway, waving to Sky and the girls as they passed on their way out. Christmas greeted him as he stepped from the truck.

"Hey, buddy. Where's your mama?"

Christmas ran to the cottage, and Grayson let them both in. He found Parker sitting at the kitchen counter wrapped in a towel. Her hair was soaking wet, and her cell phone was pressed to her ear. The box Abe had given her sat open in front of her, and a handful of empty chocolate wrappers were piled on the counter to her left. He scanned the contents of the box—a red cloth partially covered the letters Parker had left for Abe, and a pink journal lay on its side. He was glad to see she'd opened the box, but he wished he hadn't gone to work so he could have been with her when she did. He leaned down and kissed her cheek.

She turned a smile his way and held up a finger, mouthing, *One sec. Don't go away.*

Like there was anywhere else he wanted to be? It had been hell staying away all day, but at least Sky had texted him when she arrived at the cottage to say Parker was there and the girls were with her.

"Okay, thank you," Parker said into the phone. "I look forward to meeting you, too." After she ended the call, she jumped to her feet and hugged Grayson. "I'm so glad you're here. It's been a crazy day."

"Looks like it. So, you're okay?"

She looked down at her towel and her smile widened. "The girls initiated me into their group, and I looked through the box, and now I have to go to New Jersey."

"Whoa, towel girl. New Jersey?"

She pressed her hands to his chest. "Yes! I have so much to tell you."

"I can't wait to hear. I'm glad you're okay. I was worried

about you."

"I know you were. Thank you for not coming back to rescue me. I love that you wanted to."

"Not rescue you, baby. Be with you. Comfort you. And my sister has a big mouth."

"I love her! I love all the girls, and, Grayson?" She grabbed his face, her eyes dancing with excitement. "I love you. So very much."

"Now, that's what I like to hear." He pressed his lips to hers, and felt her melting against him, and just as quickly, she broke the connection.

"Stop kissing me for a second or I won't be able to think."

"What's wrong with that?"

"Grayson," she pleaded.

He put his hands behind his back. "Okay. Start at the beginning, but I'm not sure how long I can resist you."

She went up on her tiptoes. "Me either." She kissed him again. "Darn it. This always happens. Act unsexy or something!"

He laughed and tugged her against him. "This is as unsexy as it gets. Say your piece so I can take mine."

"You're so bad." She bit her lip, and the darkening of her eyes told him she was thinking about how good it would feel to be close, just as he was.

"What was I saying?" she asked breathlessly.

"Something about an initiation that looks like it included

nakedness and chocolate, you looked in the box, and you need to go to New Jersey."

"Oh, right," she said. "You make me forget everything." She shook her head, completely unaware of the effect seeing her flustered over him had on every part of him. Finally she said, "Did you know the girls chunky-dunked?"

"Everyone knows they do, but usually only at night at their community pool." His eyes narrowed. "Did you skinny-dip here?" Thank God they had no neighbors.

"Uh-huh. It was so much fun. I'd never done it before, but…I love them so much, Grayson. It's like having the sisters I always dreamed of. I wasn't going to do it, but they were having so much fun, and they could probably convince me to do anything."

"That sounds like trouble," he teased. "Tell me the rest, baby. The box? New Jersey?"

She grabbed the box and told him about what she'd found, what she'd read, and how she felt compelled to return the diary to Abe's ex-wife.

"I called Helga. She did some poking around, and she found his ex-wife, Sarah. I asked Helga why she didn't just return the diary to her directly. She said she'd never go against Abe's wishes, but that she'd hoped I'd come to this conclusion on my own. Can you imagine? That's loyalty."

"She loved him, baby," he explained. "She told me she'd been his nurse for the past seven years, and for several years before that she was his personal assistant. Unrequited love is a powerful thing."

"Oh no. Poor Helga. She must be so sad."

"She has family to help her through. They live in Hyannis, and she's returning there after she ties up things here."

"Good. I'm glad she has family." She pressed her hands to his chest again. "I'm so glad I have you, Grayson. Will you come with me to see Sarah? I was going to mail the diary to her, but when I called and told her I had it, she broke down and could barely get a word out. I really want to be the one to hand it to her. Mail is so impersonal."

Marveling at her generous and caring spirit, he couldn't imagine ever loving her more than he did right then. "Of course you should be the one to give it to her."

"She's in Rocky Hill, New Jersey. I'm not sure where that is, but it can't be *that* far from here."

"That's not far from where Matt lives. When do you want to go?"

"As soon as we can. Will you come with me? Please?"

The hope in her big blue eyes made his insides go soft. "What do you think?"

"With that bear of a client breathing down your back, I wasn't sure if you could get away," she teased.

Sliding his hands beneath her hair, he kissed the corners of her mouth. "Maybe I can convince her to give me a little time off."

CHAPTER TWENTY-THREE

"I DON'T KNOW why I'm so nervous," Parker admitted as Grayson parked in front of Sarah Stein's house Friday afternoon. She hadn't been nervous on the drive over, but now that they'd arrived, her stomach twisted and turned. They were staying with Matt tonight, and they'd left Christmas with Hunter and Jana. Jana had fallen in love with him at first sight, so Parker knew her boy would be well cared for.

"It's because you care," Grayson said with the soothing confidence that always put her at ease. "You know this is going to be hard for her, and maybe hard for you, too. You were up until almost two in the morning rereading the diary."

She'd held the diary in her lap during the entire drive, and now she pressed it to her chest. "I had to read it again. There are so many conflicting emotions in here. I longed for parents my whole life, and I dreamed about how wonderful it would be to do the silliest things with them. Have breakfast, go shopping, tell them about my friends at school."

His eyes warmed as he took her hand and squeezed it reassuringly. "I'm sorry you didn't have those things. But one day you'll be able to do all those things with your own child."

Her throat thickened. They hadn't talked about children since they had breakfast at Seaside, but she knew in her heart Grayson wanted a family as much as she did.

"I hope so. But Miriam had parents who had the means to give her everything, and all she wanted was to be noticed and loved and for them to support her passion for music. I know everything in this diary is from a teenage perspective, which can be skewed and self-centered, but still. These were *her* feelings, regardless of how anyone else perceived the things she wrote about. In her head, her father was loyal only to himself, her mother was loving but overly loyal to Abe—so who was loyal to Miriam?"

"Maybe Sarah can shed some light on that for you."

As he came around the car and offered her a hand, she was reminded of their first trip to see Abe, when Grayson had climbed into the car without giving her a choice—and he'd stuck by her side ever since.

On the front porch, he hesitated before knocking. "Ready?"

She nodded and tried to slip into her actress armor, rolling her shoulders back and lifting her chin, but not for the first time since she'd come to Wellfleet, it made her feel like she was wearing someone else's skin. This wasn't the time to pretend. She shook off the ill-fitting costume. This was Sarah Stein's *real* life, and Parker hoped that when she handed Sarah her daughter's diary, it would make her life better and not worse.

She managed a nervous smile. "I'm ready."

Every rap of his knuckles on the door echoed inside her like a countdown. She held her breath as the door opened and Sarah Stein came into view. Her hair was a stunning mix of white-blond and silver, cut just above her shoulders, with natural curl and heavy bangs that gave her a surprisingly youthful appearance. Sarah pressed her hand to her chest and her mouth opened, but no words came.

"Sarah? I'm Parker, and this is my boyfriend, Grayson. It's such a pleasure to meet you."

Sarah nodded, then shook her head, looking slightly confused. Parker wondered if she had forgotten they were coming, or perhaps Sarah recognized her as an actress.

"Parker," Sarah said with a warm smile and less confusion in her eyes. "Forgive me. Yes, it is a pleasure. Please, come in."

"Thank you." Parker stepped inside. The scent of cinnamon and freshly baked bread hung in the air. "Mm. It smells like a bakery."

A nervous smile lifted Sarah's lips. "I bake when I'm nervous."

"It's nice to meet you, Sarah," Grayson said.

"You as well. Thank you for coming all this way. Grayson, why, that's a nice, strong name." She led them through the foyer to a spacious living room and motioned toward an olive-green sofa beneath the windows on the far wall. Paintings of trees hung on butter-yellow walls above another couch on the adjacent wall. A vase of fresh flowers sat atop a glass table beside an upholstered wing chair. Parker glanced at Sarah, with her peach top and black slacks, and thought the simple but elegant room suited her perfectly.

"Please," Sarah said, "make yourself comfortable."

"Thank you," Grayson said.

Sarah nervously smoothed her black slacks. "Can I get you something to drink? Tea? Coffee? Water? Or something to eat? I have an abundance of cinnamon rolls and tarts at the moment."

"No, thank you." Parker was too nervous to eat.

"Sure. I'd love anything you baked, thank you." Grayson rose from the couch. "Would you like help?"

"Oh no," she said. "I'll be just a moment." She disappeared through the dining room.

Grayson whispered, "I thought she needed a reason to move. She's as nervous as you are." He put his arm around Parker. "You okay?"

"Yes. Or I will be. She looked at me funny when she first saw me, and I worried she didn't remember our phone conversation."

"I'm sure it's a lot for her to take."

Sarah returned from the kitchen carrying a tray with plates, several cinnamon buns that smelled like heaven, and three glasses of water. Grayson was quick to take it from her and set it on the table.

"Thank you, Grayson," Sarah said as she sat on the sofa. "Such a gentleman."

There was a brief moment of uncomfortable silence. Sarah folded her hands in her lap. Her lips twitched nervously, tugging at Parker's heart. She wanted to soothe Sarah's nerves, and while she hoped the diary might someday do that, she knew today was probably not the day. Today was probably going to bring a torrent of emotions, just as their phone call had.

"Sarah, as I mentioned on the phone, Abe left me Miriam's diary." She got up and handed the diary to Sarah.

Sarah placed her hand on Parker's, nodding toward the seat beside her. "Join me? Please?"

Parker sat beside her.

Sarah's gaze was trained on the diary. "The police found this under Miriam's mattress when we reported her missing. They went through all of her belongings, looking for clues, something to tell them if she was indeed a runaway, or if something awful had happened to her." She sighed and shook her head. "I knew she'd left of her own volition, even before the police found her diary. She was only sixteen, but so wise for her age. Stubborn and confident, like her father. Nothing could have held her back, and if she didn't want to be found, I knew she'd find a way to stay hidden. When the police returned the diary to us, Abe whisked it away. I wasn't sure I'd ever see it again." She looked at Parker. "Did you read it?"

Despite her embarrassment for peering into Sarah's family's privacy, she told the truth. "I did. I'm sorry. When I first saw it—"

Sarah patted Parker's hand. "It's okay, dear. I would have done the same."

"I'm really sorry, for everything."

Sarah nodded. "Me too. I failed my own daughter, and not a day goes by that I don't wish I could go back and relive those years. Do things right this time."

"I can only imagine how hard that must be," Parker said.

"It was hard to see clearly back then. Despite what you've read in Miriam's diary, Abe was a *good* man with good intentions. He poured himself into his family's business in order to save it."

"Yes, that's what he told us." Parker didn't want to talk about Abe too much, given their unfriendly divorce, but she wanted to validate Sarah's thoughts.

"He was so business savvy." Sarah stared down at the diary as she spoke. "He was incredibly smart, determined. Unfortunately, he wasn't as well equipped when it came to people. He handled things poorly, pushing everyone who loved him out of his life. The guilt of it ate at him, but he was a prideful man. So prideful he lost himself somewhere along the way." She met Parker's gaze. "You were a friend of Bert's?"

"Yes. We were very close," Parker said.

"He was a wonderful man. I'm sorry he's gone," Sarah said in a thoughtful tone. "I would have liked to remain close to Bert, but I would never have gone against my husband's wishes. I loved that man too much." She looked at Grayson. "I didn't know a person could love too much, but I did. I lost Miriam because of that love. I thought she was going through a phase, wanting to join a band and angry all the time. She never stuck with anything. When she wanted to dance, we got her lessons. The next month it was horses, and a few months later singing. Wasn't that what teenagers did? Talked about becoming the next this or that but never followed through? When we first read her diary, I thought, 'If only we'd bought the guitar...' But she didn't leave because of the guitar." She lowered her gaze to the diary again and pulled a wad of tissues from the box beside her, wiping tears as they slipped down her cheeks. "We gave every ounce of ourselves to searching for our daughter, until there was nothing left—no more leads to follow and no more *us* to hold on to."

"It must have been very painful," Parker said.

"It was. It is. You mentioned on the phone that you were surprised I'd kept my name. Abe must have told you that I left him for another man."

"Yes. He did." She hated admitting she'd been privy to that part of their history as well.

"There was never another man. I loved Abe even after he

became so hateful no one else could stand to be around him. I was only twenty-five when we met. He was eleven years older, and I thought he walked on water. He had big dreams, and I knew he'd accomplish every one of them."

"He was a very confident man." *Confidence. Control.*

"Yes. And he became mean as a snake. We were both so broken, so depleted of anything good. If I'd stayed, I would have turned into the wretched person he'd become, and I still had hope that Miriam would one day come back. That's what carried me out the door. I'd failed her once. She thought I was weak for staying with a man who didn't know how to show his affection to anyone but me, and only in private. I tried to teach him, to tell him his daughter needed him, but that just brought arguments about how there wasn't enough time in the day. God knows what type of hold he had on my heart—truth be known, he still does."

Sarah laughed under her breath. "Even from beyond the grave he still has a hold over me. When I finally got the courage to leave him, I knew he'd come for me if I didn't do something so evil he would no longer be able to stand the sight of me."

"So you made it up?" Parker asked, exchanging a look of disbelief with Grayson.

"I had to. For Miriam. I knew she'd never come near Abe again. On her eighteenth birthday I moved out in the meanest, ugliest way I could. And then I prayed, day and night, that Miriam would come back." Sarah sat back, and a genuine smile climbed all the way to her eyes. "And then, five years after Miriam left, on October 15, 1989, I received a phone call from her. My heart nearly stopped. I thought it was a prank, because we'd had our fair share of those over the years. But it was my Miriam. There were lots of apologies on both sides and tears, which made it hard to talk, but she was alive and well and happy. She sounded truly happy." She wiped her steadily flowing tears.

"Here, baby." Grayson handed Parker a tissue for the tears she didn't realize she was shedding.

"She said she was living out west and had a surprise for me. She said she'd be here on the eighteenth. I never even thought to ask how she'd found me, or for her phone number. I was so overwhelmed, but I felt so *good* after that call. I was afraid to leave the house, in case she called again, so I waited. Throughout that week and the next. When she didn't call and didn't show up, I wondered if I'd imagined the call. I waited for weeks, which turned to months, then years."

Parker felt Grayson's steady gaze on her, but she couldn't take her eyes off of Sarah as she revealed the anguish she'd suffered.

"Every October fifteenth I remember our call. At least now I only allow myself to dissect every word we said on that *one* day. For years I went over it in my head *every* day, wondering what I'd said that made her not want to come back."

"I'm sure it wasn't anything you said," Parker reassured her.

"Did you try to have the call traced?" Grayson asked. "To track her down?"

Sarah shook her head. "If I had done that, Abe would have been notified because her case had never been resolved, and then there would be no chance of her returning. I still have hope." She turned to Parker again. "When I saw you standing on my porch, my mind reached for Miriam. That happens a lot. I search the face of every blond-haired, blue-eyed woman, wondering if that's what my daughter might have looked like at that age."

She reached for a frame on the table beside her and showed it to Parker. "This was taken a few weeks before she went missing."

Parker took in the girl's straight honey-colored hair and vacant blue eyes. She looked sad despite her smile. Parker saw a hint of that vacancy in Sarah's eyes, like the missing pieces of their lives reflecting back at the world—a look Parker recognized all too well, having seen it in her own reflection for so many years.

GRAYSON HAD LEARNED many things from his father, but perhaps the most important lesson was when to hold his tongue. He applied that lesson now, sitting on the front stoop of Matt's home, waiting for him to arrive, as Parker paced the yard, rehashing their visit with Sarah. She'd been taking apart every sentence, every facial expression, every unspoken emotion, for a half hour.

"Do you think she had the same thoughts we did after the call when Miriam never showed up? That it wasn't really her daughter after all? Or if it was, maybe something had happened to her? I couldn't live like that, without knowing the answers."

He forced himself not to move from the step, because if he held her in his arms, he knew he wouldn't be able to keep from saying what had been eating at him since he saw the picture of Miriam.

"She has no choice," he finally answered.

"Not now she doesn't. But back then? She could have done *something*."

"She was afraid of Abe finding out. Besides, it was 1989. How advanced was technology back then?"

"I don't know. I was only a year old." Her eyes filled with sadness.

Damn, he could take her angst, but he was no match for her sad baby blues. Unable to stay away, he pushed from the stoop. Taking her in his arms, he gazed into her eyes, loving her so much he ached.

"She did what she felt was right, sweetheart. I know you

want to help her, and I'm sure you're wondering how you can help track down her daughter, but you've done all that you can. You've given her back something she went years without."

"Yeah, a diary full of bad feelings." She touched her forehead to his chest. "Did I make a mistake? Should I have left well enough alone? Do you think she'll be okay, or do you think she's falling apart right this very second because of the diary?"

He lifted her face again, unable to concentrate on her questions as love for his caring, thoughtful girlfriend obliterated every other thought. "Do you have any idea how much I love you?"

"You're not answering my questions."

He cocked a brow, having already answered the same questions at least four times since she'd begun analyzing their visit.

She sighed.

"We've gone through this, sweetheart. She's doing whatever it is she needs to do to deal with having the diary after all these years." But he wondered if there was something else *she* could do, and decided to feel her out. "Did Miriam's picture look familiar to you? Did the timing of her call and the fact that she never showed up ring any bells?"

"What do you mean?"

Was it possible he'd seen only what he wanted to see, and

he was barking up the wrong tree?

"Her daughter called days before the San Francisco earthquake."

"You think she..." She swallowed hard.

He shrugged. The picture of Miriam flashed in his mind again, so similar to the picture Bert had taken of Parker at eighteen.

"Oh no. I hope not," she said. "That would be terrible."

"Baby, the picture she showed us? Don't you think it looked similar to the one Bert took of you?"

"What? No. She..." She stepped away and paced. "What are you saying?"

"I'm not *saying* anything. I'm thinking out loud."

"Well, don't," she snapped. "Whatever it is you think you're putting together, don't."

"Baby." He reached for her and she stepped back, her face a mask of hurt and anger. "I'm sorry, but the dates, the picture. Maybe I'm reading too much into it, but what if I'm not?"

"You definitely are," she snapped. "My mom's gone, Grayson. And I hope Sarah's daughter isn't."

He reached for her again, and she let him hold her this time. "I'm sorry. I don't mean to upset you, but what if the dots connect? What if your birth mother was Miriam Stein? A genetic reconstruction DNA test could give you the answer."

"What? No. Absolutely not. My mother was *Sherry Col-*

lins, not Miriam Stein. You're grasping at straws. Do you know how big of an area the *west* is? She could have been anywhere out there, not just in California. I just...I don't want that for her. I don't want that for me. What if I get my hopes up, and then it's not her?"

He softened his tone. "But what if it is? It would mean you have a grandmother you could get to know. You'd have your family."

"No." She shook her head. "It would mean my mother ran away from parents who didn't love her enough. It would mean she was killed because she was in the wrong place at the wrong time, all because her father was too self-centered to love her or incapable—"

She was shaking all over, and he realized just how big of a mistake he'd made.

"I'm sorry. Shh. It's okay." *Goddamn it.* He couldn't put her through this. He could be *way* off base, and she didn't need another thing to worry about. But what if this was the link she'd always hoped for? How could he turn his back on that possibility?

Parker exhaled loudly. "I trust your judgment, Grayson, but I think you're way off on this. I can't even begin to give it serious consideration. I don't want her daughter to be dead. I want her to be off somewhere living her life, angry or confused or whatever, but *alive*."

CHaPTeR TWeNTY-FOUR

PARKER SAT ON the stoop beside Grayson and rested her head on his shoulder. It had been twenty minutes since he'd mentioned the similarities between the picture of Miriam and her younger self and the coincidence of the dates of Miriam's call and her mother's death. Now it was all she could think about—and she didn't want to think about it for another second.

"I'm sorry I pushed the issue about Miriam," he said for the tenth time. "I probably saw something that wasn't there."

She wasn't sure if he'd seen similarities that didn't exist, or if she didn't want to see whatever he claimed to—and she didn't really *want* to know.

"I'm sorry I got so upset. It's been a stressful afternoon, but you didn't deserve that." She leaned into him, and he put his arm around her, which settled some of her anxiety.

"I don't know what's taking Matt so long. He's never late, and he's not the kind of guy to blow us off without a phone call."

She was thankful for the change in subject, but she knew

he was still thinking about the picture, wondering if there was a connection and keeping those thoughts to himself. He loved her enough to suffer through his questions in silence, and she loved him even more for it.

"I'm sure he'll be here when he can. Maybe he got hung up with a student or something. At least it's nice out and we're together. Thank you for being here. It means a lot to me."

"Always, baby." He pulled her onto his lap and kissed her.

She pushed away all the troubling thoughts and surrendered to the blissful feeling that always accompanied their kisses. A car door closed, startling Parker. She jumped from Grayson's lap.

"Matt's seen people kiss before." Grayson rose to greet his brother.

Parker had seen pictures of Matt in Grayson's house, but she barely recognized him in the disheveled man stepping around the car. His hair was going every which way, as if he'd been stuck in a crosswind. His button-down shirt was untucked, torn at the shoulder seam and across the chest. Smears of what looked like blood stained his arm and streaked his face.

Grayson embraced him. "Missed you," he said, as if this were Matt's everyday appearance, which was unfitting of a Princeton professor.

"You too. Sorry I'm late." Matt flashed a crooked smile at Parker, which softened his chiseled features. "It's nice to finally meet the woman who's got my brother's head in the clouds." He embraced Parker.

"Nice to meet you, too." She followed him to the door, stunned by their lack of conversation about Matt's torn and bloody clothes. She mouthed, *What happened?* to Grayson. He lifted his shoulder in a casual shrug. This was a great distraction from her worries about Miriam, but now she had all sorts of new concerns racing through her mind.

"Come on in." Matt tossed his keys on a table by the door and began unbuttoning the few remaining buttons on his shirt. He nodded to the living room. Cardboard boxes were stacked two and three high. The framed picture of Parker and Grayson kissing sat atop one of the boxes, and two couches sat at odd angles near the back wall.

"Did you just move in?" Parker asked.

"No." Matt wrinkled his brow like she'd asked a ridiculous question. "Make yourselves at home." He hiked his thumb over his shoulder toward the staircase. "I'm going to shower and change, and then we can head out to dinner."

"Sounds good," Grayson said to his brother's back as Matt ascended the stairs. "Sweetheart," he said to Parker. "I'm going to grab our stuff."

She followed him out. "What do you think happened to him?"

"Who knows." He pulled their suitcase from the trunk and headed back toward the house.

"Grayson? He was bloody and his clothes were torn. Aren't you worried?"

"About him?" He laughed. "Matt's like Clark Kent. Clean-cut professor by day, superhero by night."

She stopped cold. "What does that mean? He beats up bad guys? Flies through the air with a cape?"

He reached for her hand, bringing her into the house with him. "Not usually."

"How can you be so nonchalant about this?"

He shrugged again, and she followed him downstairs to a bedroom, where he set their things down and wrapped her in his arms again.

"Sweetheart, he's not a dangerous guy. Matt's as straitlaced as they come. But if there's trouble—a car accident, an unfair fight, an old lady needing help crossing the street—Matt jumps in. Always has. No big deal."

She could easily imagine Grayson doing every one of those things and coming out of the fight with the same calm demeanor he'd possessed since she'd known him.

"It's not a big deal. Don't overthink it." Grayson stripped down to his briefs to change for dinner, making it easy for her to stop thinking about Matt.

Matt joined them a little while later, freshly showered and dressed in a neatly pressed white button-down and a pair of dark slacks, looking very professorial. Now that Parker wasn't focused on his torn clothing, she saw that where Grayson was broad and thick chested with muscles that rivaled that of a bodybuilder, Matt was athletically built, but leaner and slimmer at the waist. His features were more angular than Grayson's. He was handsome, as all the Lacrouxs were, but he didn't hold a candle to *her* man, who took her breath away in a pair of low-slung jeans and a black button-down rolled up to his elbows, exposing the muscular forearms she loved to touch.

Matt jiggled the keys hanging from his finger. "Dinner?"

Parker wondered what type of spell their parents had cast that enabled them to remain calm in the face of any storm— and how she could get some of that potion.

LATER THAT EVENING Grayson sat on the edge of the bed in Matt's guest room, rationalizing the calls he'd made to Hunter and Caden when Parker had been on the phone with Luce. No matter how hard he tried not to think about the possible connection between Parker and Miriam Stein, it was right there, refusing to be ignored. He loved Parker too damn much to let even a remote possibility of finding her family go *and* he loved her too much to cause her the anguish of false hope.

He looked across the room at her now, sorting through her toiletries, still wearing the little black dress she'd worn to dinner, and he hoped he'd done the right thing.

"I had a nice time tonight," Parker said. "That was crazy about the cat in the sewer."

"Leave it to Matt to get tangled up in something." Matt had told Parker he'd rescued a cat that had been stuck in a sewer after work, calming her concerns about his roughed-up appearance. Grayson had seen a shadowed look in his brother's eyes, and when Parker had gone to the ladies' room, Grayson had called him on it. Matt admitted to stopping a carjacking and not wanting to worry Parker, which made him appreciate his brother's careful thought process even more.

Grayson had taken advantage of their brief moment alone to tell Matt about the similarities in the photos and the dates surrounding Miriam's last call and Parker's mother's death. Matt's response mirrored Grayson's thoughts. *They have DNA tests for that.* It sounded so easy, but Parker had been vehement in wanting no part of it, taking easy out of the equation.

They'd had a nice evening despite the rocky beginning. After dinner Matt had given them a tour of Princeton's campus. Grayson had almost forgotten how being with Matt was like spending time with both their mother and father. Matt possessed their father's innate ability to remember everything he'd ever read or heard and their mother's ability to get to the heart of any issue with just a few words. In the first few minutes of their walk, Matt had learned about Bert, Abe, *and* Christmas. Grayson had to admit he was a little jealous, considering it had taken him ten months to learn as much, but he took that as a good sign. Parker had been on such an emotional roller coaster lately, he hadn't expected her to share much of herself with Matt. The fact that she had proved just how strong she was.

Parker put her toiletries in the bathroom and glanced at him over her shoulder. "I'm going to take a quick shower."

She was so beautiful, standing inside the open bathroom doorway with her back to him. She stepped from her dress, purposely giving Grayson an eyeful—and wiping his brain clean of anything but thoughts of loving her, body, mind, and soul. She unhooked her bra and let it fall to the floor. She hooked her fingers in the sliver-like sides of her thong and wiggled her ass as she stepped out of it. Then she stepped out of sight and turned on the shower.

Grayson undressed as he walked toward the bathroom. He drank in her gorgeous silhouette through the foggy glass doors. Her head was back, her hands moving over her breasts, her ribs, and down her belly. Hard as steel and hungry for *her*, he squeezed the base of his cock as he slid the door open and stepped inside, pressing his chest to her back.

His hands slid over her wet skin, and he filled his palms with her breasts, teasing her nipples into taut peaks beneath the warm spray of the shower.

"Mm. I was wondering when you were going to join me." She ground her ass against his erection, sending lust to his core.

"I'll make up for taking so long." He moved one hand down her taut stomach, to the wetness between her legs. "You're so ready, baby. Did you start without me?"

"No." She lifted up on her toes. "I was waiting for you. Knowing you were watching me through the glass turned me on."

"Damn, baby. You drive me crazy." Lowering his hips, he aligned the head of his cock between her legs and pushed in slowly. She was tighter when he entered her this way, and when he was buried balls deep, they both stilled. "Love how tight you are."

He lowered his mouth to her shoulder, sucking and biting just hard enough to cause her to gasp with pleasure. She reached behind her and gripped his hips as he began to move. She was so tight, so hot, so eager, the way she rose on her toes and sank down in fast succession as she rode him.

"Faster. Harder." She braced her hands against the tile wall as he pounded into her.

He squeezed her nipple, knowing just how to give her what she wanted, and moved his thumb over her clit.

"Grayson. Oh God, right there. Gonna…Oh Go—"

Her hips bucked, her sex clenched in pulse after mind-blowing pulse around his cock, nearly drawing the come right out of him. Clenching his teeth against his own release, they rode out her climax.

"I've got to see you, baby."

Turning her in his arms, he lifted her easily and lowered her onto his throbbing shaft. They both moaned at the intense pleasure. Their mouths crashed together in a feverish game of take and take and take some more. She clawed at his shoulders as he buried himself to the root time and time again. He was too lost in her to slow down. The sounds escaping her lungs and careening into his told him she was right there with him.

Tearing his mouth away, he growled, "Come with me," and claimed her in another possessive kiss.

She cried out and her head tipped back. Knowing she came harder when they kissed, he brought her mouth back to his. Her sex pulsated around his shaft, shattering his last ounce of control, and he surrendered to the pure, explosive pleasure.

Grayson held her in his arms beneath the warm shower spray until their breathing calmed. He loved that she trusted him enough to give herself so completely to him when they made love, but nothing touched him more deeply than when she went soft in his arms, knowing he'd take care of her.

She was leaving for California in four days, and he wouldn't be there to take care of her. He had three more nights to hold her in his arms. Four mornings to wake up with her by his side. The timeline felt more like a time bomb. He'd worried about living on opposite sides of the country, but their intimacy ran beyond sex and secrets, and when he looked into their future, he knew there was no distance vast enough to keep them apart.

CHAPTER TWENTY-FIVE

"WALK WITH ME." Parker reached for Grayson's hand, and they walked to the end of the bluff with Christmas by their side. They'd returned to pack Parker's things for her flight home and were due to leave for the airport in twenty minutes.

It had been four days since they'd met Sarah. Four days since he'd made the phone call that set his secret plan into action. Four days since guilt had begun eating him alive. He'd tried to bring up the DNA test every day since he'd made the arrangements, and again last night after their friends had thrown Parker a goodbye party on Cahoon Hollow Beach. They'd had a bonfire. Sawyer had played his guitar. They'd laughed and danced, and Parker had hugged the girls so many times, he'd half expected her not to leave.

He'd tried to bring up the test again yesterday evening, but it was their last night together for a few weeks, and he couldn't do it. If the results were negative, she'd never have to know, and telling her would only make her worry. But if they were positive, she'd have the family she'd always wished for. He was doing the right thing, or at least he thought he was, but the guilt of keeping a secret from Parker was killing him.

"This is where you first kissed me." Parker turned to face him. Her smile reached her eyes, radiating in the reflection of the sun. She was dressed to the nines, in a classy skirt and top with sky-high heels. Beyond gorgeous, she was back to the Parker Collins the world knew and loved. But he saw more than what everyone else saw, and he'd fallen in love with all of her—the Parker Collins that was just as much a down-to-earth woman as she was a famous actress. The way she could morph into her public persona in the blink of an eye or cuddle beside him on a sandy beach in a pair of shorts, with her hair in a ponytail and no makeup. He loved hearing her on the phone with directors and actors and her agent and Luce, moving between personalities with the grace and expertise she'd used to build her fabulous career.

The sound of the bay floated up from below, and behind her, Christmas bounded across the grass after a bird. They were his life now. In just a few weeks they'd become the most important parts of his life. How could they be leaving?

He drew her against him. "Sweetheart, was the kiss in the elevator that forgettable?"

She shook her head. "But I meant really kissed me, like I was yours."

She had him there. In the elevator, he was still hoping. Now he knew.

"Christmas will miss you," she said softly.

"You won't?" He fought against the claws of guilt trying to pull him away.

She held up her finger and thumb less than an inch apart, laughing as his mouth descended on hers, and he kissed that laugh right out of her, reveling in her warmth, her taste, her eagerness. When they parted, she had the look of love in her eyes he saw in his dreams. And it was that look that brought guilt so crushing he could barely breathe.

"I already miss you," she said.

Tell her. Just tell her. "Hm?"

"I already miss you. Are you okay? You look a little green."

"Yes. No." He couldn't let her leave until he came clean, no matter how good his intentions were and regardless of the results not being in yet. He was beginning to think he'd made the biggest mistake of his life.

"No?" Her brows knitted.

He extracted his hands from hers and scrubbed a hand down his face, wishing he'd never made the fucking call—and in the next breath, knowing that if the results were positive, he'd damn well done the right thing.

"Grayson, you're worrying me."

Conflicted didn't begin to describe the way he felt, and now the worry on Parker's face made him feel like he'd swallowed a pound of lead.

"I'm sorry, baby." He reached for her hand, and she trustingly took it, which made this even harder. "I have to tell you something, and I should have told you days ago, but I couldn't. I know you didn't want to pursue the idea of Miriam being related to you."

"Grayson?" She shook her head.

He tightened his hold on it. "I know you didn't want to pursue it because you were scared of having false hope and you want Sarah's daughter to be alive. But, baby, sweetheart, all you've ever wanted was to have a family, and no matter how remote the chance, I couldn't let it go."

She tore her hand from his and crossed her arms. Her eyes narrowed with fear and anger and hurt that cut like a knife. "What did you do?"

He held her gaze, owning the pain and accepting her anger, and gave her the truth. "When we got back from Jersey I gave Caden your blue hairbrush, and he sent it in for a DNA test."

"You…?" She stumbled backward, shaking her head. "I don't understand. Why would you do that?"

He stepped forward, but she held up a hand, warding him off, and he reluctantly stopped. "I couldn't let it go."

"I *told* you to let it go. It wasn't your decision to make." Tears streamed down her cheeks, piercing his heart even deeper. "Did you…? Does she know? Sarah? God, poor Sarah."

"No. Parker—"

"No, Grayson!" she shouted. Christmas sprinted over and

stood between them, his big head moving back and forth, as if he didn't know where his loyalty should lie. "I trusted you. I trusted you wholly and completely and you—"

He closed the distance between them. "I messed up big time, Parker, and I'm sorry. I wasn't even going to tell you if the results were negative. You wouldn't have had to worry at all."

"Like that's any better? Lying to me *forever?*" She spun around and stormed toward the house.

He kept pace beside her. "It's not better, but I'm telling you now. I couldn't live with the guilt."

"Apparently you lived with it pretty well for the last few days."

"No, it was killing me. But if the results are positive, then you have a family, Parker. You have a *grandmother.*"

She stopped cold and turned a lethal gaze on him. "I trusted you," she seethed. "I told you I didn't want this."

"I know, and I'm sorry. I should have told you sooner. I should have gotten your permission." Goddamn it. In his head, he had done it for all the right reasons. Couldn't she see that? "I hoped to find a family connection. Maybe I went about it the wrong way."

"Maybe?" She scoffed and grabbed her phone from the patio table. "You should have *told me* sooner? I can't deal with this right now. I need space. Time. You're..." She shook her head. "You're unbelievable."

"Unbelievable?" Anger and confusion whirled inside him. This couldn't be happening. He had to stop this fight, to make her understand, but he could tell she was way past understanding. He'd done this to them—to her. Something inside him snapped, and he was powerless to stop the words from coming out.

"Goddamn it, Parker! I get that I fucked up. I love you *too* much to cause you the anguish of false hope—and I love you *too* much to let go of the remote possibility of finding your family. It was wrong. I broke your trust. But I stand behind it, because I love you. I want to give you everything, but I couldn't with you standing in my way. I had to go around you. Can't you see that?"

She lifted her chin and drew her shoulders back, gaining composure in the righting of her spine and the unfurling of her fingers. "You won't have to go around me anymore." She punched a few numbers on her phone and lifted it to her ear.

"Parker...? What are you saying? I'm taking you to the airport."

"No, you're not. Goodbye, Grayson."

THE CAR SERVICE showed up late and Parker missed her flight out of Boston. She was too upset to sit around an airport for hours and did what she'd sworn she would never do, and damn it to hell, she didn't care who saw her. A few phone calls later, she and Christmas were on a private jet, flying across the country toward the land of beautiful people and scenic beaches. To her secluded home in Malibu, her life, and back-to-back meetings beginning tomorrow morning. She had the airliner to herself, having told the stewards not to bother her, which was perfect, because she didn't know how much longer she could keep up the act of diva actress.

Not very long, it turned out. As Boston faded away in the distance, tears tumbled down her cheeks. Christmas put his front paws on her legs and licked her tears away.

Perfect.

Flipping perfect.

She was right back where she'd started a month ago.

Only worse.

Now she knew what it felt like to be in love, and whether she liked it or not, she was truly, deeply in love with Grayson. He'd taught her that it was okay to be herself and to honor her sadness and grief without feeling bad about it. He'd respected her worries about her reputation, and he'd done his best to protect her. *I'll be your bodyguard.* He'd brought her into his circle of friends and family, and he'd supported her in every single thing she'd gone through. Even Abe. And Sarah.

And he loved her dog as much as she did.

Christmas whimpered and rested his chin on her legs, looking up at her like he was missing Grayson, too.

"Stop it. We can't miss him. We can't trust him. He hurt us."

Christmas lifted his head, and she knew he was waiting for more tears, but she refused to let them fall.

Unfortunately, Grayson had taught her how to move on, too.

This is my real life now.

CHAPTER TWENTY-SIX

PARKER LOOKED AT her watch for the fifth time, wondering where in the hell Luce was. They were supposed to meet more than an hour ago, and Parker needed her support today more than ever. Not as a public-relations rep but as a friend. Today was her big audition for the lead role in the romantic comedy. Every time Parker auditioned for a role, her stomach knotted, her chest constricted, and she worried she'd wet her pants, throw up, or pass out—or maybe all of the above. Bert used to tell her that was because she cared so much about being great at her job. It was true she cared about excelling as an actress, and she always gave one hundred and ten percent to every audition and, subsequently, to every role. But that wasn't what was causing her such panic. It was the feeling that at any moment someone would out her for being someone she wasn't, which was silly, she knew. She was *acting*. She was *supposed* to be someone she wasn't. That was the very thing she adored about her job, becoming someone else—and she was damn good at it.

But auditions had always felt different, like those first few days in a foster home. When the pressure was on to learn how to act, how to fit in, *and* how to go unnoticed.

"I'm here! Sorry I'm late." Luce flew into the waiting room, her blond hair pulled back in a clip at the base of her neck, her usual enormous tote over her right shoulder. She eyed Parker as she fell into the seat beside her. "You sure you want to do this?"

"Yes. Why are you so late? You're never late." She was barely holding her shit together. She'd spent the last two days going in and out of meetings, doing her best impression of a happy actress. She wasn't just good at it; she was one of the best. Then again, not giving herself time to think had always worked in the past, and it was doing a fair job of keeping her distracted now. Or at least it had been, until last night, when she'd realized it had been *two days* and she hadn't heard from Grayson. Not a text. Not an email. Not a phone call.

"Sorry. I got an urgent call from a client who was in trouble, and I had to sort a few things out. You look like shit. You sure you want to do this? We can put it off."

Parker rolled her eyes. Luce pulled a makeup bag out of her tote and dragged Parker into the ladies' room. She could always count on Luce to be blatantly honest and prepared.

"I already did my makeup," Parker complained.

"Yeah, but you did it like you didn't give a shit." Luce took the clip out of her hair, freeing her thick mane, and used it to pull Parker's hair into a low ponytail, securing it at the nape of her neck.

"Maybe I don't." She definitely hadn't taken the time to do her makeup the way she usually did. Every time she looked in the mirror, she saw someone she didn't like. Grayson had been so good to her, so patient and loving, and she'd barely given him a chance to explain.

"You do care. You're just in that crazy fucked-up place women go when their hearts have been broken." Luce put makeup beneath Parker's eyes. "You're becoming beautiful again, thanks to me."

She'd been up half the night studying her lines and trying to convince herself that she'd done the right thing by walking away from Grayson. Okay, maybe she'd spent the night trying to study her lines and thinking about how much she missed Grayson.

Luce snapped her fingers in front of Parker's eyes.

Parker blinked several times. "What?"

"You are totally zoning out. You cannot do this audition." Luce shoved her makeup back into her tote and crossed her arms. She was about as cutthroat and sharp as they came, and she could turn a rat bastard's reputation into Prince Charming within a few highly strategized days.

Parker knew if Luce didn't think she should do the audition, she was probably right, but she wasn't in a compliant mood. "You're not here as my PR rep," she reminded her.

"Right. Let me say this as your friend instead." With one

hand on her hip and a bitchy look on her face, she said, "Your incredibly amazing boyfriend did you a solid by trying to find your family. He went about it ass backward, because that's what *real* men do. They don't always think before taking action. Not that you would know, because you're never around normal men. You're around quasi-men who wax their entire bodies, have less muscle than me, and trade testosterone for paychecks."

Parker couldn't help but laugh. "They really do wax all over, don't they? *Blech*. Grayson has this sexy dusting of chest hair, and he's *loaded* with testosterone. He's so confident and in control and always watching, you know? Watching other people watching me, like he'd step in if someone approached."

Luce raised her brows. "You sound dreamy, like you did when you were back at the Cape."

"I do not." *I totally do.*

"You love him, Parker, and there's no shame in that."

"He broke my trust." She turned away, but she couldn't escape the pain that chased the memory. "I can't love him."

"Okay, you're right. You can't love him, because people don't make mistakes. That's why I'll be out of a job tomorrow. No mistakes, no need for PR."

Parker glared at her. Nothing felt right since she'd come back home. Her house felt vacant, her bed was lonely, and her heart ached so badly every time she thought of Grayson she wanted to cry and punch something in equal measure. And

Christmas? Her poor boy had been moping around for two days, whimpering, sleeping beside the bed, like he was waiting for Grayson to climb into his spot beside her. She wished he would.

"Well, if you're really over him, then you won't mind seeing this." Luce dug in her tote and pulled out a screenshot of Perez Hilton's website. Beneath the headline, WHEN PARKER'S AWAY LACROUX WILL PLAY, there was a picture of Grayson sitting in a dark restaurant with an arm around Bailey Bray, one of the hottest female rock stars around. He was leaning in, like he was whispering in her ear.

Like he used to do to her.

She could practically feel his warm breath on her skin. Hear him whispering, *I love you, sweetheart.*

Parker dropped the paper. Her lungs refused to work. She couldn't believe Grayson would move on that fast. She had been bitchy and upset, but still. He'd said he loved her. He'd touched her *like* he loved her.

"I didn't show you before because, well, you know. I thought it might make you fall apart." Luce pulled a handful of tissues from her tote and shoved them into Parker's hand. "So much for the makeup. I'm canceling your audition."

"No!" Parker finally managed. She wiped her eyes, sniffling, and trying her damnedest to pull her shit together. "I need this role."

"Like you need a hole in your head," Luce said flatly. "If

you never worked again you'd have enough money to live a very elaborate life."

"I don't need it for the money." Tears tumbled down her cheeks. "I need it so I can forget…"

Luce opened her arms, and Parker fell into her warm and welcome embrace.

"Feel that?" Luce asked.

"The man I love killing me? Yeah. I do. Thanks. And I hate you *so* much right now."

Luce stroked Parker's back. "No, honey. You're not dying. You're finally living."

"You're messed up."

Luce laughed. "Probably, considering I can fix everyone's life but my own." She pulled Parker from her shoulder and leveled her with a serious stare. "You need a mom."

"You're full of hateful things today. I think I need to re-think this friendship."

"I'm being serious. You've never had a mother figure, so I'm stepping in. Here's what my mom told me when I was about thirteen: Boys can be stupid. And they can be smart. And sometimes they can be stupid when they think they're being smart. It's very confusing to be a boy."

"That's not very helpful," Parker said. "Grayson isn't stupid. He *knew* I needed to go see Abe when I wasn't so sure myself. And he knew I'd have a hard time if I didn't get to give Abe one last hug before he passed away." *And roots. He knew I needed stable, unbreakable roots.*

"He's not stupid, because he's not a boy," Luce said evenly. "When I was eighteen my mother told me guys could be assholes, but usually they didn't realize when they were being assholes. That was the year my boyfriend cheated on me with the class slut."

"Are you calling Grayson an asshole? Because he's *not* an asshole. He thought he was doing the right thing. He wasn't trying to hurt me, Luce. He was trying to connect the stupid dots that probably don't connect at all, but that doesn't matter." Her head was spinning, and her thoughts kept falling out. "He didn't want to give up on finding my family, and he was trying to keep me from worrying about it just in case, so *don't* call him an asshole. And you know what else? I don't know what kind of cockamamy bullshit that was on Perez Hilton, but I know Grayson, and he wouldn't…" She turned away, unable to say the words. He wouldn't *cheat?* Would it even be considered cheating anymore? Were they still together? Did she break up with him? She didn't even know how they'd left things.

Luce spun her around again. "Don't turn away from your mother."

"Then don't call him an asshole," she fumed.

"He's not an asshole," Luce agreed. "Grayson's not a guy. He's a man. When I graduated from college and all my friends were falling in love, and then falling apart, my mother told me this: Men lose their minds when they fall in love. They will do everything and anything to protect the woman they love. Sometimes, they get it wrong, and they do stupid things that make them look like assholes because they're so in love they can't see straight."

"Luce!" Parker threw her hands up in the air and groaned. "He would do *anything* for me. He *did* everything for me. He…" *Oh God, what have I done?* She looked at Luce, whose gratified smile told her she'd been leading Parker down this path like a horse following a carrot. "What kind of friend are you? Why didn't you just slap me and tell me I was being a stupid asshole?"

"I tried, but you're stubborn." Luce opened her arms.

"I'm too annoyed to hug you. Fuck the audition. Please can you cancel it, or reschedule, or whatever needs to be done? I don't even care right now. And fuck Perez Hilton, the gossipmonger. Do something to him, too, please."

"Anything for you, dear daughter," Luce teased.

Parker pulled the clip from her hair and handed it to Luce. "Thank you for trying to make me beautiful, but I'm not feeling *Parker* beautiful at the moment, and I don't want to fake it to make it. And you know what? That's okay."

She grabbed her purse and headed out the bathroom door.

"Where are you going?" Luce called after her.

"To call my man and tell him he's a stupid crazy asshole who loves me too much."

PARKER HOOKED UP her Bluetooth and called Grayson as she drove toward her house. *Pick up. Please pick up.* Her heart raced and her mind spun. What if he didn't answer? What if the picture on Perez Hilton was from last night, and he really was with Bailey Bray? How did he even know her?

Her call went to voicemail. "Grayson, it's Parker." *Duh.* "I...Can we talk? Please? Call me." She called Grunter's, hoping he was there.

"Grunter's Ironworks."

"Hi. Is Grayson around? This is Parker."

"Hey, Parker. It's Clark. He's out at meetings."

Meetings. Great. That sounded like an excuse. "Okay, thanks."

She ended the call and tried Grayson's number again. It rang three times and went to voicemail. In all the time they'd been together he hadn't had a single meeting. He was definitely avoiding her. She was sure of it. She could feel it in her gut. Maybe she'd already lost him for good.

Twenty minutes, and way too many bad thoughts later, she pulled into her driveway. Her phone rang as she stepped from the car. Her heart skipped a beat when Grayson's name appeared on the screen.

"Grayson?"

"Hey." He sounded tentative.

He never sounded tentative.

She froze. *He's given up on me. Please, please, don't give up on me.* "Grayson, I'm sorry I overreacted. I know you were trying to do the right thing."

He was quiet for a long moment, and just as she began to panic, he said, "I'm sorry, sweetheart. I never should have gone against your wishes. I'll never, *ever* do that again."

Sweetheart. Tears filled her eyes. "Thank you, because even if you were being a stupid crazy asshole who loves me too much, it's no excuse to go behind my back. Ever."

"A stupid, crazy…I promise, baby. Never again. I… Aw, *hell.*"

"What?" Her stomach lurched.

"I might have gone behind your back one other time."

"Oh God, Grayson." Praying he hadn't done something else as bad, she walked up the slate steps to her front door. "What did you do? Wait. Don't tell me yet. Tell me over Skype, so if it's really, really bad, I can turn off Skype, which is about as good as slamming a phone down."

He laughed at that. "It's not really, really bad, baby. But yes, let's Skype."

"Promise it's not that bad?"

"Yes."

She froze. "Grayson, does this have to do with Bailey Bray?"

"Bailey? Leanna's little sister? No. Why would it? I haven't seen her in more than a year. When she came down to play at the Beachcomber last time, we all went to see her."

Leanna's little sister? "A year ago? I saw a picture on Perez Hilton of you two sitting together."

He laughed. "Then your goddamn LA photogs hijacked it from last year, and just so you know, I've never gone out with Bailey."

Breathing easier, and harder, she was even more anxious to see him now.

"Okay. Stay on the phone with me. I need two minutes to get inside."

"I'm here, sweetheart. Take your time. I can't wait to see your beautiful face."

She unlocked the door, threw it open, and stepped inside. "Hold on. I—"

Her purse and phone dropped to the floor. Grayson stood in the center of the room with his arm draped possessively around Christmas, who looked happier than he had in days, and Grayson—beautiful, crazy, loved-too-hard Grayson— looked like he hadn't slept in days. He sported at least three days' scruff, with dark crescents underscoring tired, loving eyes, bringing tears to hers.

"GRAYSON."

Christmas *woofed* and went to greet Parker.

It was all Grayson could do to try to find his voice at the sight of the woman he'd thought he'd lost. His throat was already thick with emotion from their phone call, and then she said his name in that way that answered all the questions he'd spent the past two days worrying over—she loved him. She was hurt, sad, and angry, but she loved him, and God knew he loved her.

"You're here," she said softly.

He cleared his throat, hoping to find his voice. "I told you if we weren't physically in the same place when you needed me, I'd be there as fast as I could."

She wiped her tears. "You told me at the very beginning, when something comes up, not to pull away, because issues seem bigger when we're alone. I pulled away, Grayson, and you were right. It was worse."

He drew her into his arms, and his heart swelled. Christmas tried to nose between them, but just this once Grayson needed Parker close. He reached down and petted her boy, hoping she knew there was no way he was letting either of them go again.

"I might have been right about that, but I was wrong to do what I did. I'm so sorry, sweetheart, and if you'll forgive me, I..." He framed her beautiful face with his hands and gazed into her eyes, recognizing how big of a gift she was giving him by taking him back.

"I've spent the last two days trying to figure out what I could give you or what I could say to signify that I truly understand how badly I've messed up. That's why I didn't come on the next plane out of town after you left. But no matter how many times I went over it in my head, or tried to make you something that would prove to you how sorry I am, nothing came close. I finally gave up and got on a plane, and here I am." He took her hand in his and laid his heart out before them.

"I don't expect you to trust me again for a long time, but please know I love you. It's not an excuse, and what I did was wrong on many levels, but I really did do it out of love. It was stupid and overprotective in the wrong way, and I will never make that mistake again. We can call and cancel the test. You'll never have to think about it again."

"Thank you," she said softly. "When you brought up having a DNA test done after we saw Sarah, I was so scared. I didn't want to think about Miriam not being alive. I was scared for Sarah, and for myself, about what connecting those dots would mean if the test came back positive. I didn't want to think that my mother could have been in the wrong place at the wrong time because Abe had driven her away or because her mother didn't fight hard enough for her."

She swallowed hard, and he tightened his hold on her hand, wanting so badly to take her in his arms, but he knew she needed to get this out—and he needed to hear everything she had to say.

"I can't change the circumstances that brought me into this world or that took my mother away. But I had Bert, and in a sense I had Abe, even if it was only for a short time. And, Grayson, I have you. I thought that was enough. But it wasn't enough for you. You wanted to give me everything, even if the possibilities were nearly nonexistent, just like you tried to tell me."

"I do, sweetheart. I want to give you everything. But I'll never make the mistake of going around you again."

"I know you won't. You made sure I've had the opportunity to do things that I needed or wanted to do, even when I was scared and wanted to walk away. You've always known what I needed, Grayson. I don't know how or why, but you have."

"Sky would say it's not me or you knowing anything. It's the universe stepping in when we needed it most," he said.

"I think she'd be right. She said I needed to be loved so I could heal, and she said you were *ready*. I didn't understand what she meant before, but I think I do now. You were ready to love me, to be my rock, even if it meant doing hard things. I don't want to cancel the DNA test. I need to know the truth. Thank you for not giving up on me."

"I'll never give up on you, baby. Not in a million years." He leaned in for a kiss, and she pressed her hand to his chest, holding him an inch away.

"Wait. How did you get in here?"

"Luce."

Her eyes widened. "Luce? You were her urgent call?"

He was indeed her urgent call. She'd read him the riot act before agreeing to meet him and let him into Parker's house. "She's wonderful."

"She's sneaky." She wound her arms around his neck. "Like you."

"Never again, sweetheart. From now on I'm an open book."

Her eyes filled with wickedness. "Tell me about the juicy pages."

"I've got a better idea." He kissed her softly. "How about if I show you?"

CHAPTER TWENTY-SEVEN

PARKER LAY IN bed staring up at the ceiling, listening to what she lovingly deemed as her boys' morning ritual—the familiar tapping of Christmas's nails on the hardwood floor and Grayson's sleepy, and always delightful, voice as he reminded Christmas to stay out of trouble and told their big dog he loved him before letting him outside each morning. Grayson spoiled *their boy* rotten. And she loved him even more for it. It had been eight weeks since she'd returned to California, six weeks since they'd received the DNA test results and learned that Miriam had indeed been Parker's mother, and one week since she'd come back home to Wellfleet. In the span of a few weeks, she'd lost a man she loved and gained more than she'd ever imagined possible—a grandmother whom she was enjoying getting to know, a boyfriend who loved and adored her, and a sense of peace and belonging.

As if his ears were burning, Grayson sauntered into the bedroom wearing only a pair of black briefs and a sleepy, sexy-as-sin smile. "Hey, baby. Miss me?"

He leaned down to kiss her, and her heart turned over in

her chest. She hadn't fully comprehended how deeply a person could love another human being. But she was learning, because every single day she fell even more in love with Grayson.

Christmas leaped onto the bed and licked her face.

Parker fanned his breath away. "Did you give him peanut butter again?"

"Just one cookie," Grayson said with wide, anything-but-innocent eyes. "You can't blame me. He gave me those eyes again."

She laughed as he sat down beside her on the bed. "Those are the only eyes he has."

He leaned in for another kiss. "I'm a sucker for them, the same way I'm a sucker for you."

"Lucky us." She giggled, and he kissed her again. "Did you decide what you want to do today?" She'd wanted to go to Martha's Vineyard, but Grayson needed to meet with a client later in the afternoon. They'd been batting around other ideas, but he seemed a bit distracted.

"You mean besides *you*?" He lifted her onto his lap and took her in a long, languid kiss, drugging her with his affection. He deepened the kiss, drawing hungry moans from both of them.

"Do you think we're turning into sex maniacs?" she teased.

"I'm not sure." He nipped her neck. "But I think we should investigate the possibility." He waggled his brows and

Christmas barked, then whimpered.

"He wants another cookie. You've spoiled him."

Grayson laughed. "Actually, I think he had a burr beneath his collar. Can you check? I tried, but I had a hard time dodging his tongue long enough to get a good look."

She rolled off his lap and began feeling Christmas's neck. "Come here, you big peanut-butter-loving mutt—" She felt something odd under his chin. "What the heck?" She lifted Christmas's face and spotted a little silver pouch dangling from his collar. She whipped her head around, her eyes filling with tears as she met Grayson's loving gaze. Shivers raced down her spine, and she *knew*—before he had a chance to say a word, before he had a chance to blink, she threw her arms around Grayson's neck and kissed him square on the lips.

Christmas barked, and she laughed and kissed Grayson again. Her heart didn't just turn over. It tumbled inside her chest.

"What is all this for? Did you find the burr?"

She swatted him, laughing as their mouths came together again and Christmas pushed in between them.

"All this for a little silver pouch?" Grayson teased. "Damn. What would you give me for a peanut-butter cookie?" He wiped tears of joy from her eyes and, thankfully—because she was shaking too badly to move and clinging to him so tightly not even air could fit between them—he removed the pouch from Christmas's collar.

"I really wanted to get down on one knee and do this right," he said with the biggest, most loving smile she'd ever seen. He rose with Parker in his arms, dropped to one knee, and set her on the other. Christmas jumped off the bed and stood beside them, his tongue lolling out of his mouth.

"Parker Polly Collins, my sweet, amazing girl." His voice was thick with emotion. He swallowed hard, his eyes suspiciously glassy, while a river of joy flowed from Parker's. She didn't even try to wipe her tears away. She didn't want to miss one second of seeing the love on Grayson's face.

"I had a whole speech memorized, but, baby, you're looking at me like that, and I'm so nervous I feel like I'm going to pass out."

"Don't pass out," she said quickly. "Not until you ask me!"

"Don't worry. I brought backup." He opened the silver pouch and handed her a slip of paper.

Fresh tears spilled down her cheeks as she read it. "Parker Polly Collins, my sweet amazing girl, if you're reading this, I must be out cold. I'm sorry." She looked up and smiled.

He covered the note. "Don't read the rest. I think I can cover it. Parker, I spent months falling in love with you from thousands of miles away, and the minute I saw you, in your sexy sweatpants, with tequila breath and your badass guard dog, I knew I was a goner."

A half laugh, half sob burst from her lips. "*Ohmygod,*

Grayson," she whispered.

"Every day I learn more about you and fall in love with you all over again."

"Grayson," she said through her tears. "I'm not going to be able to speak by the time you're done. Will you marry me?"

"Christ, baby," he muttered with a smile. "I wanted to make this perfect for you."

"Don't you see? You already have. You gave me the family I never knew existed, and now you've given me something even better. A chance for *our own* family."

He gazed deeply into her eyes, and her throat clogged with emotions. "Baby, will you marry me? Crazy cross-country schedules and all?"

"Yes!"

He pressed his lips to hers, half kissing, half laughing, and said, "I love you so much."

"Good, then shut up and kiss me. I've never kissed a fiancé before, and I want to see if he's as good as my boyfriend was."

"Don't you want to see your ring…?"

There went her thoughtful man again, trying to make her life wonderful.

"Later," she said as their mouths came together and he carried her to the bed.

GRAYSON STOOD IN his yard, listening to the sounds of love surrounding him. Summer and Hannah giggled at the water's edge. The other Seaside babies played on blankets on the shore, while their parents chatted happily around them. On the other side of the dock, Mira watched her son chase Christmas, Pepper, and Joey, who were too busy running after birds to notice. Occasional barks floated in the breezy summer afternoon.

Sawyer, Sky, and Grayson's brothers and father were talking on the grass a few feet from him, their deep voices similar and comforting. Matt's arm was draped lazily over their father's shoulder. It was wonderful seeing everyone together. Grayson's and Parker's schedules were a little chaotic. They had two homes now, their cottage on the pond and Parker's home in Malibu, as well as a gazebo for each; Grayson intended to keep his promise of giving Parker *everything*. He'd built the gazebos with the same theme as the railing he'd installed in the house on the bay: thick, stable roots with lots of branches and a few birds thrown in for Christmas. It didn't matter how chaotic their schedules were or how many homes they had. As long as they were together, wherever they were became *home*.

Hunter broke away from the group, watching Jana cross the grass toward the gazebo as he came to Grayson's side. "You finally figured out how to get Matt to visit."

"It was a nice side effect to the engagement party," Grayson admitted, though he would have rescheduled if Matt couldn't be there.

"He's had his eye on Mira all afternoon." Hunter nodded toward Matt, who was watching Mira and her son like a hawk.

"Good. Maybe he'll have a reason to stay." Grayson shifted his gaze back to Parker. She'd been sitting in the gazebo for the past hour, talking with Luce, Sarah Stein, and Jamie's grandmother, Vera, who had come back for the engagement party. After the DNA results had come back, he and Parker had visited Sarah and gently broken the news about Miriam and about Parker. Sarah had cried tears of sadness over losing her daughter and tears of joy for the granddaughter she now had a chance to get to know.

Parker leaned in and hugged Sarah. She talked with Jana for a few minutes, both of them stealing glances in Grayson's and Hunter's direction. Then they stepped out of the gazebo and headed over to them. Parker's eyes connected with Grayson's, sending an electrical charge through the air. He knew he'd never get used to the effect she had on him.

"It's a shame Reggie wasn't able to find out any more details about her mother," Hunter said. They'd hired private investigator Reggie Steele, who had come highly recommended by Kurt's friend Treat Braden. There was no record of Miriam Stein after she left home and no record of Sherry Collins until she took a job at a music store while she was pregnant with Parker. She'd worked there until the day she was killed. Apparently her boss was a good guy and had allowed her to bring Parker—*Polly*—to work with her. Reggie assumed Miriam had secured several false identities in the years in between when she'd left her family and when she'd become Sherry Collins. He'd been unable to make any connection between Miriam or Sherry and Bert, although it appeared that Bert had left the letters as a guiding light for Parker. Reggie discovered that Bert had made a few of the same inquiries he had, which indicated that Bert had at least suspected there might be a connection. He'd spoken with Sherry's boss a couple years earlier and had mentioned that Parker reminded him of his niece. They could only assume Bert hadn't told Parker of his suspicions so as not to upset her without having proof to back up his thoughts, and perhaps he was still hoping to figure it out. His attorney said Bert had notified him of the safe-deposit box several years prior to his death.

Sky insisted it was the universe stepping in once again, and Grayson thought it was probably a little bit of both. It had been as heartrending as it was a blessing for both Parker and Sarah to have the level of closure they were able to find.

"Miriam was obviously smart," Grayson said. "But that's not surprising. Look at her daughter." He couldn't take his eyes off of Parker as she crossed the grass in her cute jeans shorts and the colorful bohemian top she'd bought in Provincetown with the girls yesterday. When they were on the

Cape, she no longer fretted when she left the house. She'd always have to be careful in more media-centric areas, but she finally seemed comfortable in her own skin, as evident in everything about her, from her more relaxed aura, to her gorgeous smile, bright eyes, and loving nature.

"Hey, sweetheart," he said as she came to his side. "Everything okay with the ladies?"

"Couldn't be better. Sarah and Vera have so much in common. They're talking about the *old* days." Parker's eyes filled with mischief. "Jana and I were just thinking…"

"Oh no. This can't be good." Hunter pulled Jana against him.

"You're right," Jana said, poking his abs. "It's not good; it's great."

"What would you guys think about a double wedding?" The hope in Parker's eyes tweaked every part of Grayson's heart.

Grayson looked at Hunter, who rolled his eyes, but Grayson knew his brother well. That eye roll was to keep up his macho image. Hunter would do anything for Jana. The same way Grayson would for Parker. Before either of them could say a word, Sky ran across the grass and barreled into the group.

"Oh my God, you guys! I have the *best* idea!" Sky grabbed Jana's and Parker's arms. "A triple wedding!"

The girls screamed and hugged each other.

"Yes!" Parker said.

"Definitely!" Jana added.

"Wait, wait, wait." Hunter waved his hands, silencing them. "Parker and Grayson don't even know where they're living from one week to the next. He's going to Texas, she's going to be filming in some undetermined location, and then he's in Georgia. How can you guys plan a wedding?"

"We're engaged! Of course we're going to plan a wedding." Parker waved her engagement ring, which Grayson had made. He'd poured his love into the intricate rose-gold setting, creating tiny birds and flowers surrounding a two-karat pear-shaped diamond.

"If my girl wants a triple wedding, we'll make it happen," Grayson said as Parker came to his side. He draped his arm over her shoulder, soaking in her radiant smile. "Right, baby?"

"Definitely. So we do a little more traveling than most couples. This is our life now, Hunter. This moment here, and our time in Texas and California, and wherever else life leads us. There's nothing we can't figure out, so let's not overthink it."

Parker gazed up at Grayson and added, "Besides, how can you doubt your brother's ability to do anything? He said he'd give me everything, and he's already given me more than I ever dreamed of."

Ready for more Seaside fun?

Fall in love with Matt and Mira in SEASIDE WHISPERS

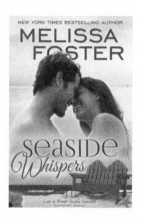

Having a mad crush on her boss's son, Matt Lacroux—*an intriguing mix of proper gentleman and flirtatious bad boy*—is probably not the smartest idea for single mother Mira Savage. Especially when the company, and her job, is already on shaky ground. But as a Princeton professor, Matt's life is hours away from Mira's home on Cape Cod, keeping him safely in the fantasy-only zone. And as a single mother to six-year-old Hagen, with a floundering company to save, fantasies are all she has time for.

With hopes of becoming dean off the table, and too many months of longing for a woman who lived too far away to pursue, Matt's publishing contract couldn't have come at a better time. He heads home to Cape Cod on a brief sabbatical, intent on starting his book, and finally getting his arms around sweet, seductive Mira.

A surprise encounter leads to white-hot passions and midnight confessions. The more time Matt and Mira spend together, the deeper their relationship grows, and the love and attention Matt showers on Hagen is more than she has ever dreamed of. But Matt's sabbatical is only temporary, and Mira's not saving his father's company so she can leave it behind. Will their whispers of love be enough for one of them to change their life forever?

Have you met the Ryders?

Fall in love with actress Trish & rock star Boone

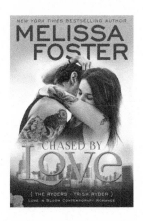

Actress Trish Ryder takes her job seriously and has no time for those who don't. When she's awarded a major role in a new movie featuring America's hottest rock star, Boone Stryker, she's beyond excited. The six-two, tattooed hunk of burning desire is known for his dedication to his craft—but when he ditches their first meeting, she begins to wonder if he's just another rocker with a great PR team.

Sex, booze, women, and music pretty much sums up Boone Stryker's private world. He's coasted through life playing by his own rules with plenty of people willing to cover his tracks, and he's not likely to change—until he meets a woman who refuses to give him the time of day, much less anything more.

Sparks fly from the first moment Trish and Boone meet—tensions run hot and desire runs hotter when they're trapped together on a remote location with no place to hide. Will sparks ignite, or will a hurricane douse the flames?

Have you met the Bradens at Peaceful Harbor?

Fall in love with Shannon Braden and Steve Johnson

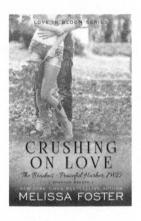

Steve Johnson is living his life's passion watching over the Colorado Mountains as a ranger and wildlife consultant. But his peaceful life is upended when overzealous and insanely beautiful Shannon Braden flits back into his life after returning from a brief trip home to Maryland. He thought his attraction to her was under control—after all, she's only in Colorado temporarily, and he doesn't do casual affairs.

Shannon's return to Colorado has as much to do with the game of cat and mouse she and Steve have been playing as it does the data she's been hired to collect. But despite her efforts to explore the undeniable heat simmering between them,

Steve's intent on keeping his distance.

When a ranch abutting the national park goes up for sale, Steve will do whatever it takes to keep it from falling into the wrong hands. And when all his attempts fail, he's left with no alternative but to follow Shannon's guidance into the online world he abhors in order to raise the funds. The more time they spend together, the deeper their attraction becomes, and a game of cat and mouse turns into an unstoppable connection. But when Shannon's assignment comes to an end, will it mean an end to them, too?

Do you enjoy M/M romance?

Fall in love with Alex and Tristan, two sexy, lovable heroes

Fresh off the heels of yet another bad relationship, Tristan Brewer is taking a break from men to try and figure out where he keeps going wrong. He knows his biggest fault—he leads with his heart, not his head—and that's never going to change. But after several introspective weeks, he's beginning to get a handle on things. That is, until badass heartthrob Alex Wells walks into his bar...

Alex has spent eight years in the Army, months in a hospital bed, and far too long hiding his sexual identity. He's guilt-ridden, damaged, pissed off, and up for a Silver Star—for the incident that nearly cost him his life, and kept him from his grandmother's funeral. But all he wants to do is forget his stint with the institution that allows but doesn't necessarily accept, and live the life he's always dreamed of.

The chemistry between Tristan and Alex ignites from the moment they meet, and the more time they spend together the hotter the flames become. But the closer Tristan gets, the more Alex's walls go up, and when the two walk onto a military base, Tristan finds out Alex's physical scars aren't the ones that run the deepest.

SWEET TEMPTATION JAM RECIPE

2 pounds strawberries

1 tablespoon lemon juice

1 1.75-ounce box powdered pectin

7 cups sugar

1 cup dark chocolate

Blend strawberries until chunky. Place strawberries and lemon juice in a large saucepan and heat to a boil, continually stirring the strawberries so they don't burn to the bottom of the pan, then add chocolate and bring back to a boil for one minute. Slowly stir in the pectin and bring to a boil. Add sugar one cup at a time while stirring and bring to a boil for one minute. Place your jars and lids in a large saucepan filled with water and bring to a hard boil. Remove jars from the hot water one at a time and fill with the hot jam mixture. Place the lid on the top tightly and invert the jars upside down for 30 seconds, then turn upright and let set so they can seal.

This recipe makes seven to eight 8-ounce jars of jam.

Available at www.AlsBackwoodsBerrie.com, Amazon, and other retailers.

MORE BOOKS BY MELISSA FOSTER

LOVE IN BLOOM SERIES

SNOW SISTERS

Sisters in Love

Sisters in Bloom

Sisters in White

THE BRADENS at Weston

Lovers at Heart, Reimagined

Destined for Love

Friendship on Fire

Sea of Love

Bursting with Love

Hearts at Play

THE BRADENS at Trusty

Taken by Love

Fated for Love

Romancing My Love

Flirting with Love

Dreaming of Love

Crashing into Love

THE BRADENS at Peaceful Harbor

Healed by Love

Surrender My Love

River of Love
Crushing on Love
Whisper of Love
Thrill of Love

THE BRADENS & MONTGOMERYS at Pleasant Hill – Oak Falls

Embracing Her Heart
Anything For Love
Trails of Love
Wild, Crazy Hearts
Making You Mine
Searching For Love

THE BRADEN NOVELLAS

Promise My Love
Our New Love
Daring Her Love
Story of Love
Love at Last
A Very Braden Christmas

THE REMINGTONS

Game of Love
Stroke of Love
Flames of Love
Slope of Love
Read, Write, Love
Touched by Love

SEASIDE SUMMERS

Seaside Dreams

Seaside Hearts

Seaside Sunsets

Seaside Secrets

Seaside Nights

Seaside Embrace

Seaside Lovers

Seaside Whispers

Seaside Serenade

BAYSIDE SUMMERS

Bayside Desires

Bayside Passions

Bayside Heat

Bayside Escape

Bayside Romance

Bayside Fantasies

THE RYDERS

Seized by Love

Claimed by Love

Chased by Love

Rescued by Love

Swept Into Love

THE WHISKEYS: DARK KNIGHTS AT PEACEFUL HARBOR

Tru Blue
Truly, Madly, Whiskey
Driving Whiskey Wild
Wicked Whiskey Love
Mad About Moon
Taming My Whiskey
The Gritty Truth

SUGAR LAKE

The Real Thing
Only for You
Love Like Ours
Finding My Girl

HARMONY POINTE

Call Her Mine
This is Love
She Loves Me

THE WICKEDS: DARK KNIGHTS AT BAYSIDE

A Little Bit Wicked
Wicked Aftermath

WILD BOYS AFTER DARK (Billionaires After Dark)

Logan

Heath

Jackson

Cooper

BAD BOYS AFTER DARK (Billionaires After Dark)

Mick

Dylan

Carson

Brett

HARBORSIDE NIGHTS SERIES

Includes characters from the Love in Bloom series

Catching Cassidy

Discovering Delilah

Tempting Tristan

More Books by Melissa

Chasing Amanda (mystery/suspense)

Come Back to Me (mystery/suspense)

Have No Shame (historical fiction/romance)

Love, Lies & Mystery (3-book bundle)

Megan's Way (literary fiction)

Traces of Kara (psychological thriller)

Where Petals Fall (suspense)

ACKNOWLEDGMENTS

When I first met Parker Collins, I was writing Hunter Lacroux's book, *Seaside Embrace*, and although she wasn't heavily entrenched in that story, she made it very clear to me that she had eyes for Grayson—and she wasn't about to let me give him to anyone else. Creating Parker and Grayson's story was a joy, not only because of their super-hot chemistry, but also because it enabled me to bring a little of my mystery mind into play. I hope you enjoyed their fated love story as much as I enjoyed writing it.

Sign up for my newsletter to keep up to date with releases and series news.
www.MelissaFoster.com/Newsletter

There's nothing more exciting for me than hearing from my fans and knowing you love my stories as much as I enjoy writing them. Please keep your emails and your posts on social media coming. If you haven't joined my Street Team, what are you waiting for? We have loads of fun, chat about books, and members get special sneak peeks of upcoming publications.
www.facebook.com/groups/MelissaFosterFans

I am indebted to my meticulous and talented editorial team. Thank you, Kristen, Penina, Jenna, Juliette, Marlene, Lynn, and Justinn for all you do for me and for our readers.

Meet Melissa

www.MelissaFoster.com

Melissa Foster is a *New York Times* and *USA Today* bestselling and award-winning author. Her books have been recommended by *USA Today's* book blog, *Hagerstown* magazine, *The Patriot*, and several other print venues. Melissa has painted and donated several murals to the Hospital for Sick Children in Washington, DC.

Visit Melissa on her website or chat with her on social media. Melissa enjoys discussing her books with book clubs and reader groups and welcomes an invitation to your event. Melissa's books are available through most online retailers in paperback, digital, and audio formats.

Melissa also writes sweet romance under the pen name, Addison Cole.

Made in the USA
Coppell, TX
04 April 2022